Beacon

S J Richards

BEACON OF BLIGHT

Published worldwide by Apple Loft Press

This edition published in 2025

Copyright © 2025 by S J Richards

S J Richards has asserted his right to be identified as the author of this work in accordance with the Copyright, Design and Patents Act 1988.

All rights reserved. This book or any portion thereof may not be reproduced or used in any manner whatsoever without the express written permission of the author, except for quotes or short extracts for the purpose of reviews.

www.sjrichardsauthor.com

*For Dee, Marcie and Sarah
…who've been supporting me with their invaluable feedback since my first book*

The Luke Sackville Crime Thriller Series

Taken to the Hills
Black Money
Fog of Silence
The Corruption Code
Lethal Odds
Sow the Wind
Beacon of Blight
Tiger Bait

Chapter 1

Fern's mother was driving her up the wall.

It wasn't the constant questioning of her actions, although that was bad enough. No, what was frustrating was her failure to comprehend the value that Beacon was bringing to her daughter's life.

She had been depressed and contemplating self-harm before running into Wynna in a potions shop in Glastonbury. All that was now well in the past and she felt like a new woman. She had purpose and was well and truly on the path to spiritual enlightenment.

Beacon had saved her from herself.

It was a relief that she didn't live with her parents any more. Moving out of the rooms above the family-owned pub in Maidenhead had been one of the best decisions she had made. Okay, her accommodation was uncomfortable, and sharing a dormitory bedroom with three other women was far from ideal, but Beacon provided it free of charge which meant the money her father sent could go to the group's numerous charities, helping those around the world who needed it the most.

The other benefit of moving away was that it gave her more independence and time to do the studying necessary to make progress. It was hard work, and intense too, but she had learned so much. She was still at Level Origin, but Wynna had made it clear that she was only a hair's breadth away from Level Rising Sun. Once she had achieved that then Level Final Harvest would be within her grasp, and with it inner fulfilment.

Only a few had made it to that level but she was almost there. She needed to concentrate harder, that was all.

"How are you doing, Fern?" Wynna asked. "You look

as though you're daydreaming."

Fern looked up and blinked her eyes. She hadn't noticed Wynna come into the room.

"Sorry, I… Yes, I suppose I was."

Wynna smiled but there was an edge to it.

"You are so close, Fern, but if you don't pick up the pace I fear you will fall back. You don't want that, do you?"

Fern was aware that the others were staring at her.

"No."

"You don't want to let yourself down."

"No."

"Have you prepared for the call with Skylar?"

"I think so."

"To say you think so is not enough, Fern. You need to be sure. Skylar will be the decision-maker on your elevation to Level Rising Sun and you need to ensure he is happy with your progress."

"But you said that Erebus would decide."

Wynna shook her head. "No, it will be Skylar. Have you been speaking to your mother again?"

"She rang me this morning."

"And before that?"

"Yesterday afternoon. She rings me every day."

"Mmm. You should reduce contact. She is in danger of leading you astray."

"But how can I do that?"

"Next time she rings tell her you have too many studies and that you will call her when you get the chance, which will be no more than once a week. We'll see how that works."

"Okay."

Wynna raised her voice to make it clear that she was addressing everyone in the room.

"The call will be at three."

"But that's only an hour," Celestina said, a note of panic in her voice. She was the oldest of the group but the most timid, a slight woman in her early thirties with mousey-brown hair. "You said it would be at five and I won't be ready."

"Then work harder."

Wynna left the room and Fern could see that Celestina was close to tears.

"Be strong, Celestina," Brenonna said without looking up from her notepad. "All we can do is our best."

"She said five," Celestina said. "I still have thirty empowerments to work through. I can't do it in that time."

"Brenonna's right," Valmoria said. "You need to stop whinging and get on with it."

Fern felt she ought to stand up for the older woman. However, she knew what Valmoria was like and the last thing she wanted was an argument. Besides, she didn't have time to waste. She was only marginally better off with twenty-two empowerments still to complete. An hour was nowhere near long enough.

The room fell silent and Fern returned her attention to her pad. The next on her list was Reverence and she needed to list ten ways in which it could be demonstrated and then write down three real-life examples of each.

*

"Skylar is ready," Wynna said.

Fern looked up from her pad and then at the wall clock, surprised to see that it was almost 4 pm. She had completed all bar five of the empowerments and was pleased with what she had achieved.

"You said it would be at three o'clock," Celestina complained.

Wynna ignored her, opened up the laptop and summoned the four women to sit facing it in a semicircle. She clicked a button and Skylar's face appeared on the screen. As always, he was smiling, but Fern knew that his temperament could change in a second. He was their guide and mentor and she had learned much from him. However, his anger and disappointment could be hard to bear. Celestina found it particularly difficult to cope.

"Good afternoon," he began in his soft Australian drawl. "I will talk through the empowerments one by one and you must note down everything I say. Your well-being depends on your understanding of their impact and importance. Once you fully comprehend them you will move one step further on your path to spiritual enlightenment."

"Don't you want an update on our progress?" Valmoria said, before adding cockily, "I completed all forty empowerments."

"After this session, you will need to reflect on what was missing from your analysis, Valmoria. It is important to be self-critical. Tomorrow, we will work through them again and we will repeat the process as often as is necessary." He paused. "We will begin with Morality. This is one of the six raised empowerments, the others being…" He hesitated. "Celestina, why aren't you writing?"

"Sorry, Skylar. I was concentrating on what you were saying."

She picked up her pen.

"As I said," he went on, "Morality is a raised empowerment alongside Tolerance, Compassion, Respect, Love and Wisdom. Morality is vital if we are to truly…"

He talked quickly and Fern struggled to keep up. The others were also bent over their writing pads as Skylar continued, repeating points where emphasis was needed.

It was over four and a half hours before he finished.

Chapter 2

"I'm going to call Shannon," Yvonne said.

She was sitting at the table closest to the bar. It was another half an hour until opening time and she and her husband had the pub to themselves.

Patrick put away the wine glass he'd been drying and looked across at his wife.

"You rang her yesterday. Don't you think you're over-analysing things?"

"I'm worried."

"But why? Think of how she was a few months ago. She was always miserable and down on herself but since she met Wynna she seems much more content."

"I don't know, Patrick. Sure it's lifted her spirits, but she's become very intense."

"She's got direction in her life, that's all."

Yvonne shook her head. "I'm not sure this Beacon mentoring group is a good thing." She held her hand up before he could speak. "Yes, I know they do a lot for charitable causes, but they seem so full on."

"Ring her by all means, but think of how she is now compared to how she was before she joined Beacon." He smiled. "If she gets that job she's applied for she'll have everything going for her: a career, a beautiful apartment and, most important of all, a better outlook on life."

Yvonne looked at him for a few seconds as he continued drying glasses. He might be right, but there was something about the way her daughter had changed that made her uncomfortable. She found it hard to put her finger on it, but she seemed somehow distant.

She placed the call and Shannon picked up after a few seconds.

"Hi, Darling."

"Hello, Mum. How are you and Dad?"

"Same as ever. The pub's busy."

"That's good."

"How are you, Shannon?"

"Fern. You need to call me Fern."

"You've said that before, but…"

"Please. It's important."

Yvonne felt a tear come to her eye.

She wasn't sure why, but it seemed like the name change would create a gap between them. They'd always been close and the thought of calling her daughter Fern made her stomach queasy.

"Any news on the job?"

"The what?"

"The job you applied for?"

"Oh, that. Ah… not yet. Mum, we need to speak less often."

"What do you mean?" Yvonne wiped beneath both eyes with the side of her hand.

"I have too many studies. Speaking to you takes up valuable time."

"But I…"

"It's better if I ring you. I'll try to call once a week."

Yvonne looked briefly across at Patrick who had stopped what he was doing and was watching her intently.

"I'd like to speak to you more often than that, darling. I worry about you."

"There's no need to worry. I really must go now. I have a lot to do."

"Oh… How is the flat?"

"It's lovely. Bye, Mum."

The line went dead before Yvonne could respond.

Patrick walked around the bar and passed her a tissue. She dabbed beneath her eyes and looked up at him.

"She was so distant, Patrick. It wasn't like Shannon.

These Beacon people have changed her."

"She's busy, that's all."

"Busy with what? She hasn't got a job yet. What are all these so-called studies they've got her doing? Oh Patrick, I wish she'd never met that Wynna woman."

"Look, let's drive to Bath, take her out for a meal and have a proper conversation. That'll set your mind at ease. Why don't you give her a call back and suggest it?"

"What about the pub?"

"That's not a problem. If it makes you feel better, we could go this afternoon. I'm sure Alice can manage without us for one evening."

Yvonne tried to force a smile.

"Thanks."

She dialled her daughter back but it went straight to voicemail.

Chapter 3

Fern was sitting on the edge of her bed while Brenonna and Valmoria were at either end of the battered pine table in the centre of the bedroom. They were bent over their notepads and scribbling away, trying to complete their assignment before being summoned to meet with Skylar.

She should have been doing the same, but her mind kept returning to the phone call with her mother. Wynna was right of course. She would never reach her full potential if she allowed herself to be pressured.

And yet there was something niggling at her. Her mother didn't understand, could never understand, but hearing her upset like that was horrible.

She looked down at her phone and wondered if she should turn it back on and call back.

"What are you doing?"

Fern's eyes widened as she looked up at her mentor who was scowling down at her.

"Have you completed your preparation?"

"No, I…"

Wynna held her hand out. "I think I should take that. It is clearly a distraction."

Fern passed the phone over.

"I suggest you clear your head and return to your studies, Fern. It's only thirty minutes until Skylar calls."

"I thought it was at seven."

Wynna ignored her.

"You need to work harder and stop letting your mind wander."

Fern gestured to the table. "Where is Celestina?"

"She has been elevated."

"To Level Rising Sun? That's good news."

"Come on, Fern. You're wasting time."

Fern picked up her notepad and pen and took it to the table.

"Your session will begin in an hour," Wynna said as she left.

"Didn't she say thirty minutes a moment ago?" Fern said after she'd gone.

"Be quiet," Valmoria said. "There isn't much time."

Chapter 4

Yvonne was worried, but not unduly so. Okay, Shannon wasn't answering her phone but it could just be that the battery had died. Anyway, they were nearly at her apartment.

It had been six months since they had moved her in. Within days she had found herself a waitressing job and had assured them that she would be okay, that independence was what she needed to sort her head out.

Yvonne had wanted to visit but Patrick had assured her that space was what their daughter needed. He'd been proved right when, after a month or so, she started counselling sessions with Beacon. Her spirits had lifted immediately. Gone were her frequent bouts of despair and all had seemed to be on the up.

It was only in the last few weeks that Yvonne had sensed a change that wasn't for the better. Somehow, Shannon wasn't acting like her daughter. She hadn't regressed to her previous near-suicidal state, but she seemed to have gone beyond enjoying and benefiting from her counselling sessions and into a state of utterly and totally depending on them.

There was this stupid name change too.

It was as if Beacon had a hold over her.

Which was nonsense. It was only a counselling group.

"We're here," Patrick announced.

Yvonne looked over at the large detached house. Shannon's flat occupied the whole of the first floor and had a lovely view onto Lansdowne Cricket Club. The rental cost was eating into their savings but they had both felt it was money well spent.

"I hope she doesn't mind us surprising her like this,

Patrick."

"She'll love it. Come on."

They walked through the gate and rang the middle of the three buzzers. After a minute or so there was a click and a female voice came through the speaker.

"Hello."

"Hi," Yvonne said. "Is Shannon there?"

"I think you've got the wrong address."

"She might be calling herself Fern."

"No, I'm afraid… Hang on. Did you say Shannon?"

"Yes. Shannon Wilson."

"I'll come right down."

A few seconds later they heard footsteps and the door was pulled open to reveal a tall woman in her mid-thirties.

She smiled at both of them. "I'm sorry about that. I'd forgotten her name."

Yvonne and Patrick exchanged a look.

"Forgotten her name?" Yvonne asked.

"Yes. She was the previous occupant and I didn't meet her."

"She's moved out?"

"Four months ago. I've got a forwarding address for her though. She moved to Glastonbury." She held out a piece of paper but Yvonne was too dumbstruck to react.

"Thanks," Patrick said as he took it from her.

"No problem."

The woman shut the door.

Chapter 5

"The call with Skylar will be at eight," Wynna said, "which means you have another two hours to finish your preparation. We will take our meal afterwards."

Fern sighed. If they weren't starting until eight it would be gone midnight before they ate and she was starving.

She should be more self-disciplined, she knew that. It was weakness of the fourth order to allow gluttony to pervade the mind.

But this wasn't gluttony, this was simple hunger. Surely a packet of crisps wouldn't do any harm. She had a five-pound note hidden in her bedside drawer that she could use.

She stood up from the table, retrieved the money and stepped as quietly as she could out of the room.

Brenonna and Valmoria hardly seemed to notice.

Once in the corridor she tip-toed to the front door and pressed down on the handle.

"Where are you going?"

Fern almost leapt into the air. "I, ah… I need some fresh air, Wynna."

Wynna looked at her watch. "Ten minutes, no more."

Fern tried to smile but it was a poor attempt. "I'll be quick."

"Good."

Wynna turned and returned to the front room.

Fern had second thoughts as she stepped out into the warm summer evening. She had lied, a sin of the second order. It compounded the weakness of gluttony and demonstrated frailty.

She turned to go back in and grasped the door handle.

"Shannon!"

She was shocked by the sound of her mother's voice and panic hit. Gulping, she quickly pushed the handle down. She had to go back in, tell her mentor what had happened and get her to lock the door.

"Darling."

Fern hesitated and in that second her mother grabbed her arm. She tried to jerk away, her eyes darting from the door to her mother and back.

Her father was there too, marching towards them both.

She shook her head violently.

"You have to go, both of you. I can't speak now. I have a session in a few minutes."

"Surely, you can miss it," Patrick said, in that calm and implacable way of his. "We've driven here to surprise you, and we thought we'd treat you to a meal."

"No." Fern swallowed. "I can't leave." She looked back at the partly open door and pulled it closed as softly as possible. "You don't understand." She was whispering now. "I have a Zoom call with Skylar and I can't afford to miss it."

Her father gave a dry laugh. "What sort of a name is that?"

"Please, darling," Yvonne said, her voice shaking with emotion. "We want to make sure you're okay."

Fern saw her mother's lips were trembling and that she seemed close to tears.

But why?

Couldn't she see that her daughter was in a happy place?

"There's a cafe around the corner," Patrick said. "We'll only keep you five minutes and then you can return to Skybar."

He smiled as he said this, deliberately getting the name wrong.

Fern almost rose to the bait, almost corrected him, but she saw what he was doing. In his gentle, laid-back way he was trying to take the tension out of the situation.

But why was there tension?

These were her parents and she should be comfortable in their presence, especially so since she was on the path to self-fulfilment, almost at Level Rising Sun. She was now a strong, independent woman who was frightened of no one.

Fern looked back at the door, afraid that Wynna might appear at any moment.

It was then that realisation hit.

She felt weak at the knees.

She wasn't strong, she was weak.

Neither was she independent, far from it in fact. She did everything Wynna, Skylar or Erebus told her to do without question or hesitation.

And they scared her too.

She reached for her mother's hand and looked into her eyes.

"Save me, Mummy," she said, her voice so quiet the words were barely audible. "Please save me."

Chapter 6

NOW (18 months later)

Luke turned the BMW's ignition on and retreated to the warmth of the farmhouse for the short time it would take for the car to warm up and the windows to defrost.

As soon as he entered the boot room Wilkins rushed forwards as if he hadn't seen his master for months.

Luke bent down to tickle the cocker spaniel's chin.

"I've been gone all of two minutes, you silly mutt."

Wilkins flicked his eyes towards the cupboard.

"Okay. Only one though."

He retrieved a bone-shaped biscuit from the drawer.

"Sit."

Wilkins obediently sat back, his eyes firmly fixed on the treat.

Luke fed it to him, then gestured for the dog to enter his crate.

"Marjorie will be here in a couple of hours," he said as he fastened the latch, "and I'll see you this evening."

The dog cocked his head to one side as if trying to understand his master's words then appeared to give up, rotated twice and flopped down onto his side.

Luke returned to the Beemer and set off for the office, his thoughts immediately going to the weekend just gone and to Saturday in particular.

A smile came to his face as he reflected on how much he had enjoyed the evening. It was early days, heck it was only four weeks earlier that he'd told Sam how he felt about her, but everything seemed to be going well.

She'd insisted they take things slowly at first, and he understood why, given the relationship challenges she'd had in the nine months or so that he'd known her. Tony was bad enough but Ollie beggared belief. He hoped to goodness he never saw him again, because if he did…

The phone rang and he saw that it was Detective Inspector Pete Gilmore, a long-term friend and Luke's number two when he'd been a DCI at Avon and Somerset Police.

"Morning, Pete. Good weekend?"

"It was okay until I got called in yesterday afternoon."

"What happened?"

"A body was found. Young man, thirty or so. Sally Croft is doing the post-mortem this morning."

"Suspicious circumstances I take it."

Pete gave a dry laugh. "He was found in a suitcase so yes, I'd say it's suspicious all right. Naked and curled up in a foetal position."

"Nasty. Any ID?"

"Nothing. He'd been dead for a while, that much is clear. It was the smell that made someone at Bath Spa open the case to see what was inside."

"Bath Spa?"

"Lost property. The suitcase was left on the London train six days ago."

"And you're telling me this because?"

"I want your help interviewing someone."

"You've got a suspect already? That's quick work, Pete."

"He's not a suspect, he's one of the staff in Lost Property. He's being evasive and I'm not sure why. Could you make it to HQ this afternoon?"

"I should be able to. Is 2 pm okay?"

"That would be great. I'll clear your involvement with the chief."

Luke ended the call and his thoughts turned to the Ethics Team workload. They had a lot on, and Monday mornings were particularly difficult because his attendance at the weekly Internal Affairs meeting was deemed compulsory by his boss Edward Filcher.

He briefly considered asking Sam to deputise for him but decided that would be unfair, especially since she'd be leading the team in his absence while he was in Portishead. No, he'd have to go and hope that for once Filcher kept it brief.

Helen was the only one in the Ethics Room when he walked in. She looked up from what looked to be a lengthy printout and he saw that there was a twinkle in her eye.

"Morning, Luke. Good weekend?"

"Excellent, thanks."

"I trust you and Sam had a good time on Saturday?"

"We did, yes."

"Ach, that's good news."

She returned to her document and Luke sat behind his desk.

A few seconds later the youngest member of the team walked in.

"Morning, Helen," Josh said then turned to Luke. "Morning, guv." He grinned. "Did it all go well on Saturday?"

Luke glared at him and he held his hands up.

"Sorry. Just asking."

"Well, don't."

Luke turned his laptop on and was about to check his emails when Maj walked in.

"Good morning, everyone," he said. "Saturday go okay, Luke?"

"I wouldn't go there," Josh hissed. "He doesn't want to talk about it."

Luke sighed.

"It isn't that I don't want to talk about it, Josh. It's the fact that you're all acting like you're my mother. Yes, Sam and I had a great time on Saturday. There, now you know. Can you get back to your work please?"

Helen, Maj and Josh grinned at each other and sat at

their desks.

A few minutes later Sam walked in. "Good morning, everyone," she said. "Did you all have a good weekend?"

"Not as good as yours," Josh said under his breath.

She looked over at Luke and he saw that her cheeks were ever so slightly pink.

"Right, everyone," he said. "We've got a lot on and I've got to go to Portishead after lunch so can we have a quick catch-up please?"

They wheeled their chairs to the table in the centre of the room.

"You on a case, guv?" Josh asked.

Luke nodded. "Pete Gilmore rang me on my way in." He turned to Sam. "Are you okay to cover for me while I'm out, Sam? At the moment it's only this afternoon but you know how it can go."

"No problem." She smiled and he looked at her for a moment, then cleared his throat before continuing. "Helen, do you mind starting? How's it going with the Cuthberts contract?"

Twenty minutes later they were done and, not for the first time, Luke found himself reflecting on what a great bunch of people he had working for him. They brought complementary skills and together formed an excellent team.

It went further than that though. He would trust any of them with his life if he had to.

Helen was the most experienced by far. She had studied law in her home town of Edinburgh back in the early 1980s and had spent several decades as a paralegal. Give her any document and she was more than capable of seeing through the fog of legalese and corporate bullshit.

Maj had proven himself to be a real technical whizz, able to find his way around computer systems, CCTV and the like with ease.

Sam, an accountant by trade, was a natural people

person. She had a warm personality and he automatically thought of her first when it came to cases where bullying or harassment were involved.

And Josh was…

Well, Josh was Josh. Wildly enthusiastic, and sometimes immature, but smart too and always keen to learn.

Which was good given what Luke had in mind for him.

"Josh," he called. "Have you got a minute?"

"Sure, guv."

He wheeled his chair over and the eager look on his face reminded Luke of Wilkins' expression when he'd held the dog biscuit out for him.

Luke passed over a pamphlet.

"I think it would be good for your personal development if you went on this Criminology and Ethics course."

"Gucci!" Josh cast his eyes down the leaflet. "When?"

"It's a week-long residential training programme and there's a vacancy on the course starting next Monday. Could you do that?"

"Sure. I'll have to check with Leanne obviously but yes, should be fine." He was beaming from ear to ear. "Thanks, guv."

"No problem." Luke looked at his watch. "Right, I'll have to be off or I'll be late for Filchers' meeting. Get HR to book your place once you've okay-ed it with Leanne."

"Will do."

Chapter 7

"You're a few minutes early," Gloria, Filcher's secretary, said when Luke arrived outside his boss's office on the Executive Floor.

"Is he in?"

"Yes. He's with Glen who wanted a private word."

"Any idea what about?"

"He's asking for a pay rise." She smiled and half-whispered. "He'll be lucky."

Glen Baxter was Filchers' Head of Security and one of Luke's least favourite people. They had had numerous run-ins when they had both worked for Avon and Somerset Police.

Luke walked to the office door, knocked gently and pushed it open without waiting for an answer.

"Fifty-three," Glen said before spotting him.

Filcher was in his normal, especially elevated, chair at his desk and was shifting from side to side, looking distinctly uncomfortable. Glen was standing with his back to the window, his tight short-sleeved shirt serving to emphasise the steroid-fuelled muscles in his neck and arms.

Glen waved his hand towards the door. "You need to wait outside, Luke. This is a private conversation."

"I heard you say fifty-three. Is that your IQ?"

The sarcasm flew straight over Glen's slightly-greying buzz-cut.

"It's the number of staff in my team," he growled, then gestured towards the door again. "Go on. Out."

Luke ignored him and took a seat at the table. "It's gone up. The last I heard it was fifty-two."

"It's fifty-three including me."

"Ah, I see. A full pack of cards plus a Joker."

"That's right."

"And you're the Joker?"

"Correct. They're down here..." He held his left hand flat at waist-height. "...and I'm up here." He raised his right hand until it was level with his eyes.

"You've risen to the top in the way scum always does."

"Exactly."

"And if you've got fifty-two staff and I've got four, I guess that makes you thirteen times more important than me."

He could almost see the cogs whirring as Glen did the mental calculation. After a few seconds, he nodded.

Luke sat back in his chair.

"Don't mind me. Please continue."

"No!" Filcher said emphatically. "Finished. Done. No more to be said."

"Then you agree?" Glen said.

Filcher harrumphed and squirmed in his seat for a few seconds before answering.

"Ah... Almost."

"Almost?"

"Yes, but let's take it offline. We can circle back later." He swallowed. "Need to drill down and evaluate." He heard a noise and added, with what seemed like palpable relief, "Ah, James."

Luke turned to see that James McDonald, Head of HR, and Fred Tanner, Head of Marketing, had arrived. He nodded hello and they sat at the table, followed a few seconds later by a scowling Glen.

"James," Filcher said. "We need to talk." He sniffed and nodded his head towards Glen. "After this meeting."

James smiled. "What about?"

"Compensatory limits. We need to touch base in my thought shower."

Fred snorted.

"In your thought shower?" James asked, managing

somehow to keep a straight face.

Filcher bobbed his head up and down a couple of times. "Yes. In my thought shower." He paused, picked up a pile of paper from the desk and walked around to the head of the table. "Short meeting today." He sat down and handed the sheets out.

Luke saw with horror that there were fourteen agenda items.

"First," Filcher went on, "Fred, what is…"

The door started to open and Filcher changed tack mid-sentence.

"Gloria!" he barked, "We are in a meeting!"

He scowled at the door ready to berate his secretary further, but gulped audibly when the person pushing the door open was revealed to be the silver-haired Ambrose Filcher, the company's founder and Chief Executive.

"Oh, ah…" Filcher leapt to his feet and seemed to be fighting the urge to salute. "Uncle Ambrose. I didn't… I mean, I…"

"Stop blabbering, Edward, and sit down."

"Right. I, ah…" He sat down. "Private word. I see." He waved to his four subordinates. "Off you go. Speak later."

Ambrose smiled. "They don't need to leave. I have something I want to ask the four of them."

"The four of them?"

"Yes."

"Surely me first. One-to-one. Then I'll tell them. I report to you. They work for me. Hierarchy. Management line."

Ambrose ignored him and addressed his next comments to the others.

"I have been telling the Company Board how important Internal Affairs is. They tend to focus on the revenue-earning parts of the business, but I want them to appreciate the excellent job you all do."

"My department," Filcher said, thrusting his chest out.

"Excellent job."

"To that end," Ambrose went on, ignoring him again, "I want you to present at our next Board Meeting."

Filcher beamed. "Delighted to."

"Not you, Edward. James, Fred, Luke, Glen… would you be happy to present on each of your operations? It'll have to be brief I'm afraid. Ten to fifteen minutes each."

"Anything you want us to focus on in particular?" Luke asked.

"I'll brief you all," Filcher said, then turned to his Uncle and tapped the side of his long hooked nose. "Keep them in line."

"No, Edward. That is not the way I want it done."

"Indeed. You brief them. Sensible approach."

"They are grown men. I'm sure they know better than anyone what to say. And in answer to your question, Luke, no there's nothing in particular I want you to focus on."

Filcher shook his head. "Too much trust," he said under his breath.

Ambrose turned towards his nephew. "Are you saying you don't trust your team, Edward?"

"No."

"You don't trust them?"

"No! I didn't… Ah… I mean, yes."

"Because if you have a bad relationship with your staff perhaps it would be better if you moved on. To head up Audit perhaps?"

"What?" Filcher sucked his chin in. "I trust them all. No question. Absolutely. Immense trust. Always."

"I'm pleased to hear it. Oh, and Luke, would you mind popping over to my office when this meeting is over."

"Not at all, Ambrose," Luke said, then a thought occurred to him. "Or I could come now if it's convenient. I'm sure Mr Filcher wouldn't mind me missing the weekly catch-up."

Filcher looked first at Ambrose, then at Luke, and then

back at his Uncle again. He attempted to smile but his lips were unaccustomed to the movement and he ended up pursing them together as if he'd sucked on a particularly acidic lemon.

"Ah, no," he said. "Not for you, Uncle. Of course not." He waved his hand. "Off you go, Luke."

Luke stood up and followed Ambrose out of the room, hearing a whispered 'Lucky bastard' in Fred's distinctive Yorkshire twang as the door closed behind them.

Chapter 8

Ambrose's PA looked up and smiled as they approached her desk outside the CEO's office.

"Good morning, Luke."

He returned her smile. "Morning, Ellie."

"Ellie," Ambrose said. "Please can you retrieve the 'What' file from the safe and bring it in?"

"Of course, Ambrose. I'll bring coffees as well."

"Thanks." He turned to Luke. "You like it strong and black, don't you?"

"Yes, please."

He turned back to Ellie. "A latte for me, please."

Luke followed Ambrose into his office and, as on previous visits, was struck immediately by the elegance of the room, the soft colours of the William Morris-covered sofas seeming to complement the company founder's relaxed and friendly manner. It was in complete contrast to the mahogany stuffiness of Edward Filcher's private enclave.

Ambrose walked to the furthest settee and gestured for Luke to sit on the other one.

He was intrigued by what the CEO had said.

"Did I hear you ask Ellie for the 'What' file, Ambrose?"

Ambrose smiled. "The contents are very sensitive and I needed to assign a project name. You'll understand why in a minute."

The door opened and Ellie walked in, handed a manila folder to Ambrose and placed their drinks down on the coffee table.

"No interruptions please, Ellie."

"I understand."

She left the room and Ambrose opened the folder,

leafed quickly through the sheets of paper inside and then placed it down on the table.

He sighed.

"I've learned many lessons during my seventy-five years on this planet, Luke, and one of them is to be careful who I trust." He paused. "But then, as an ex-policeman, I imagine you're the same."

Luke nodded. "Trust has to be earned."

"Indeed it does." He paused. "Sad to say, there are only four people in Filchers who I have complete faith in. Ellie is one, then there's you of course, and also James."

"James McDonald?"

"Yes. I needed his help a while back, before you joined the company, and as a result I have complete faith in him."

"And the fourth person?"

"My nephew." He held his hand up as if Luke was about to interrupt. "He might be a bumbling, pompous fool, but Edward is an honest man and I would trust him with my life."

"But surely there are others? What about your colleagues on the Board of Filchers?"

"Ah, there's the rub." He picked the folder up and passed it over to Luke. "Have a look at this and tell me what you think."

Luke took the contents out and placed the folder back on the table.

The first sheet was a printout of an email. It was dated a week or so earlier.

To: *Ambrose Filcher*
From: *abtweeing@me.com*
Subject: *Clothing*

Mr Filcher,

In The Emporer's New Clothes, two dishonest weavers fool their ruler into wearing only his underwear. They tell him, and he tells his entourage, that it is a wonderful fabric that cannot be seen by people who are stupid and unfit for their role.

As a result, his followers lie that it is beautiful, and it is a young boy who eventually reveals the truth.

Think of me as that boy.

You are the emporer and you are being fooled.

There are one, possibly two, weavers. I do not have names but know that he/she/they are members of Filchers' Board of Directors.

In this instance the clothes are real and it is their manufacture that is dishonest. More than that, it is immoral and exploititive.

I beg you to investigate. Begin with Tease, but please keep my message to yourself. If my identity is revealed I may be in danger.

If I find out more I will be in touch.

Regards
A Friend

Luke looked up from the sheet. "I take it that the email address means nothing to you?"

Ambrose shook his head. "Not a thing." He gestured to the other sheets of paper. "I asked Ellie to find out what she could and those are her notes. She immediately recognised 'Tease' as a brand of clothing targeted at young women, but hasn't been able to find any link between the company and members of the Board. I need you to take the investigation on." He hesitated. "I told you who I trust in the organisation. Who in Filchers do you trust?"

Luke considered this for a moment. "The four

members of my team above all others."

"Excellent. Please involve all of them in this investigation. Is there anyone else?"

"Leanne Kemp."

"Leanne on reception?"

"Yes. She and Josh Ogden are an item."

"I see. I didn't know that. How is young Josh faring? I was pleased when he joined your team. Working for Edward was never going to be good for him."

"He's doing excellently, Ambrose. I'm thinking of booking him on a course next week on Criminology and Ethics."

Ambrose thought about this for a second or two. "And he and Leanne are partners, you say?"

"That's right. They're living together."

"Mmm." After a few seconds, he nodded to himself and Luke could see that he'd reached a conclusion and was happy with it. "I think we might have to defer his course."

"For what reason?"

"One of the next steps should be to visit the place where Tease makes their clothes. I can't do it, of course, and I worry that most of the Board members know you too. It needs to be someone they wouldn't recognise, someone who can visit and remain under the radar."

"And you're thinking Josh might be a good choice?"

"Yes. He and Leanne could visit under the guise of being on holiday."

"I take it it's not in this country?"

Ambrose gave a little laugh. "My project name is a play on words. I called it 'What' because of the country's most famous monument."

Luke remembered that 'Wat' was the name for a Buddhist temple, and recalled Sam saying she'd been to Wat Pho in Bangkok.

"Are you talking about Thailand, Ambrose?"

"You're not a million miles away but no, not Thailand.

Tease's clothes are made in Siem Reap, not far from Angkor Wat. I want Josh and Leanne to travel to Cambodia."

Chapter 9

Luke returned to the Ethics Room, called the team together and asked Helen to clean the whiteboard.

"Have we got a new investigation for the crazy wall?" Josh asked.

Luke nodded. "It's highly confidential, and I've been asked by Ambrose to make it our top priority."

"What's it about, guv?" He was practically bouncing on his chair with excitement. "We'll need a project name. I want to choose it. Bags I choose it."

"You're not coming up with a project title, Josh. Ambrose has already given it a name."

Disappointment was written all over his face. "What?"

"Exactly."

"Eh?"

"What."

Josh's eyebrows went up. "What?"

"That's the project name."

"What is?"

"Yes."

"Eh?"

Sam held her hand up. "It's not only Josh who's confused, Luke. You've lost me as well."

"Sorry." Luke looked at Helen. "Please can you write the project name at the top of the board, Helen? It's Project What, spelt W-H-A-T."

Helen picked up a marker and added it.

"Ambrose gave it that name because, well, it'll become clear in a moment. Also, someone else is joining our team for this investigation."

"Who, guv?" Josh was still excited and in full squeal mode. "Is he an expert in something?"

"It's a she." Luke smiled. "And yes, her particular expertise is handling difficult and troublesome people. I gave her a ring on the way down and she should be here any moment."

There was a knock at the Ethics Room door.

"That'll be her now. Can you let her in please, Josh?"

"Sure."

Josh stood up, walked to the door, opened it, saw who it was, looked briefly at the others and then turned back to his girlfriend. "Not now, Leanne," he whispered. "We've got an expert coming for What."

"For what?"

"Yes."

She raised an eyebrow. "Have you been drinking, Joshy?"

"Come on in," Luke called.

Leanne walked over to the others leaving Josh at the door. He stepped out into the corridor and looked first left and then right.

"There's no one else, guv."

"Come back in, son," Luke said. "I'm not expecting anyone else. Leanne is our new team member."

"I am?" Leanne said.

"Eh?" Josh said for the umpteenth time.

"Both of you sit down and I'll explain."

"I haven't asked her about the course yet, if that's got anything to do with it."

"It's just as well, because you're not going."

He explained about the email sent anonymously to their Chief Executive.

"I've bought clothes from Tease," Leanne said when he'd finished. "They've become very popular in the last couple of years."

"I've heard of them," Sam said, "but they're a bit young for me. Very trendy though, and inexpensive too."

"Can I have a look at the email, Luke?" Maj asked.

"Sure." He passed it over.

Maj took the sheet to his desk, bashed away on his keyboard for a few seconds and then returned to the table.

"As I suspected, it's a temporary email address. However, if I can access the email itself I might be able to identify where it was sent from."

"How will you do that?" Helen asked.

Maj smiled. "It's not difficult. I'll locate the domain name in the header then use a DNS lookup and an IP geolocation service."

"Ach, right." She turned to Luke and smiled. "I think I'll stick to five-hundred-page contracts. They're much simpler."

"Maj," Luke said, "go up and see Ellie, Ambrose's Personal Assistant, when we're finished. She can give you access to the email."

"I still don't understand why Leanne's joining the team," Josh said. "You said she was an expert in handling difficult and troublesome… Oh, hang on. You meant me, didn't you?"

Luke grinned. "I couldn't possibly comment."

"And why can't I go on that course?"

"I want the two of you to visit Tease's factory under the guise of being fans of their clothes."

"Couldn't we do it this week though, guv? It'll only take a day, won't it?"

"It's a bit of a hike."

"Is it in Scotland?"

"And what's wrong with Scotland?" Helen said.

"Ah, nothing, but…"

"It's in Cambodia," Luke said.

"Cambodia!" Josh's voice was a couple of octaves higher than normal now. "But isn't that… I mean, that's…"

"Further than Scotland," Helen said, a wicked grin on her face.

He fired a finger gun at her. "Exactly. Isn't it in Asia?"

"Southeast Asia to be precise," Leanne said. "It's between Thailand and Vietnam. I've always wanted to go there." She looked up at the two words on the otherwise unmarked whiteboard. "I see why it's called Project What now."

"Why?" Josh asked.

"Angkor."

Josh drew his face back in horror at what she had said. "Sorry, Leanne. I was only asking."

Leanne laughed. "No, Joshy. I wasn't calling you names. Cambodia is where Angkor Wat is."

"I assume you've both got passports?" Luke asked.

They nodded.

"The furthest I've ever been is Malaga though, guv. I mean, Southeast Asia. That's a long way. How will we get there?"

"I'm guessing aeroplane," Helen said.

"Ha, ha."

"Filchers will be paying," Luke said, "and you'll be flying business class."

"Wowza! Wait until I tell Noah and my mum."

"You can tell them where you're going, but if it comes up you'll have to say that you're travelling economy. Everyone needs to think the two of you are on holiday." He paused. "Outside of the six of us, plus Ambrose and Ellie, his PA, the only other person in the know is James McDonald. The two of you need to speak to James to arrange flights, visas, accommodation and so on."

"When do you want us to go?" Leanne asked.

"This weekend would be good."

"Can I have a look at the email please, Maj?" Sam asked.

He passed it over.

She read through it. "So," she went on, "all we know is that a whistleblower believes a member of the Board is linked to something immoral and possibly illegal at Tease."

"That about sums it up," Luke said. "We're heavily dependent on Josh and Leanne's visit to find out more. In the meantime, we need to dig up as much background on the members of Filchers' Board of Directors as we can and see if we unearth any skeletons."

"I've got a copy of the company accounts," Helen said. "They'll be listed in there."

"If it would help," Sam said, "I can prepare a spreadsheet to enable us to capture and analyse our findings."

Luke nodded. "That's a good idea. The other thing that's happening is that I'm presenting to the Board next week. It's only a fifteen-minute slot, but it'll give me the chance to meet them all."

"How many are there?" Maj asked.

Helen retrieved Filchers' annual report from her desk drawer and leafed through it until she found the names of the Board members. "There are eight," she said. "Aside from Ambrose, the only other Filchers employee on the Board is Gillian Ley, our Chief Financial Officer. The other six are Non-Executive Directors."

She wrote the seven names on the whiteboard.

"I've only met three of them," Luke said. "Gillian, Francois Lausanne and Alistair Ritchie." He turned to Leanne. "I guess you must have come across all of them at one time or another, Leanne."

"Yes, I have, but the only two I've exchanged more than a brief word with are Dame Chittock and Janice Martin."

"What do you make of them?"

"Sarah Chittock is lovely. She always makes time to talk to me and to ask how my family are. She even knows about you, Joshy."

"And what about Janice Martin?"

"She's nice too, but it somehow seems a bit forced with her, as if she knows she ought to be friendly but finds it uncomfortable."

"Any opinions on Alistair Ritchie or David Parsons?"

"Not really. They're both pleasant enough, but I don't think they see me as a person, more as an entity that hands out badges. I might as well be a computer as far as they're concerned."

Luke looked up at the whiteboard.

"I suggest that you only take one, Sam, since you're going to be covering for me when I'm at Avon and Somerset."

"That makes sense. Why don't I take Gillian?"

"That'll work. Maj, Helen and Josh, you can take two each."

He walked to the board and added their names.

PROJECT WHAT

Gillian Ley	- Sam
François Lausanne	- Maj
Meredith Holcroft	- Maj
Dame Chittock	- Helen
Janice Martin	- Helen
Alistair Ritchie	- Josh
David Parsons	- Josh

"Good luck, everyone. Leanne, I guess you'd better head back to reception. Thanks for saying you'll help."

"No problem, Luke. I'll set up a meeting with James to discuss our travel arrangements."

Chapter 10

Josh began with Alistair Ritchie and tried his hardest to concentrate.

But it was difficult.

He kept thinking about Cambodia.

He and Leanne were going to Southeast Asia.

Wowza!

He'd take it in his stride, of course, and be super-cool. They were on a mission, he had to remember that, there to visit Tease's manufacturing site and see whether there was anything in what the whistleblower was claiming.

But still!

Cambodia.

He wondered what it was like. What language did they even speak? Was it Cambodian? And if none of them spoke English, how would he and Leanne get by? She was proficient in Russian. Would that help?

He had a ton of questions and decided he'd do some searching on the internet when he got home.

With an effort, Josh forced his mind back to Alistair Ritchie and called up his entry in Filchers' annual report.

> Alistair Ritchie (62) founded Nebox, a hub that provides strategy consulting for senior executives, in 2014. He helps companies grow by taking advantage of the opportunities offered by digital, social and environmental transitions.
> A graduate of Yale, and holder of a PhD in political science, Alistair began his career in strategy consulting (at Accenture) working for...

It was at this point that he realised the report might send

send him to sleep but wasn't going to tell him anything useful. It was dry and there was nothing that told him what motivated the man or how he had made his money.

David Parsons was the other Non-Executive Director Josh had been assigned. He called up his entry and it was almost a carbon copy of Alistair Ritchie's. Here was another smiling man in a suit, this time marginally younger at 58, with a track record of super-duper employment and entrepreneurship.

Perhaps his old friend Google would help.

He started with David Parsons this time but, again, all he got were photos and vapid descriptions of his business career. Alistair Ritchie was the same.

He moved to Facebook, then LinkedIn, X, Threads and Instagram.

After a couple of hours, he realised he had learned absolutely nothing of value.

He looked up at the whiteboard to check who Maj was researching and called over. "How are you getting on with Francois Lausanne and Meredith Holcroft, Maj? Found anything useful?"

Maj shook his head. "Very little. Meredith Holcroft is divorced, and her ex-husband is a Non-Exec at one of our competitors, but that's about it."

Helen heard this and looked across. "Same story here. We've got to get a real feel for what makes them tick. Is there any way we could meet them?"

Sam came into the office at that moment.

"Sam," Maj said. "We're struggling and wondering if we can find a way of meeting these Non-Executive Directors. Is Luke still here?"

"No. He's headed off for Portishead." She paused. "I'm luckier than you three because Gillian Ley is an employee. I've booked a slot in her diary for later this week on the pretence of needing to discuss our budget forecasts."

"What about Leanne?" Helen said.

"What about her?" Josh asked.

"She's at least met these people. I know she said the only ones she'd talked to beyond a polite hello were Dame Chittock and Janice Martin, but it might be worth exploring it further, see if she recalls anything else that might be useful."

"That's a good idea," Sam said. "Josh, can you ask her if she can spare us an hour?"

"Sure. She and I are seeing James at 3 pm. I'll ask her then."

"Thanks. In the meantime, I suggest you all plough on with your desk research. You never know what you might turn up. I'll have a word with Luke after he's finished at Avon and Somerset HQ and see if he's got any ideas."

Helen smiled. "Will that be at his place or at yours?"

"Golly," Josh said. "I didn't realise you'd moved in together. That was quick."

Sam glanced at Helen. "Thanks a bunch for that." She addressed her next comment to Josh. "We haven't moved in together, not that it's any of your business."

"But you're still…" He hesitated, not knowing how best to phrase it. "…a couple?"

Sam sighed. "Yes, we're still seeing each other, but we're taking things slowly."

"So you're not seeing him this evening?"

"Enough!"

Josh grinned. "Gotcha!" He lowered his voice to a stage whisper. "They're seeing each other this evening."

"Right," Helen said. "I'm hungry. Anyone fancy joining me for a sandwich in the canteen?"

*

Josh continued his research after lunch but was relieved when he looked at his watch and saw that it was nearly 3 pm. He made his way to James McDonald's office, but when he arrived was surprised to find a very striking and confident-looking woman in her mid-thirties standing outside.

"Oh. Ah… Hi. I was expecting Leanne."

"No Leanne I'm afraid. I'm joining you instead." She smiled and held out her hand. "I'm Ellie."

"Hi, Ellie. I'm Josh."

"I know. It's nice to meet you. I guess we'll get to know each other quite well." She lowered her voice to a whisper. "With the trip to Cambodia and everything."

"And everything?"

"Yes. There's a lot to think about."

"And you're going to be with me? Not Leanne?"

"No. She's needed on reception and, well…" She touched him gently on the arm. "I'm sure you and I will get along just fine."

"So it's you and me? Not Leanne?"

She raised her eyebrows. "That's the third time you've asked. Yes, it's you and me. Don't be nervous. I'm very experienced."

He swallowed. "You're very experienced. Right, ah…" He jerked his head around in the hope there might be someone who could save him. "Where's James?" he squealed.

"He popped out. Said he had to see Ambrose about something. Actually, if we keep our voices down we could start thinking about arrangements now."

"Arrangements. Ah… Right."

"I've been looking at hotels. I take it you want a king bed, or would you prefer a queen to be closer together?"

"Closer together?" His swallow was more of a gulp this time. "Ah…"

She touched his arm again and he almost recoiled in fright.

"You're going to love travelling business class. I'll see if

I can get the honeymoon seats. They transform into a double bed."

He shook his head violently. "I don't think so. Window or aisle please."

"You're sure Leanne wouldn't want me to book the honeymoon seats?"

"No way, Jose. She'd crucify me."

"Why would I crucify you?"

His eyes widened as he recognised his girlfriend's voice. He turned around and tried his best to smile. "Ah, Leanne. I thought…"

"Mark said he'd cover for me. Hi, Ellie."

"Hi, Leanne. I was telling Josh I'll try for Emirates' honeymoon seats."

"Oh. How lovely." She turned to Josh. "It'll be very romantic."

"Eh?"

"Sorry I'm late," James said as he walked up to them. He opened his office door and gestured for the others to go inside. "Thanks for saying you'll make all the arrangements, Ellie," he added as they took their seats around the small meeting table in front of his desk.

"I've made a list," Ellie said. "I gather you've both got passports?"

"Both of us?" Josh asked.

He looked at Ellie, then at his girlfriend and suddenly put two and two together.

"Riiii-ght," he said, drawing the word out as the penny dropped. "The king bed is for Leanne and me."

"Of course," Ellie said. "Did you think it was just for you?"

"Um, ah…"

"Joshy," Leanne said. "You are silly."

"There are two parts to the list," Ellie went on. "There's the logistics of arranging flights, visas, hotels and so on, and then there's getting you two into Tease's manufacturing facility."

"Could we say we're fans?' Leanne suggested. "I could contact them, say I'm a big fan of their clothing line and, given we're in Cambodia for a holiday, could we visit?"

"That sounds like an excellent idea," James said.

Ellie made a note on her pad. "I'll see if I can find a contact name and number."

Chapter 11

Luke was driving out of Filchers' car park when Pete rang.

"Everything okay, Pete?"

"Would you mind meeting me in Flax Bourton? Sally wants to see us."

"Sure. Are we still interviewing the man from Bath Spa Lost Property?"

"We are, but I've had to say it'll be in Bath so we'll need to double back afterwards. He's being bloody difficult, to be honest. His shift finishes at four and he said he'll come to Redbridge House straight from the station."

Fifty minutes later, Luke walked into Sally Croft's office to find the pathologist in typical pose, her pink-slack-encased legs up on her desk while she leaned back and took bites out of a Golden Delicious that was almost as bright a green as her blouse.

"Ah, the ever-gorgeous Mr Sackville," she said between mouthfuls. "Thank you for gracing us with your towering presence, Luke."

Pete was pinned to a chair in the corner of the room looking for all the world like he was trying to force his way backwards through the solid wall behind him.

"It's been too long, darling," she went on, putting the apple down on her desk and swinging her legs off in one swift movement, "How's your love life?"

"A vacuum without you in it," Luke said with a smile, knowing that she liked nothing better than to play this mock-flirtation game.

"He won't consider me," she said, gesturing in Pete's direction. "Gets too much at home, that's his trouble."

"Fat chance," Pete muttered.

She stood, picked the apple up again, took another bite

and then waved it around in a circular motion. "But seriously, boys, you've brought me a doozy this time." She returned the apple to the table and gestured to a cupboard in the corner of the room. "PPE is in there. Please put it on and follow me."

She donned scrubs and mask and, when Luke and Pete were ready, led them from the office to the examination room.

Two of the three metal tables were scrubbed clean while a blanket covered the body on the central one.

Sally stood at one end and gestured for the two men to stand on either side.

"Have you got a name for this poor man yet, DI Gilmore?"

Pete shook his head. "Nothing. His fingerprints aren't on our database. We'll have to see if there's a DNA match, or perhaps we can check dental records."

"Do you have access to records in Saudi Arabia?"

"Saudi Arabia?"

"Probably not, actually, but he's from an Arab-speaking country, I'm fairly sure of that."

"How?"

She lifted the blanket to reveal the man's body. He was lying flat on his back, his glassy eyes staring up at the ceiling.

"He was found curled in a foetal position, but his body had already relaxed from rigor mortis. The presence of eggs here..." she pointed to the man's mouth "...and here..." she indicated the man's ears "...tell me that he'd been dead for seven to ten days when he was found." She paused. "Pete, you'll need to come over here."

Pete walked around to join Luke.

Sally pointed to a tattoo on the left side of the man's thigh. "This is what points to him being from an Arab-speaking country. I'm afraid my Arabic is a bit rusty, well non-existent if I'm honest, but even my untrained eye can see it's Arab script. Do you agree?"

"It looks like it to me," Luke said. "We'll need to get an Arab speaker to tell us what it says."

Sally smiled. "That's where we're in luck. A close friend of mine is Egyptian and I took the liberty of sending her a photo. She hasn't got back to me yet, but as soon as she does I'll be in touch."

"Did you find anything else of interest?" Luke asked.

"I did, indeed I did."

She leaned forward and turned the dead man's hands over.

"See those hard, raised areas of skin here…" She pointed to the base of the man's left palm. "…and here…" She indicated the top of the palm. "…and also here." She pointed to the ends of the fingers. "These calluses have been caused by repeated friction and rubbing. You'll also have noticed the bruises and grazes on both his knees."

"Are they recent?" Luke asked.

"I believe so, yes, and whatever this poor man was doing was very rough on his hands. These…" She pointed to small scratches in the middle of the left palm. "…are no more than a couple of weeks old."

"Can you tell how he died?"

"Not with certainty, but I'm inclined to believe that he suffered an acute myocardial infarction."

"Isn't a heart attack unlikely given his age?"

"Normally, yes, but it's clear from the marks on his hands that he'd been doing extremely heavy labour which could have caused stress. That, coupled with the drugs in his system, could have blocked the flow of blood bringing oxygen to his heart muscle. Hence the infarction."

"Did you say drugs?"

"I found traces of methylphenidate in his urine. It's an amphetamine most commonly used to treat attention deficit hyperactivity disorder."

"So you think he suffered from ADHD?"

She shook her head. "No. Finding these traces after he had been dead for over a week suggests to me that he had taken an excessive amount. A massive amount in fact."

"Or been given a large dose by whoever put him into the suitcase?"

"That has to be a possibility."

She led them back to her office where they all removed their protective clothing.

"Ah," she said as she retrieved her phone from the top of her desk. "Shoshana has replied." She read the message and looked across at Luke and Pete. "I wasn't too far away with my guess of Saudi Arabia."

She handed Luke her phone.

"'Idlib is my Freedom'," he read before passing the phone to Pete. "I can't say I'm any clearer. I take it you know what Idlib means?"

She smiled. "It doesn't mean anything. It's a place, one of the few regions controlled by anti-government forces in a country that was in a civil war for over a decade." She paused. "I'd bet my bottom dollar on that poor man being from Syria."

Chapter 12

"PC Warwick, isn't it?" Luke said as the young uniformed constable opened the door to Redbridge House.

"Well remembered, Mr Sackville."

"Call me Luke, please."

"Mr Simpson hasn't arrived yet, ah…" She blushed slightly as she added, "…Luke."

"That's okay. I'll wait in the interview room. DI Gilmore should be here at any minute."

"Can I fetch you a coffee?"

"I can get my own."

"No, please let me." She grimaced. "To be honest, it'll be something to do. It's boring as hell here on a weekday. The only action all morning was a techie coming in to sort Dave out, but he got nowhere."

"Who's Dave?"

She laughed. "Dave's not a person. Dave's our interview recording kit. It stopped working last week."

There was a knock at the door and she opened it to let Pete in.

"Pete," Luke said, "the audio recording machine's bust. What do you think about PC Warwick joining us in the interview to take notes?"

"I don't see why not."

She smiled, clearly pleased with this. "What's Mr Simpson done?"

"He's not suspected of anything," Pete said, "but he found a body and we want to talk to him about it."

"Intriguing. Right, if you make yourselves comfortable in the interview room, I'll get the coffees in."

Two rounds of drinks later, Luke was beginning to think their interviewee was going to be a no-show.

"I'll give him a call," Pete said, picking his phone up from the table.

He rang and after thirty seconds or so it went to voicemail. Pete started to leave a message when a voice came on the line, shouting loudly enough for Luke to hear every word.

"Get off my back! I'm outside."

Pete was about to respond when there was a click and the line went dead.

"Charming." He looked across at Luke. "I told you he was a difficult sod."

A couple of minutes later, PC Warwick opened the door, stepped in and then closed it behind her.

"This is embarrassing," she said in a whisper.

"What is?" Luke asked.

"Mr Simpson's arrived and the thing is, I know him, although I'm pretty sure he doesn't remember me."

"How do you know him?"

"He used to drive our school bus. We called him Skiver Simpson."

"Why was that?"

She was about to answer when there was a click behind her and the door was pushed violently open, swinging 180 degrees and smashing against the wall.

The man who strode in was grossly overweight. He was also perspiring heavily despite it being mid-January.

"Are we getting on with this or what?" he demanded.

"We'll be with you in a moment, Mr Simpson," Pete said.

The man grunted and left the room.

PC Warwick closed the door after him.

"Are you okay to take the lead, Pete?" Luke asked.

"Sure, but feel free to leap in if you need to ask anything."

"I suggest we start before he blows a gasket. Would you mind asking him to come in, PC Warwick?"

She went out and returned a few seconds later.

Simpson followed her in and sneered, clearly pleased with himself. "I thought that would get you moving."

"Please take a seat, Mr Simpson," Pete said, gesturing to the seat opposite him.

Luke sat next to their interviewee and the constable sat opposite him next to Pete.

"Why does this need three of you?" Simpson demanded.

"Mr Sackville and I will conduct the interview," Pete said, "and PC Warwick will take notes."

"Haven't you got a machine to record everything?"

"Unfortunately, it's broken."

"Typical." He sniffed and looked scornfully at the PC before returning his attention to Pete. "How do I know she's writing things down accurately?"

"I assure you, Mr Simpson, that when the notes are typed up you'll have a chance to review everything and make changes before signing your witness statement."

"Does that mean I have to come in again?"

"If you don't mind?"

"And if I do mind?"

"If I may say so, Mr Simpson," Luke said, "you seem on edge. Are you worried about this interview for some reason?"

Simpson glared at Luke but ignored the question. He indicated Pete with his thumb. "He called you Mr Sackville. What are you doing here if you're not a policeman?"

"Luke is a police consultant," Pete said. "Now, I'm sure you're a busy man, Mr Simpson, so let's get on, shall we?"

Simpson wiped the sweat off his brow with the back of his hand and grunted again.

Pete took this as agreement.

"I'd like to start with your personal details, Mr Simpson."

"Why?"

"Purely for the record. What's your full name?"

"Barry Simpson."

"Address?"

"3 Fullington Court, Twerton."

"Date of birth?"

Simpson sighed and said, almost sulkily, "Third of August, 1985."

This surprised Luke. He had the man down as a decade or so older.

"Thank you," Pete said. "Now, please tell us how you found the body."

"Have you found out his name?"

"Mr Simpson, this interview is for us to collect information from you, not to share our findings." He paused. "Please tell us what happened yesterday."

"I got to Bath Spa at around two in the afternoon. "

"That's late to start a shift."

"I was in Bristol first. I'm based in Temple Meads but we're closed to the public on Sundays so most weeks I travel to one of our stations to check what's in their stores."

"I take it you arrived by train?"

Simpson gave him a disparaging look. "Obviously."

"Were you on your own in Bath Spa's Lost Property office?"

"I wouldn't call it an office. Large cupboard more like." He glanced briefly around the interview room. "It's about half the size of this."

"But you were on your own?"

"Yeah. Why are you asking?"

"Simply to understand who else was around. Go on."

"I opened the door and the smell hit me straight away. It was like rotting meat mixed with manure." He shivered at the memory. "It was horrible."

"What did you do next?"

"I thought it had to be a dead mouse or rat or something, so I decided to move everything to find it."

"Was there much to move?"

"Loads. Mainly small items, you know, handbags, briefcases, that kind of thing. The suitcase was at the back and I left it until last because it looked heavy. When I pulled it out I noticed it didn't have a tag."

"A tag?"

"Yeah. When an item's brought in, a ticket's tied to it saying when and where it was found and who found it."

"And there was no ticket?"

"That's what I said, didn't I?"

"I don't understand, Mr Simpson," Luke said. "The police were told the case was left on the London train six days ago."

"Yeah. That's what I told them."

"How did you know if there was no tag?"

"The trains through Bath Spa all go to or from London so it's hardly rocket science."

"Why six days?"

"It seemed like a good guess, given the smell."

"A good guess?"

"Yeah."

Pete sighed. "So the fact is that we don't know when or how the suitcase got into the Lost Property room?"

Simpson shrugged. "Not exactly. I could be right about the six days though. I suspect someone forgot the tag, that's all."

"What did you do after you pulled the suitcase out?"

"I opened it."

"Why?"

"The smell. I told you."

"You said you thought it was a dead rat."

"I did until I pulled the case out, but when I was close to it, well, it was obvious the smell was coming from inside."

"So you opened it?"

"Yeah. I thought it might have fruit in it. I didn't expect

there to be a body."

"Fruit? You said it smelt like rotting meat."

"Kind of, but also like fruit that had gone off."

"And when you opened it?"

"As soon as I pulled the zip a few inches it was obvious that's where the smell was coming from." He shuddered. "It was then that I saw his foot."

"You said on the phone it was a man. How did you know that just from seeing a foot?"

Simpson grunted. "It was obvious from the size, wasn't it?"

"What did you do next?"

"I phoned the police."

"What did you do with the suitcase?"

"Nothing. Look at the CCTV if you don't believe me."

"It's not that I don't believe you, Mr Simpson. I'm merely trying to clarify what happened."

"I told you. I didn't do nothing to the suitcase after I found him. I rang 999 then went home."

"You didn't wait for the police to arrive?"

"No." He sniffed again. "Is that everything? Can I go now?"

Pete looked over at Luke. "Have you got more questions?"

"Just one." He smiled across at the interviewee. "Mr Simpson, six days seems very precise. Why six and not seven or eight? For that matter, why even hazard a guess?"

For the first time, Simpson looked cagey.

"I told you, it was just a guess."

"I see."

"Okay," Pete said. "Thank you for coming in, Mr Simpson. We'll let you know when the statement is ready for you to check and sign. Please can you show our visitor out, PC Warwick?"

She returned to the interview room after seeing him to the front door.

"He hasn't changed," she said. "He was always abrasive and none of my school friends liked him."

"You said he was known as Skiver Simpson," Luke said. "How did he get that nickname?"

She chuckled. "At least once a week we'd have another driver, Mr Patel. He was lovely. One of the girls asked him if Mr Simpson had some kind of illness because he was off so often, and he told her there was nothing wrong with him other than being lazy and liking a lie-in. The name came from that."

"I see." He thought about this for a second. "You know, Pete, I wouldn't mind betting that Barry Simpson told his boss he was working in Bath Spa two Sundays running, but on the first Sunday went straight home. That's why he told the police the suitcase had been there six days."

"I see what you're getting at. If it had been there longer and he hadn't been AWOL he'd have seen it the previous weekend."

"Exactly. We also don't know that it was found on a train." He paused. "Simpson said there's a CCTV camera outside the Lost Property room. I suggest you ask one of your team to look through the recordings to see who put the suitcase in there and when."

"Good idea. I'll do that."

Chapter 13

Sam was looking forward to seeing Hannah but she had to admit she was disappointed that she and Luke were spending the evening apart.

It had been her idea to limit the time they spent together socially, but doing so was harder than she had expected. He was amusing and great company, plus he'd revealed a romantic side to his character that she hadn't seen coming. Bringing her gorgeous flowers on Saturday evening had been a lovely surprise.

Right now, all she wanted to do was sink into his arms and let the worries of the world fade away.

However, she felt it was important to take things slowly.

Why, she wasn't quite sure.

No, that wasn't true.

She knew damn well why she didn't want their relationship to move too quickly.

It was for fear of rejection, or worse that he would turn out to be a disappointment, to have a hidden, dark side to his personality.

She'd been burned before and she couldn't bear for it to happen again.

Tony had been a pain but wasn't all bad. She didn't seem to be able to eliminate him from her life but he was innocuous enough. Stupid but harmless.

Ollie, on the other hand, had been a nightmare. He had seemed wonderful at first, and they'd even talked about moving in together, but he'd turned out to be intensely jealous. Ironically, he had been fanatically jealous of Luke when there had been nothing between him and Sam.

Those men were in her past though. Right now she was in a relationship with Luke and loving every minute.

It dawned on her that although it might be sensible not to see each other every evening, there was no reason not to ring him.

"Hi," he said when he answered. "How was your day?"

"Okay." She didn't want to discuss work. That could wait for the morning. "Fancy coming to mine for dinner tomorrow? I was thinking steak."

"I'd love to. Anything planned for tonight?"

"Yes. I'm seeing Hannah."

They carried on talking, subjects ranging from her mother's latest paramour, to how Luke's children were faring at University, and on to the latest TV crime series she'd become hooked on. As always, conversation flowed easily and twenty minutes had passed before she knew it.

"I'll have to go, Luke. I'm supposed to be meeting Hannah in half an hour and I need to get ready."

"You look beautiful whatever you wear, Sam."

"Stop it."

"I'll see you in the morning."

"Take care, Luke."

It was a couple of seconds before he replied.

"You too, Sam."

She hung up and found herself wondering why he had hesitated. Was there something else he was thinking of saying?

She shook her head. No point in trying to guess what was on his mind. She needed to have a quick shower and get on her way.

Fifteen minutes later she messaged Hannah to say she was running late and set off for the pub. It was cold, but she was well wrapped up and The Curfew was only a mile or so from her flat. A brisk walk would do her good.

After a couple of minutes, she turned off Cleveland Walk to head down Bathwick Hill towards the roundabout. It was quiet, though that wasn't surprising given the chill in the air and the fact that it was a Monday, not a common going-out day.

She was halfway down the hill when she registered that someone had been walking behind her for several minutes. Nothing odd in that, but after the stunt Ollie had pulled the last time she'd seen him she had the ridiculous idea that it might be him.

She kept walking, thinking how stupid she was being. It doubtless wasn't Ollie, just some stranger walking into Bath as she was doing.

Odd that he or she was exactly keeping pace with her though.

She walked faster, but whoever it was sped up to maintain the gap between them.

They were no more than twenty yards behind. Perhaps fifteen.

Rather than Ollie, could it be a mugger? Some drugged-up individual who was desperate for their next fix and prepared to attack a woman on her own. They might even be armed. Knives were frighteningly common these days.

What was normally a busy road now struck her as ominously quiet. There was no one on the opposite side, and the occasional car drove past but she could hardly wave one down.

Should she stop and wait for him or her to walk by? Or would that only serve to force their hand?

Perhaps she should ring someone. Luke perhaps? But what could he do? Even if she rang the police they would take several minutes to get there.

And besides, all it was was someone walking closely behind her.

Much too close.

She needed to act before it was too late. Her karate had come to her rescue before and if necessary she would have to rely on it now.

She turned to confront whoever it was.

Chapter 14

"FUCK OFF AND STOP FOLLOWING ME!"

As she shouted these words Sam moved her feet so that they were shoulder-width apart, turned her toes inward at an angle and tensed her knees.

This was soto-hachiji-dachi, a classic ready stance in karate.

She'd been wrong about the distance. Her pursuer was no more than ten yards away. It had felt like more than that because she'd heard the footsteps and had been thinking in terms of someone Ollie's size.

But this was no Ollie.

Although clad in a heavy-duty coat, it was clear from her build that this was a woman, and a slight woman at that, but that didn't make her any less of a threat. If she was high on drugs who knew what she might do?

Her hood was up and her face was hidden.

"Why are you following me?" Sam demanded.

A car passed and the headlights illuminated the woman's face for a split-second making it clear that she was young, late twenties perhaps. Although her eyes were wide and staring she didn't look dosed-up.

Her hands were in her coat pockets.

Sam kept her voice strong and strident.

"Take your hands out where I can see them, but take them out slowly."

The woman took two paces forward.

"Why, Sammy?" she said, her words rasping, gravelly and almost, but not quite, Marilyn-Monroe-husky. "I ain't carrying nuffin."

Those six words were enough to dissolve away Sam's fears. She'd never met the woman but she'd recognise the voice anywhere.

"For fuck's sake, Jazelle," she said, her words a hissed whisper this time.

"Why do ya keep swearin', Sammy? Tone says you ain't the swearin' type."

"I'm not normally."

"You abnormal today then?"

Sam ignored the question. "Why have you been following me, Jazelle?"

"I weren't followin'. I was trying to catch up. Trouble is, you kept rushing off every time I went faster."

"But why?"

"Tone sent me. He needs a favour."

"Why couldn't he talk to me himself?"

"You told him not to contact you."

"So he sent you instead so that you could frighten me half to death by creeping up behind me?"

She shrugged. "Yeah."

"Okay. What's the favour?"

Jazelle lowered her voice to a whisper. "He's got a problem with his vestibules."

"His vestibules?"

"Yeah, the right one. It's swollen." She held out her right hand, curved her thumb and fingers as if she was clutching a football and then lowered it to her groin. "All swollen up like a basketball."

"Like a basketball?"

"Well not quite, but big. We ain't had Posh and Becks for over a week."

Sam was pretty sure she knew what Jazelle meant by 'Posh and Becks' and didn't want to go there.

"But I don't understand. Why come to me?"

"Well, he's all magna carta, ain't he? Doctor banned him from the surgery."

"You mean persona non grata."

"That as well. He says you'll have the special lotion

from when it happened before."

"Jazelle, this never happened when I was going out with Tony."

"Yeah, it did, only he didn't tell you."

"I think I would have noticed if he had a swollen testicle."

"He said it happened while your Aunt Flo was visiting. You know, code red in your lady garden."

Sam held her hand up. "I understand what you mean, Jazelle."

"He says he hid his nut butter behind the bath panel."

"Did you say 'nut butter'?"

"Yeah. It's called 'Tame the Beast'."

Sam sighed. "Jazelle, he really ought to see a nurse or a doctor. I'm not sure nut butter will solve his problem."

"I told you. He's magna carta at the surgery."

"What about A&E at the Royal United? They'll see him."

"Oh yeah. We hadn't thought of that."

This latest example of Tony and Jazelle's stupidity made Sam feel like swearing again but she decided to let it ride.

"Well," she lied, "it's been nice meeting you, Jazelle."

"Yeah. You too. The offer's still open you know."

"If you mean what I believe you referred to as a 'mange a twa', the answer's a definitive no."

"Nah. Not that. Tone and I are inclusive now."

"Exclusive."

"Yeah. It's just me and him. We're, like, forever."

"That's good to hear."

"What I meant was the offer to come to our wedding. I sent you an invitation."

"You did?"

"Yeah." Jazelle hesitated. "At least I think I did. Maybe I didn't post it. I wrote it though."

"I think I'll have to say no."

"Fair enough. But please, if you talk to Tone, don't tell

him."

"I'm sure he won't mind if I don't come."

"I meant don't tell him about the wedding. He doesn't know we're getting married yet."

Sam shook her head. "I'd better get on, Jazelle. I'm meeting someone."

"What about the lotion?"

"If you need it give me a ring, but I'm sure A&E will be able to sort him out."

"Okay. Byesies."

"Goodnight, Jazelle."

Chapter 15

"Thanks for coming up again, Leanne," Sam said as she opened the door. "We'd better get your fingerprints on the system so you can access the Ethics Room without one of us having to let you in."

"I can do that," Josh said.

"Great."

A few seconds later Luke walked in.

"Clever that," Josh said, looking first at Luke and then at Sam. "Coming in separately. Keeps it a secret."

"We're not keeping anything a secret, son," Luke said.

Josh fired double finger guns at him and grinned. "Course not, guv."

"Right everyone," Sam said. "Let's make a start."

Helen walked to the whiteboard while the others sat around the table in the centre of the room.

Luke looked across at Sam. "Are you okay to take the lead?"

"Happy to." She turned to Leanne. "Leanne, Josh has probably told you that we struggled to find out much about Filchers' Board members online. We know the companies they've worked for but not a whole lot more. We're hoping you can give us a bit of insight into what they're like."

Leanne smiled. "I'll do my best."

"I've printed off photos of each of them," Maj said. He went over to his desk, picked up the printouts and passed them to Helen.

"Let's start at the top with our Finance Director," Sam said.

Helen found her photo and stuck it on the whiteboard next to her name.

"And before you start, Leanne," Luke said, "Let's be

clear that we want you to be candid. We want your opinions more than anything. Anything you say stays in the room."

Josh nodded. "Pretend we're in Las Vegas."

Everyone turned to look at him.

"Why would that help?" Luke asked.

"It's a saying, isn't it? What happens in Vegas stays in Vegas. It can be like that with the Ethics Room. What happens in Ethics stays in Ethics."

"Like Colchester," Helen said.

"Eh?"

"Colchester stays in Essex."

"I said Ethics not…"

Luke raised his voice. "Enough! Leanne, please continue."

"Gillian Ley is a stereotypical accountant," Leanne began.

"Like me," Sam suggested with a smile.

"Sorry, Sam, I forgot. No, she's absolutely nothing like you, although she's about your height. What are you, 5ft 7?"

"About that, yes."

"She's very quiet and…" she pointed to the photo "…she always wears those horn-rimmed glasses. To be honest, if you met her out of work you'd never dream she was so senior in the organisation."

"I'm with you on that," Luke said. "I've only met her a few times but she's a genuine introvert. Very smart though."

They continued discussing Gillian Ley for several minutes before moving onto Francois Lausanne.

The team spent the next hour working their way through all seven members of the Board, combining what they had found on the internet and social media with information Leanne, and in some cases Luke, had gleaned from talking to them.

Sam took copious notes throughout.

"Thanks very much, Leanne," she said when they'd finished. She looked up at the board, and the brief summaries Helen had added under each name. "That's added a bit of colour which is useful. I'll email my notes to everyone."

PROJECT WHAT

Gillian Ley
- 48, Finance Director, Introvert, very high IQ, married, 2 grown-up children

Francois Lausanne
- 55, poor English, narcissistic, single

Meredith Holcroft
- 49, self-made woman, brought up in poverty, divorced, no children

Dame Chittock
- 69, friendly, Labour Party supporter, president of numerous charities, single

Janice Martin
- 56, outgoing, quick-tempered, trained as a doctor, on 2nd marriage, 2 children

Alistair Ritchie

- 62, ex-MP, technology expert, married, 2 children

David Parsons
- 58, ex-barrister, founded right-wing think tank, married, 1 child

Once everyone had returned to their desks, and Leanne to reception, Luke called Sam over.

"Did you have a good time with Hannah last night?"

She smiled as she remembered her encounter with Jazelle. "Yes, thanks."

"Why are you smiling?"

"Something that happened on the way to the pub. I'll tell you about it this evening." She paused and lowered her voice. "That session was useful, but I'm not sure it moved us very far forward."

"I agree, but I've had a thought. You know I've got to present to the Board next week?"

"Yes."

"I'm not sure you're going to like this idea much, but I was thinking of it not just being me presenting. That way it would give others in the team a chance to see the Board members in action."

"Why wouldn't I like the idea?"

"Well, my thinking is that I present with Maj and Helen."

"Why would I mind that?"

"If there are three of us, then it would be unfair to ask Glen to stand up on his own, and I…"

Sam held her hand up. "Hang on a minute. You're not suggesting…" She looked across at him. "You can't seriously expect me to present with that jumped-up, over-inflated, steroid-fuelled…"

"It'll only be for fifteen minutes."

"Come on, Luke. Fifteen minutes in his company is fifteen minutes too many. Plus he and I will have to spend time preparing." She paused. "He's stupid, he's an out-and-out misogynist, he's…" She stuttered to a stop.

Luke smiled across at her.

"So you'll do it?"

She sighed and took a deep breath. "I'll do it."

"Thanks. I owe you."

"You certainly do."

Chapter 16

Erebus stared at the image of Wynna on her laptop, finding it hard to believe what she'd just said.

"What do you mean Fern's back?"

"I saw her when I was recruiting in Bath yesterday," Wynna said. "She's gothed up now, with black clothes, dark make-up, rings in her lips, that kind of stuff."

"I thought she'd killed herself."

"That's what we thought too."

"It was on her Facebook page," Skylar added. "Her mother posted that she'd taken an overdose."

"You're sure it was her, Wynna?" Erebus asked, ignoring Skylar.

"I'm certain."

"Did she see you?"

"I don't think so."

"You don't think so! That's not good enough. If she saw you she might decide to say something to the media. She's able to identify me, remember."

"That's not the case," Skylar said. "The AI avatar always hid your face."

Erebus moved closer to the screen.

"Don't you remember that incident where you forgot to turn it on?"

Skylar swallowed. "Oh yes," he said. "It only happened that one time though."

"Once is enough."

"I remember," Wynna said. "You joined that zoom call and the avatar was off for a couple of minutes. It was with Fern, Celestina, Brenonna and Valmoria."

"We know Celestina's not a problem," Skylar said.

Erebus sighed. "And how can you be certain in her

case? You clearly made a mistake with Fern."

"If you remember, I was, ah…" He hesitated for a second. "I was there when she jumped."

Erebus laughed. "Oh yes, of course. I'd forgotten that you'd facilitated her departure. What about Brenonna and Valmoria? Are you sure that neither of them will present us with any issues?"

"Definitely not," Skylar said. "They're 100% committed to the cause." He grinned. "They're so besotted with Beacon that they'll have completely forgotten they ever saw your face."

"Mmm. How can you be so certain? I'm high profile and the last thing I need is people spreading malicious stories about me."

"I'm with Skylar," Wynna said. "Even if they do remember seeing you, I can't see them telling anyone. They've stopped contact with their friends and families and neither of them even goes outdoors any more."

"Is that their own decision, or do you have to lock them in?"

"They're way beyond being able to make their own decisions, but we lock the outside door anyway. We don't want a repeat of what happened with Fern."

"Too right, we don't. Skylar, what about their financial contributions? It costs money to house and feed them. Are we still making enough?"

"Plenty from Brenonna. Her family are still putting £3,000 into her account every month."

"Good. And Valmoria?"

"Her situation is more challenging."

"In what way?"

"We're still receiving rental from her apartment, but the management costs are high and it looks like it needs a new boiler."

"Mmm. I think we should cut our losses before she starts to haemorrhage money. Wynna, tell Valmoria she needs to sell her apartment, that she is close to Level Rising Sun but that she needs to make a final push to remove her aura's negative influences." Erebus smiled. "Final push is an appropriate term, I think."

"Why?" Skylar asked.

"Because you, dear Skylar, will be facilitating her departure once the sale goes through in the same way that you facilitated Celestina's. Valmoria will be worthless to us once she no longer owns her flat and it will be time to wave goodbye."

Chapter 17

Wynna collapsed back into her chair as soon as the Zoom call had finished.

She needed to make sense of what had been said about Celestina's suicide.

The young woman had thrown herself off Churchill Bridge in the centre of Bath, been knocked out by the fall and drowned before her body could be recovered.

According to Erebus, Skylar had 'facilitated her departure'. Could there be an innocent explanation or was it as sinister as it sounded?

Had he persuaded her to jump?

Worse, was it conceivable that he had pushed her?

Wynna was no saint, she knew that, but the idea that Skylar had played a part in Celestina's death horrified her.

What was more, Erebus had suggested that he would need to do the same to Valmoria when her flat had been sold.

She had to speak to him and find out the truth.

He answered after a couple of rings.

"Hello."

"Skylar, I need to talk to you."

"What do you mean?" He laughed. "We've only just finished talking."

"It's…" She hesitated. "I can't do this over the phone. Can we meet? Where are you?"

"Is everything okay, Wynna? You sound troubled."

Troubled isn't the half of it, she thought, but said, "I need to understand something that was said. It's probably nothing, but…"

"I take it you're at Beacon House?"

"Yes."

She didn't know where he lived but had always assumed it was Bath, even though he looked after Beacon's 'clients' in several towns and cities across the South of England.

"Is this urgent? I have a Zoom call with Southampton this afternoon."

"Please, Skylar. It won't take long. I can get a bus to Bath if necessary."

He sighed. "Okay. Do you know the Green Rocket Cafe?"

"Yes."

"I'll see you there at 12:30."

"Thank you," she said, but he had already hung up.

She donned her coat and put her head into the dormitory where Brenonna, Valmoria and their latest female recruit, Kyris, were hard at work. It occurred to her to tell them she was going out, but there was no point. They probably wouldn't hear her anyway, so intensely were they focused on their preparations for the next day's mentoring session.

After locking the door, she walked briskly to the bus stop next to Glastonbury Town Hall.

When she got to the cafe she bought herself a cappuccino and sat down to wait for Skylar. This would be only the second time she'd met him face to face, though they talked several times a week on the phone or over Zoom.

It was two years since he had recruited her, and it had been insanely profitable. She wasn't earning as much as him she was sure, and nowhere near what Erebus, Beacon's founder, must be making, but she now had over £70,000 squirrelled away.

It was a far better money-earner than her previous work and, while also involving managing young women, it was more satisfying and felt less dirty, even though she still used drugs to keep her girls in check.

Working as a recruiter and manager for Beacon was

also much safer. In her previous role, she had had to deal with many a punter who didn't know when they'd gone too far. One poor wretch had died as a result of the beating inflicted on her.

She saw Skylar walk in and he spotted her, came directly over and sat down opposite.

"Let's keep this brief."

"Aren't you having a coffee?"

"No time. So what's troubling you, Wynna?"

She took a sip of her coffee and looked into his eyes, trying to decide how much she could trust him.

He stared back.

"Come on, out with it."

She lowered her voice. "Promise me you won't tell Erebus about this conversation."

"I promise. What's up?"

"That conversation, about Celestina."

"What about it?"

"Erebus said you facilitated her suicide."

"And you're not comfortable with that?"

"It sounds like you… well, as if you…"

He didn't let her finish. "Wynna, are you trying to tell me you've suddenly acquired scruples?"

He laughed, but it was dry and humourless and his eyes remained cold as he leaned forward so that he was only inches from her face.

"You're a pimp, Anna Grayling, nothing more, nothing less."

She was shocked by the use of her real name.

"I'm not a pimp."

"You take advantage of women. Before we met, you pimped their bodies and now you pimp their minds. You have no right to be principled."

"I managed a high-class escort agency."

"You ran a brothel."

This was an argument she wasn't going to win and she

reverted to her earlier question. "In what way did you facilitate Celestina's suicide, Skylar?"

He sat back. "That was a throw-away line. I had nothing to do with what that stupid girl did to herself."

"And what about Valmoria? Erebus said you'll need to handle her departure in the same way you handled Celestina's. What does that mean?"

He laughed his dry, humourless chuckle again. "You're getting your knickers in a twist over nothing. Once Valmoria's flat is sold she'll need to leave Beacon. I will ensure she doesn't tell anyone about us, that's all."

"How will you do that?"

"A threat or two. She has family, remember."

"And that's all?"

"Of course, that's all. What did you think I might do?"

"I don't know. I…"

"I'm going to do you a favour and not tell Erebus about this conversation. It won't go down well."

"Thank you, Skylar. I've been stupid. Sorry."

He looked at her for a moment and then stood up.

She watched as he turned and left the cafe.

Chapter 18

Skylar rang Erebus as soon as he returned home.

"What is it? I'm about to go into a meeting."

"We have a problem with Wynna."

"In what way?"

"She didn't like what you and I said about Celestina and Valmoria." He paused. "About my role in particular."

"That's ridiculous. Both women were depressed and close to killing themselves when we recruited them into Beacon. We gave them extra months of life, for heaven's sake. In Valmoria's case, she's had nearly two years."

"I know, but…"

"Do you think Wynna will do anything about it?"

"I'm not sure. She seemed very upset."

Erebus let out a deep sigh.

"She does a good job, but I can't afford to risk her telling anyone. Do we have anyone who can step in to take her place?"

"Yes. I have someone who would be ideal."

"Good. In that case please deal with Wynna."

"Deal with her?"

Erebus laughed. "You know exactly what I mean, Skylar. Please don't pretend otherwise. She's little more than a jumped-up harlot so she won't be missed, but make sure you cover your tracks."

"I will, Erebus."

"Good. Let me know when it's done."

Chapter 19

Luke parked a few yards down from The Good Bear Cafe and checked his watch. It was only 8:15 which gave him a few minutes before Pete arrived.

He ordered a double espresso from Mauro, the owner, and went to their usual table in the corner.

His daughter answered on the first ring.

"Morning, Dad."

"Hi, Chloe. I got your WhatsApp. You said your friend could do with talking to me?"

"Yes. It's Denver."

"Denver? You haven't mentioned her before."

Chloe laughed. "Denver's a man, Dad. He's one of the lecturers at Uni."

"So why does he want to talk to me?"

"He's got himself into a mess."

"What sort of a mess?"

"It's complicated and I think it would be best if he told you face-to-face. I was wondering if we could come down at the weekend?"

"For the weekend? He's obviously a very close friend." She didn't reply and that told him all he needed to know. "How long have you been seeing each other?"

"Da-aa-ad!" She stretched the word out.

"I was a detective, remember." Again, no answer. "Well? How long?"

"Only a few weeks, but he's…" She paused. "I like him a lot, Dad. I'm sure you will too."

Luke looked up to see Pete had come in. He nodded hello as Pete headed towards the counter.

"Yes of course you can come down, darling." He hesitated as a thought occurred to him. "You said Denver's a lecturer?"

"Yes, he teaches Philosophy."

"So he's a lot older than you."

"Not really. He's twenty-nine."

"Twenty-nine! But you're only nineteen."

"I'm nearly twenty, Dad."

"But that's ten years. He's ten years older."

"Dad, that's less than the gap between you and Sam."

That's different, was the thought that came into his head.

"And don't say 'that's different'."

"I wouldn't dream of it."

"So can we come down?"

"Of course you can."

"Great. We'll drive down on Saturday morning. Thanks, Dad. Oh, and no need to make up the spare bed. We'll use my room."

He swallowed. "Of course. Bye, Chloe."

"Bye, Dad. Love you."

Pete sat down opposite, mug in hand.

"You look troubled."

Luke smiled. "Not really. How old are your girls, Pete?"

"Sophie's thirteen and Grace is eleven. Why?"

"I was thinking how quickly they grow up, that's all."

"I take it that was Chloe you were on the phone to?"

"Yes."

"And she's got a boyfriend?"

"Got it in one. She's bringing him down at the weekend." He paused. "I hope he's good enough for her."

Pete laughed. "Why don't you get a lie detector? You know, like Robert de Niro did in 'Meet the Parents'."

Luke echoed his laugh. "That might be going a bit far, but I'll certainly be checking him out." He took a sip of his coffee. "So, any progress with our mysterious Syrian?"

"Not yet. One of my team's looking through CCTV this morning so hopefully that will turn something up."

"And no tie-up with missing persons?"

Pete shook his head. "Nothing."

"Have we got much of a Syrian population around here?"

"Not many. There are a few refugee families who settled in Bath back in 2021 and 2022. DS Hewitt and I are going to call in on them today, but until we turn something else up I don't think we'll need to call on your services."

"Fair enough. I'm pretty busy at Filchers anyway."

Pete's phone rang.

"Excuse me a minute, Luke." He accepted the call and listened to the caller for a few seconds. "Any ID?" He waited while the other person answered. "Okay. I'll be there as soon as I can."

He hung up and looked over at Luke.

"Sorry, I'm going to have to go." He drained his coffee and stood up.

"What is it, Pete?"

"Another body."

"Similar circumstances?"

Pete shook his head. "Completely different. This one looks like a suicide. Someone spotted a woman's body in the water beneath Churchill Bridge. They haven't checked for ID yet."

"Okay. I'll catch you later."

He watched as Pete headed out of the cafe and found himself half-wishing he was still in the police.

Not that Filchers didn't have its share of excitement, more than he'd anticipated if he was honest. Plus if he'd stayed in the police he'd never have met Sam.

Yes, on balance he was definitely better off where he was.

He drank the rest of his coffee, thanked Mauro and returned to the Beemer.

Twenty minutes later he arrived at Filchers where Leanne waved him over to the reception desk.

"Thanks again for involving me," she said.

"No problem. How's the planning for Cambodia going?"

She laughed. "Joshy's decided to learn some of the local language and his attempts are hilarious."

Luke smiled. "I bet."

He headed for the stairs and his phone rang before he reached the first floor.

"Luke Sackville."

"Luke, it's Ellie. Would you mind popping up to Ambrose's office?"

"Of course. Is there a problem?"

"Not at all. There are some people he wants you to meet."

Chapter 20

Ellie smiled at Luke as he approached.

"He says to go on in."

"Thanks, Ellie."

He went in and Ambrose immediately got to his feet.

"Ah, Luke," he said as he strode over. "Thank you so much for coming up." He turned to face the sofas. "I don't think you've met these two good ladies, have you?"

"No, I haven't." Luke smiled across at the two women.

The older of the two had neat silver hair in curls, ruddy cheeks and a beatific smile and he realised this had to be Dame Chittock.

"Hello, Luke," she said. "I'm Sarah Chittock. Sorry I can't stand up to greet you properly. Problem with the hips, I'm afraid." She gave a little chuckle. "It's what age does to you. Ambrose has been telling us what a difference you've made since you arrived."

Luke turned to the CEO. "That's very kind of you, Ambrose."

Ambrose waved this away and gestured to the younger woman sitting next to the Dame. "And this is Janice Martin, another of our Non-Execs."

"Hello," Janice said. She also smiled, though it seemed less natural, and she made no effort to stand.

"Please take a seat," Ambrose said, gesturing to the nearer sofa.

Luke sat down.

"The reason I asked you to pop up," Ambrose went on, "was to introduce you to Sarah and Janice ahead of your presentation to the Board next week."

"We're very interested in what you might have to say," Janice said. "The idea of having a Head of Ethics is novel, to say the least."

"I think it's a wonderful move," Sarah said. "Ethics is an important consideration in every aspect of our lives, and with a large organisation like Filchers it's vital we have a handle on corporate and social responsibility."

"I agree with you, Sarah, but surely it should be part of everyone's remit rather than require a dedicated department."

"And that little exchange," Ambrose said, with a twinkle in his eye, "illustrates why your presentation will be so useful, Luke. There is, I fear, a little persuading to be done."

It was clear to Luke that Ambrose had invited him up because of Project What and not because of his talk to the Board. He was allowing him to meet two of the Non-Execs and get a feel for their personalities.

He needed to make the most of the opportunity.

"You've both been associated with Filchers longer than I have," he said. "What are your views on the company's approach to ethics over the years?"

"That's a good question," Sarah began. She smiled again and it seemed very genuine. He found himself warming to the woman.

She looked at Janice. "Do you mind if I go first?"

"Not at all."

"Well, if I'm honest, Luke, I believe Filchers has been remiss. As Ambrose knows, I am associated with several charitable ventures."

"Sarah is being modest as usual," Ambrose said. "She is President of four charities, and founded one herself over a decade ago which has helped hundreds of children to escape poverty."

"Stop it, Ambrose," Sarah said, though Luke could tell she was pleased to hear these words. "You'll make me blush."

She turned back to Luke.

"The fact is, Luke, that actions which are morally

wrong, or that go against social standards, rules, or beliefs, are not only bad for the organisation, but also do intense harm to the individual." She hesitated. "I am aware of incidents that happened before you joined which, to say the least, put Filchers in a bad light." She turned to Ambrose. "You will recall that incident with the Bierhoff Finance Manager."

"I do indeed," Ambrose said. "What he did was disgraceful."

"And it went on too long."

"What did he do?" Luke asked.

Sarah shook her head. "I find it hard to talk about." She looked across at the Chief Executive. "Ambrose?"

"He used his power to seduce three young graduates, Luke, all of them men might I add. It only came to light when the mother of one of them came to me personally."

"If you had been here, Luke," Sarah said, "the first of them would have been able to flag it to you and it would have been nipped in the bud and that awful man dealt with."

"I'm not so sure," Janice said. "He could have contacted Ambrose, as the mother of the third young man did, or indeed Human Resources. I don't see how having an Ethics Team would have made a significant difference."

"We have a dedicated email address and hotline which are heavily publicised," Luke said, "and we guarantee confidentiality to any whistleblowers."

"Mmm. Do you receive many contacts through this route?"

"Several each week."

"Give us an example."

"You'll appreciate that I can't give names, or any information that might give the caller's identity away."

"Of course."

Luke glanced at Ambrose who nodded his head subtly.

"We had a caller this week who told us that someone

senior in the organisation was involved in highly unethical business offshore."

"How senior?"

"Very senior."

"This sounds fascinating," Sarah said. "Did they give detailed information enabling you to pinpoint the accused?"

"Unfortunately not, but we are investigating as I speak."

"In addition to my role at Filchers, I am on the Board of two other companies," Janice said. "Both of them are global organisations. Would that put me in the firing line?"

Luke smiled but didn't answer.

"I fear Luke is too smart to say anything to give away the level of seniority," Ambrose said.

Sarah laughed. "You were in the police weren't you, Luke?"

"Yes, I was a Detective Chief Inspector in Avon and Somerset Police."

"So I guess you've learned not to trust anyone."

"That's not strictly true, but I'm certainly of the opinion that trust has to be earned."

"And people like Sarah and me are yet to earn your trust?" Janice asked.

"That's not fair," Ambrose said.

"What about the whistleblower?" Janice went on. "Have you met him to talk through his accusations?"

"I haven't said that it's a man."

"Is it a woman then?"

Luke didn't answer and Janice smiled genuinely for the first time.

"I have to admit he's very good, Ambrose," she said. "Tell me, Luke, are your team members experts in ethics and all its ramifications?"

"Yes," he said without hesitation, "and you will meet two of them when I present to the Board." He looked at Ambrose. "I plan to present with Maj and Helen if that's okay with you, Ambrose?"

"Of course. I believe I've met Helen once, but it was a long time ago and I don't think I've ever met Maj. Would you mind booking a slot in my diary with Ellie so that you can bring them up to say hello?"

"Of course not."

"Excellent." He turned to the two women. "Any other questions, ladies, or thoughts on subjects you'd like Luke, Helen and Maj to cover when they present next week?"

"I suggest you expand on the example you've given us," Janice said. "I appreciate your need to keep identities a secret, but putting more flesh on the bones would be illuminating."

"That's an excellent idea," Sarah said. She smiled across at Luke. "It might also be useful if you describe the stages of this investigation, how you assigned people, what types of research they used, that kind of thing. It will help to convert the more cynical Board members." She laughed. "And I'm not having a dig at you there, Janice."

"I hope that's given you a couple of ideas," Ambrose said as he got to his feet. "Thanks for coming up."

"Lovely to meet you, Luke," Sarah said.

"Be prepared for some hard questions next week," Janice warned.

"I will. Thank you both for your time."

Ambrose opened the door and Luke walked over to Ellie as it closed behind him.

"How did it go?" she asked.

"Interesting. Ambrose said to book an appointment to bring Maj and Helen up to meet him."

She checked the diary and they agreed on a time.

"Are you in the office all week?" she asked.

"As far as I know."

"Good. Ambrose wants you to meet some of the other Non-Execs as well but they're busy people and I'm struggling to set meetings up. I'll let you know when I get anywhere."

"Thanks, Ellie."

Chapter 21

Luke called the team together when he returned to the Ethics Room.

"I've only got a few minutes," Sam said. "I'm seeing Glen at twelve."

Maj grinned. "That's nice for you."

She grimaced. "I can't say I'm looking forward to it."

"I don't think this'll take long," Luke said. "I've just met two of the Board members and I wanted to share my thoughts and get an update on your research. Helen, would you mind?"

She stood up and walked over to the whiteboard.

"The two I met," he went on, "were Dame Sarah Chittock and Janice Martin. Helen, you were assigned both of them and Dame Chittock mentioned her charitable endeavours. Did they come up in your research?"

Helen smiled. "Aye, they certainly did. I've found four charities so far that she's associated with. She's Honorary President of three charities and Chief Executive of the fourth."

"Do any of them have a connection with Cambodia?"

Helen shook her head. "No. Three of them, including the one she founded and is now Chief Executive of, are UK-focused. The fourth is pan-European."

"Is there a common theme to them?" Sam asked.

Helen considered this for a moment. "To an extent, yes. They're all charities helping people who are below the poverty line. The European one, SPAN, raises money for people who have involuntarily left their country for reasons of political persecution, armed conflicts or natural disasters."

"And the others?"

"The one she founded addresses the needs of agricultural workers on very low income. The other two raise money for the homeless and ex-convicts respectively."

"They're all good causes," Maj said. "What did you make of her, Luke?"

"I liked her. She's very warm. I'd even go so far as to say she's charismatic." He turned to Helen. "Aside from the charitable work, what else have you found out about her?"

"She comes from a wealthy family and she's a Labour Party donor."

"Is that how she became a Dame?" Josh asked.

Helen laughed. "Aye, probably."

"And aside from the charities?" Luke prompted.

"She inherited the family business, Chittocks, which makes pressure gauges for the shipping industry. As far as I can tell she's not very active in the business but still sits on the Board."

"And she's single?"

Helen nodded. "I haven't found a trace of any relationships."

She updated the whiteboard.

Sarah Chittock

- 69, Dame, charismatic, Labour Party donor, president of 3/4 charities, CEO of 1 charity, single

"Okay," Luke said. "Now to Janice Martin. I know Leanne said she was friendly but I found her quite cold, although that could be down to the contrast with Sarah Chittock. She wasn't as open about herself either. I alluded to Project What without giving any details and she was very keen to find out more."

"Because she's the guilty person, guv?" Josh asked.

"More likely because she's very cynical about the Ethics

Team, but I wouldn't rule her out."

"We knew she trained as a doctor," Helen said, "but in fact she's a very senior neurosurgeon. Very well-respected and has had articles published in the Lancet."

"Neurosurgeon?" Josh asked. "What's one of those?"

"She treats conditions affecting the brain, spine, and nervous system."

"Wowza! A brain surgeon. Coolio."

"What else did you discover?" Luke asked.

"I'm going to have to go," Sam said.

"Okay. Good luck."

She grimaced and touched his arm briefly as she stood up. "Thanks. I'm going to need it."

"We knew Janice Martin was on her second marriage," Helen said once Sam had left, "but what we didn't know was that her first husband was Giovanni Listello."

"The actor?" Josh said.

"The very same."

"Coolio duo!"

"They divorced in the early noughties and their break-up was acrimonious. He accused her of beating him and she was lucky to get custody of their two children. Her second marriage was to a heart surgeon in 2014."

"How did she come to be on the Board of Filchers?" Maj asked.

"It seems to be tied to the NHS contract we won three years ago."

"Any links with other companies?" Luke asked.

"None that I could find."

Helen amended the description of Janice Martin on the whiteboard.

Janice Martin
- 56, outgoing, quick-tempered, respected neurosurgeon, 1st

marriage to Giovanni Listello, 2 adult children, remarried 2014

Chapter 22

Glen was nowhere to be seen when Sam arrived at his office.

She decided to wait on the visitor's chair and immediately felt uncomfortable. His room gave off the same vibes as the man himself, over-masculinised as if he was trying to compensate for something.

She smiled.

He probably was.

On one of the walls were two framed pieces of art. One was a close-up photo of a deer's head staring into the camera, a stereotypically macho image, but the second didn't seem his type of thing at all. At the top was a black sphere containing the words 'The Man in the Arena' in vivid white script, while beneath was a lengthy quote from Theodore Roosevelt in black on white. It seemed too intellectual for Glen and she decided to ask him about it.

On the other wall was a shelf with three identical silver trophy cups. Intrigued, she wandered over to find that each was inscribed with 'Consistent Performer' and below that the words 'Glen Gloss' and the years 2022, 2023 and 2024 respectively.

She returned to the chair and found herself further bemused by the objects on his desk. There was a Newton's cradle, which doubtless gave him hours of entertainment, and beside it a pen holder in the shape of a squat rack which held 3 pens and a miniature barbell. Next to that was a wooden pendulum with the words 'Always', 'Maybe,' Yes', 'No' and 'Never' inscribed on the base.

She heard a noise and turned to see the Head of Security grinning as he closed the door.

"Ah, Sam," he said as he wandered around her to his

desk chair. "Thank you for bringing yourself to my comfortable adobe."

She knew he meant 'abode' but there was little point in correcting him. Using the wrong word was par for the course for Glen.

"Sorry, I'm late," he went on and his grin morphed into a parody of disappointment as he lowered his voice. "Don't tell anyone, but I've got a serious waterworks problem."

"Oh dear, I'm sorry to hear that. How bad is it?"

"I'll need to see a specialist." He sighed. "My hole's too big."

She swallowed. This was way too much detail.

"Your hole's too big?"

He nodded and flicked both hands outwards from the centre of his body to demonstrate spraying liquid. "It goes all over the place. Very embarrassing."

"I'm sure it is."

"It's random too. Can happen at any time."

He stood up and gestured to his groin, causing Sam to involuntarily push her chair back a foot or two.

"I've changed my trousers but I looked as though I'd wet myself." He laughed as he sat down again. "But then, I suppose I did." He hesitated before leaning forward and adding conspiratorially, "The problem was my screwing. I went on too long."

This was too much and she started to stand up.

"Glen, I…"

"If I'd stopped sooner," he went on, "I wouldn't have hit that water pipe."

She dropped back down again as his words registered.

"The water pipe?"

"Yes." He sat back down and shook his head. "I should have let one of my team fit that blessed camera. Now I'll have to call a plumber in."

Sam closed her eyes for a second while this sunk in.

Now, she decided, was the time to move on to the

reason for their meeting before they wasted even more time. She could ask him about the trophies and the Roosevelt quote at a later date.

"Have you had any thoughts about the presentation to the Board, Glen?"

He smiled, held his finger up to his lips in a shushing motion for a second and then lowered it to the miniature pendulum on his desk. He tapped it to one side and it swung for a few seconds and then stopped above the word 'Never'.

"That's wrong," he said and swung it again.

This time it stopped over the word 'Always'.

"No, that's not right either."

He tapped again and it stopped on 'Always' again.

Glen grunted and retapped. This time it stopped on 'Yes'.

He smiled and pointed to the inscription.

"Yes," he said.

"I don't think it's meant to be used like that, Glen. It's for making decisions."

His smile expanded. "Exactly, and I de-cid-ed…" He drew out the word as he said it "…to have some thoughts on our presentation."

"And those thoughts were?"

"That I should be the mainstay and you can be my glamorable assistant."

"Did you think about the content?"

"I did, yes. We should focus on my leadership, the importance of it, my role, why it's vital, why I'm pivotal."

"Surely we need to focus on security."

"The thing is," he said in his most patronising voice, "a team is only as good as its lunchmeat."

"You mean linchpin."

"Exactly. The man on top, which in my case is always me." He grinned. "Wasn't it Churchill who said, 'There's no 'I' in team but if you look carefully there's a 'me'?"

"I think that was David Brent in 'The Office'."

"There you go then." He waved at the walls of the room they were in. "And we're in an office, are we not?"

"Have you prepared any slides?"

"No." He waved his hand towards her. "I thought that perhaps you would be better. After all…" He waved vaguely in the direction of her breasts "…you are of the feminine variety."

"I'm pleased you noticed."

As ever, the sarcasm went straight over his head.

"Yes, I did. And preparing a presentation is creative work rather than intellectual and hence well suited to a person like you."

"Because I am a woman?"

"Exactly. You can use colours to brighten it up."

Sam looked at her watch. They had been talking for twenty minutes and had achieved absolutely nothing. What was worse was that she was sure another hour, or even two more, wouldn't move them any further forward.

An idea occurred to her.

"Glen, do you have a number two?"

He nodded. "Every day, regular as clockwork."

She sighed.

"Do you have a deputy?"

"I do indeed. Andy Collins."

"If it's all right with you I'll speak to Andy to find out more about the Security department. Is Andy a man or a woman?"

"A man, of course."

"Why do you say 'of course'? Andi can be a woman's name."

He laughed. "Yes, but this *is* the Security department."

"And?"

"It's mainly men who work here. Bound to be. There's a lot of physical work. Lifting heavy cameras, fitting fingerprint sensors…"

"…making holes in water pipes."

"Exactly. That camera needed to be fitted high up on the wall. I'm six foot two. A woman couldn't have done it."

"Even if she was six foot two?"

Glen looked confused for a second then started to answer but Sam held her hand up to stop him.

"Tell you what, Glen, why don't I talk to Andy, pull a presentation together and then email it to you for your approval."

"That sounds like an excellent idea. Thank you, Sam. I hope I've given you some useful guidance."

She stood up and the trophies caught her eye again.

"One thing I'm curious about, Glen." She waved at the trophies. "Why do these say Glen Gloss and not Glen Baxter?"

"Glen Gloss is the name I use for my theatrical work. It's my synonym."

"Ah yes. I remember now. You're in something called the Chippenmales aren't you?"

"That's right. I have a small part."

"That's what I'd heard. Bye, Glen."

"Bye, Sam."

Chapter 23

Luke was about to call Maj and Helen over to begin work on their presentation when his phone rang.

"Luke Sackville."

"Luke, it's Ellie."

"Hi, Ellie. Have you got more Non-Execs lined up for me to meet?"

"No, I'm ringing because we've had another email from our whistleblower. Could you come up please?"

Two minutes later he arrived at Ellie's desk where Ambrose was reading something on her screen and shaking his head. He looked up at Luke and gestured at the display.

"Take a look at this."

Luke leaned forward and read the email.

To: Ambrose Filcher
From: abtweeing@me.com
Subject: Clothing

Mr Filcher,

I have discovered that there is only one dishonest weaver of the emporer's clothes.

Moreover, I have found seperate evidence which makes it clear that the weaver is female and confirms that she is a member of Filchers' Board of Directors.

They also show that Tease is making her a lot of money.

My role gives me access to highly sensitive documents and files but I can only search them when

I am in the office. I feel I am close to discovering her name but I am worried about digging too deep.

I am frightened of what might happen to me if she discovers who I am.

Please accelarate your investigation.

I will continue as best I can.

Regards
A Friend

"Let's talk about this in my office," Ambrose said when Luke had finished reading. "You too, Ellie."

Ambrose closed the door after them. Unusually, he remained standing and didn't invite them to sit down.

"Luke," he said. "Do you believe our whistleblower is genuine?"

"I'm inclined to think so, yes, Ambrose. There's the chance it's someone with a grievance but it rings true to me."

"Ellie?"

"I agree."

"It also seems that he or she is scared," Luke went on, "which may limit their ability to uncover more information."

"Which makes our own investigation doubly important," Ambrose said. "Ellie, when are Josh and Leanne going to Cambodia?"

"Their flights are booked for Sunday but I can see if there's earlier availability."

"Luke?"

"I'll check but I'm sure they'll be fine with going sooner."

"Good." Ambrose paused. "If we believe our whistleblower is telling the truth then that narrows our list down to the four women on the Board." He shook his head. "I find it hard to believe any of them might be up to no good. You've met three of them, Luke. What do you think?"

"My opinions are neither here nor there, Ambrose. It's evidence that counts."

Ambrose sighed. "You're right, of course." He turned to his PA. "Ellie, please can you invent a reason for me to see Meredith and liaise with Luke so that he's around to meet her?"

"Will do, Ambrose."

"I'll ask Josh about bringing their trip forward, Ellie," Luke said.

"Thanks."

*

Luke returned to the Ethics Room and walked over to Sam.

"How did it go with Glen?"

She grimaced.

"We achieved absolutely nothing. I'm going to meet with his deputy to put the presentation together."

"That's a good idea. I've got a lot of time for Andy." He looked around. "Do you know where…"

He stopped as Josh walked in carrying a tray of drinks.

"Ah, there you are, Josh. I need to talk to you about Project What. In fact, I could do with updating all of you. Maj, Helen, can you join us please?"

The team wheeled their chairs to the table in the centre of the room and Josh handed out everyone's drinks then held his hand up to indicate he was about to say something important.

"Ta-lan-krong-no-when-a," he said, elucidating each syllable slowly and carefully.

"Khmer?" Luke said.

Josh slid his chair closer.

Helen snorted. "What Luke meant was, is that your attempt at Cambodian?"

Josh nodded. "Ta-lan-krong-no-when-a," he repeated.

"What does it mean?" Maj asked.

"Where is the bus?" Josh grinned. "I've been swotting ready for our trip on Sunday."

"About that," Luke said. "What do you think about going earlier?"

Josh shook his head. "I'm not sure I'll be ready. I know how to ask for the bus or the train but that's about it."

"You could take a wee phrase book," Helen suggested.

"Or an app," Maj added. "There are some excellent translation apps."

"I hadn't thought of that. Not the same as being able to converse in their language though, is it?"

"Regardless of your linguistic skills," Luke said, "we need to bring the date forward if at all possible." He explained about the latest email from the whistleblower.

Helen stood up when he'd finished, walked to the board and scrubbed out the names of the men on the Executive Board. "That leaves us with four suspects," she said. "Gillian Ley, Meredith Holcroft, Dame Sarah Chittock and Janice Martin."

Josh put his hand up. "Can I say something, Helen?"

"Sure."

"Ta-rotta-flung-no-when-a?" He grinned. "Did you notice? I said 'rotta' in place of 'lan'."

"Are you asking me where the train is?"

He grinned and fired a finger gun at her. "You betcha!"

Luke sighed. "That's enough, Josh. Forget speaking Khmer for the moment. Will you and Leanne be okay to leave earlier, possibly as soon as tomorrow?"

"I guess so, guv. I'll give her a call."

He rang, spoke briefly and then hung up.

"She's fine with it."

"Good. Let Ellie know and she can see about changing the flights and your accommodation."

"I'll do it as soon as we've finished."

Luke turned to Sam. "Sam, you're seeing Gillian Ley aren't you?"

"Yes, it's in the diary for tomorrow."

"Great. Ellie's trying to get Meredith in to see Ambrose so that I can meet her. Maj, have you got any further with your desk research?"

"Yes, I have, although I'm fairly sure I haven't got to grips with all her businesses."

"Has she got many then?"

Maj grinned. "I'm up to eleven and still counting." He looked down at his notes. "Meredith Holcroft left school when she was sixteen. I don't know what business she started in, but she was a millionaire before she was twenty-three and moved into holistic medicines. She wasn't even twenty-five when it was doing well enough to start another business offering counselling and from there she's branched out even further. Her empire now ranges from a chain of acupuncture specialists to a company offering dietary supplements."

"Definitely a theme then," Sam suggested.

Maj nodded. "Yes, all the ones she's involved in are related to complementary therapy and alternative medicines."

"All above board?" Luke asked.

"As far as I can tell."

"It's nae my cup of tea," Helen said, "but some people swear by that sort of stuff."

Luke's phone rang and he saw that it was Ambrose's PA.

"Hi, Ellie."

"I've called an Emergency Board Meeting, Luke." She laughed. "Or at least Ambrose has."

"For what reason?"

"Concerns raised about the company by a journalist."

"A fictitious journalist?"

"I couldn't possibly comment."

"When are they coming in?"

"3 pm tomorrow. Francois Lausanne is in France so he can't make it, and neither can Alistair Ritchie who's sunning himself in Barbados. But then, we're not bothered about those two are we?"

"Indeed we're not. Well done, Ellie, and thanks. Oh, and Josh and Leanne are fine to fly earlier."

"Great. There are flights out available on Friday. I'll book them now."

He hung up and updated the team.

Chapter 24

Josh arrived at Reception to find Leanne had just finished handing over to her colleague.

He'd always found Carys pleasant, but she had a reputation for being a gossip so he knew he had to be careful what he said.

"Hi, Carys. I, ah…" He hesitated for a second. "We're off on holiday on Friday." He smiled, on comfortable ground now. "Been planning it a while."

"Really?" Her Welsh accent was apparent even in that one word.

"Yes," he said confidently, then noticed Leanne over Carys' shoulder shaking her head. "Ah…" He swallowed. "Not a holiday exactly."

Leanne started nodding her head violently and mouthed 'yes it is'.

"I mean, it is a holiday, yes, of course it is, but, ah… not a long one. Only a week."

Carys raised one eyebrow and glanced at Leanne and then back at Josh. "I'm confused. You said you've been planning it a while but Leanne told me it was a last-minute decision."

"Gotcha." He looked at Leanne who was nodding again. "Yes. Ah… Cambodia was last-minute. Definito. We've been planning to go away for a while though, but somewhere closer, that's all."

"Really. Where?"

"Where?" His voice went up an octave. "You want to know where?"

His mind went blank. Where could they have been planning to go? It had to be somewhere not as far away? He looked over at Leanne who was mouthing something else. He smiled. Yes, that would do.

"Croydon."

Carys's eyebrow went up again. "You were going on holiday to Croydon?"

Leanne sighed and mouthed the destination again, widening her lips to enunciate it more clearly.

"Croatia," he said with a sigh of relief. "Sorry. I meant Croatia. We'd been planning a week in Croatia. I'm always getting those two confused."

Carys laughed. "I hope you weren't the one booking the flights."

"No, that was Ell..." He stopped himself just in time. "That was *ell...*" He emphasised the word as if that was how he normally pronounced 'all'. "...down to Leanne. She booked our flights."

Carys turned to Leanne.

"Are you flying to Siem Reap?"

Leanne nodded. "Yes, via Bangkok. We fly from Heathrow at seven tomorrow evening. The flight takes nearly twelve hours."

"I don't envy you. It'll be proper uncomfortable spending that much time in cattle class."

"Ah, but we won't be uncomfortable because..." Josh began then realised his mistake. "...we'll, ah..." He gulped as he tried to work out how to rescue the situation and then it came to him. "We'll have those soft travel pillowy, ah..."

He put his hands to his throat to demonstrate how a travel pillow would fit snugly around his neck, but widened his eyes as he did so and managed to look as if he was trying to strangle himself.

Leanne closed her eyes for a second as she watched this performance.

"Right," she said emphatically. "We'll have to be going. I haven't started packing. I'll see you next week, Carys."

"Bye, Leanne. Bye, Josh. Have a great time."

"Bye, Carys," Josh said. "I..."

Leanne grabbed her boyfriend's hand before he could dig another hole and marched him out of the building.

"I thought I handled that quite well," he said as they walked towards the bus stop.

She stopped dead in her tracks and turned to look at him.

"You thought you handled it quite well?"

"Yes. I nearly gave things away but luckily…" he tapped the side of his head. "…I can think on my feet." He hesitated. "Why are you smiling?"

She shook her head, grabbed his hand and they set off again.

About forty minutes later they reached their apartment.

"I'll prepare the meal if you don't mind packing," Josh said. "We're going to have a week of Asian cuisine so I thought I'd cook something English tonight."

"Great. What are we having?"

He grinned. "Spag Bol."

"That's not… Oh, never mind." She hesitated. "I had a reply from the Operations Manager at Tease in Siem Reap today and it's all sorted. We're visiting on Monday and she's going to show us around."

"Gucci."

"That'll give us time to get over any jet lag."

He shook his head. "I won't get that."

"How do you know?"

"I never have before."

"Joshy, the furthest you've ever flown is to Southern Spain."

"Ah, but it's the same, isn't it, just a little further? I coped with the time difference in Malaga with no problem."

"Yes, but Cambodia is seven hours ahead of us, not one. We're travelling over 6,000 miles."

"Over 6,000 miles. Wowza!" He was beaming from ear to ear. "I'm going to be an international jetsetter, embarking on an undercover mission to uncover the dastardly plans of an evil…"

He stopped talking when he realised that Leanne had left the room.

"Ah well," he said to himself and reached into the fridge for the minced beef. "Time to cookio."

Chapter 25

"I need to pop to the loo," Sam said.

Luke smiled as he watched her walk around the bar and disappear from view.

His girlfriend, he reminded himself as he took another sip of his cider.

'Wowza' as Josh would say.

He felt incredibly lucky to have such a wonderful person as his other half. She was still keen to take things slowly but he wasn't worried. The whole experience of getting to know each other better was enjoyable, and the more time they spent together the more he found her fun to be with.

He had been delighted when she accepted his invitation to come to Borrowham Hall at Christmas. His father had been stiff at first, no surprise there, but had soon relaxed, while his brother Mark had warmed to her immediately.

Mark's wife had been more offhand, but that was typical Erica, and even she had seemed to lighten up as the day progressed.

As for Marion, Erica's eight-year-old daughter, she had been all over Sam and had even cajoled her into reading her a bedtime story.

The one member of Luke's family that Sam hadn't met yet was his mother and he wasn't keen to introduce them to each other any time soon. It wasn't so much the fact that Daphne had dementia, though that didn't make things any easier. It was more that she was, and always had been, a distinctly unpleasant person. If anything, her illness made her even more argumentative and difficult.

He didn't envy the staff at the care home one tiny bit.

He looked up as Sam reappeared but the smile she had

worn all evening had vanished and she looked distinctly unhappy.

'What's up?"

She sat back down, grimaced at her phone and then slid it over the table to him.

"Read that."

The message was short and to the point.

Are you back with that policeman?

He looked over at her.

"Ollie?"

She sighed. "It has to be. I removed him from my contacts and blocked his number, but he must have bought a new phone."

She retrieved her mobile, looked at the message again, sighed and said, almost under her breath, "That bloody man."

He reached out and grasped her hand.

"Try not to let him get to you."

She tried to smile but it wasn't a very good attempt.

"The fact that he's got in touch, when I specifically told him never to contact me again, is bad enough, but asking if I'm *back* with you." She put heavy emphasis on the word 'back' as she said this. "For heaven's sake, I wasn't going out with you when I last saw him, let alone when he and I were dating." She squeezed his hand and looked into his eyes. "Do you think I should reply?"

"Definitely not. That's what he wants."

"What then? Believe me, I was pretty forceful when I told him to stay out of my life."

He grinned. "I bet you were. If you ignore him I suspect he'll stop. It's been weeks since his last contact, isn't it?"

"It was last year."

"Then ignore his message, but if he sends you another

one let me know and we'll work out what to do for the best."

"Yes, okay." She smiled and it was a full-on genuine smile this time. "Right, let's forget about that bastard and get back to our evening."

"Good idea." He drained the last of his cider and pointed at her wine glass. "Another?"

"Will you be okay to drive home if you have a second?"

"Oh, ah… right, yes… ah…"

She laughed. "Gosh, you're easy to tease."

"You can be so mean sometimes, Miss Chambers."

Chapter 26

Helen was nervous.

Which was silly, of course it was. Bob was lovely and she was sure her son would take an immediate liking to him.

But she'd held back, and now that they were finally going to meet, she and Bob were inseparable.

She smiled to herself.

They were a couple. Who'd have believed it? Helen Hogg, a widow for over thirty years, finds love in her late-fifties.

It was the stuff of dreams.

But then Bob was the stuff of dreams as far as she was concerned. She found him hellishly attractive with his trim build, bright blue eyes and full head of salt-and-pepper hair. She smiled. Even in the month or so they'd known each other she'd noticed the salt content increasing.

Okay, he could be outspoken. Bob wore his feelings on his sleeve and was very political, albeit with a small 'p'. However, regardless of all that, he was a wee darling. She was smitten, absolutely smitten, and he seemed to feel the same way about her.

They were more or less living together now, splitting time between her home in Bath and 'Smoke and Mirrors', his narrowboat. Their relationship had moved forward at breakneck speed but what the hell? You only lived once.

"How are you doing?" she called.

"Just about there."

A few seconds later he emerged into the small lounge-cum-galley.

"What do you think?"

She looked him up and down and smiled. "You look

good enough to eat, that's what I think."

He gestured to his colourful shirt. "You don't think this is too much?"

"It's bright, but there's nothing wrong with that." She smiled. "It's not like you to worry about what you wear. Ronnie won't bite, you know."

"I want to make a good impression. He's a big part of your life and he'll be a big part of mine going forward. What if he doesn't like me?"

"Ach, don't be a wee ditherhead. Come on, let's get going."

Twenty minutes later they pulled up outside Ronnie and Becky's flat.

"Hi Mum," Ronnie said as he opened the door. He put his arms around her and then stood back as Bob put his hand out. "Great to meet you, Bob."

Bob shook his hand and smiled. "You too, Ronnie."

Becky walked up behind her boyfriend, kissed Helen on the cheek, looked up at Bob and raised an eyebrow.

"Have we met?"

Bob shook his head. "I don't think so."

"Come on in," Ronnie said. "We've done roast chicken. I hope that's okay."

"Sounds great," Bob said.

Once they were in the lounge, Ronnie poured drinks and Becky retreated to the kitchen to put the vegetables on to boil.

Five minutes later she reappeared.

"I know why I recognise you, Bob."

He looked at her, then at Helen, and then back at Becky, a slightly edgy look on his face. "I'm sure I'd remember if we'd met."

She laughed. "You wouldn't. It was you that was the centre of attention. I was just one person among a hundred or so onlookers."

"Come on, Becky," Helen said. "Put us out of our

misery."

"It was last Spring. April maybe. A friend of mine persuaded a couple of us to go to the Little Theatre to watch a live interview with an ex-Sky newsreader. She said he's got a name for being humorous."

"I know what you're talking about," Bob said. "It wasn't my proudest moment."

"Were you the person being interviewed?" Ronnie asked.

Both Bob and Becky laughed.

"Far from it," Becky said.

"I knew more about him than Becky did," Bob said. "He intends standing as an Independent MP but I'd heard some of the things he'd said and I went along intending to call him out."

Becky smiled. "Which you definitely did. This ex-newsreader....What was his name?"

"Leonard Marshall."

She nodded. "I remember now. Marshall started off well, and cracked a few one-liners that made us laugh, but then he started to get more and more extreme. He was still couching everything in jokey terms, but it was clear his views were out there, and I mean really out there. You could sense the mood of the audience changing and then…" She smiled as she remembered and looked at Bob. "…and then you stood up."

"I'd had enough. I wasn't going to let him say that kind of thing."

"What did you say, Bob?" Helen asked.

Bob sighed. "I might have used an expletive or two so I don't like to repeat it."

"I think you used one, Bob," Becky said, "but no one in the audience minded in the least. What you said was what we were all feeling."

"I suppose so." He turned to Helen. "He told a story he seemed to find amusing which involved several migrants dying trying to cross the channel in a boat. He then went on to call them scum and said that they were the lowest of the low and that they'd brought their suffering on themselves. It was disgraceful and I wasn't going to let him get away with it so I stood up and challenged him."

"You were great, Bob. You laid out the facts and he didn't have a decent comeback." Becky turned to Helen. "He got a standing ovation for it." A timer went off. "That's the veg ready. Come on, Ronnie, let's get this served up."

Chapter 27

Nabi stepped out from behind the oak tree and approached the older man as he emerged from the battered Toyota.

"When will we be able to cross?" he asked, his accent thick but the words clearly enunciated. He had completed an English course before the Taliban regained control of his country and it was now proving invaluable.

The man grunted, put a cigarette in his mouth and curled his hand to shield the flame of his lighter. He sucked in greedily, not bothering to look at Nabi, and blew out a stream of smoke before responding.

"Tonight, in one or two hours."

His voice was deep and he too spoke English with an accent, though in his case it was European. Possibly French, Nabi thought, although he couldn't be certain.

"Where do we need to wait?"

"How many of you?"

"Three. You know there are three. I told you this yesterday. My wife and small child are with me."

"Have you paid for three?"

"Yes. I paid the money-handler before we left. Five thousand."

"Euros?"

Nabi nodded. "The money will be transferred when our employer picks us up after we land safely."

The man's lips turned up slightly as if Nabi had cracked a joke, then he took another deep draw on his cigarette and let it drop to the ground where he stubbed it out with the end of his shoe. He turned to walk back to his car.

Nabi put his arm on the man's shoulder and he immediately jerked around and thrust his face forward.

"Do not touch me!" he shouted, spittle striking Nabi

on the cheek.

Nabi took a pace back and wiped the side of his face with his sleeve. "You haven't told me where we go. Where does the boat leave from?"

The man laughed. "From the beach, idiot."

"But the beach is long."

"Look for the crowd of people. It will be obvious."

The man returned to the Toyota and said something to the driver. They both laughed and after a short exchange of words he walked to the passenger side, climbed in and they drove away.

Nabi returned to his wife and reverted to Dari. She hadn't been lucky enough to study English and the only word in the language that she knew was 'Hello'. She was bright though, and he was confident that she would learn quickly once they settled down.

"Not long now, Jamila. Soon we will be able to cross and the three of us will be safe."

His wife looked up at him as she cradled their sleeping two-year-old daughter in her arms.

"These are bad men, Nabi." Her eyes were wide and she was shaking slightly. "They scare me."

"I don't like them either, but we have paid good money and they know what they are doing." He tried to keep his voice light and confident. "Their dinghies are well-made. I believe they come from China."

"How many others will be on the boat with us?"

"Ten or so I suspect, but they are large and it is only thirty kilometres to England. I met a man yesterday who told me that the crossing takes five or six hours. Once we land our employer will drive us to a place where we will be safe from the authorities and paid to work."

"You are an experienced electrician, Nabi. Will they use your skills?"

"Hopefully." He kissed the top of Jamila's head. "Even if they don't, life will be a lot better than if we had stayed in

Kandahar."

"Did the man say when the boat will leave?"

"In an hour or two. We need to move closer to the beach. Hopefully, we can find shelter from the cold there."

The beach was only a few hundred metres away but he was disappointed to find when they got there that there were no trees. He led his wife to some shrubs on the edge of a low sand dune.

"You lie at the base of these bushes with Bibi, Jamila. I will walk along the beach to see if I can find anyone."

He wrapped their only blanket around his wife and daughter. It was thin cotton, but it at least afforded some protection from the bitter wind which was even stronger now that they were close to the sea.

"Don't go too far, Nabi."

He smiled and kissed his wife on the forehead. "No, I won't go far."

He strode away along the beach. After twenty paces he turned, but there was only a pale crescent moon to light the sky and he was unable to see his family. He hated having to leave them but knew he had no choice.

He continued for another five or six minutes but stopped abruptly when he heard sounds ahead. After a few seconds, he realised it was people talking. He walked on.

"Hello," he called. There was no response and he raised his voice as he repeated the word. "Hello."

Someone flicked their phone up and shone it into Nabi's face. He shielded his eyes and walked towards the light.

A man spoke but the language wasn't one he recognised.

"Do you speak English?" Nabi asked.

It was a second man who answered.

"I speak a little."

Now that Nabi was close to the group he saw that there were three men, all about his own age or perhaps slightly older. They looked to be Asian.

"Are you and your friends waiting for the boat?"

"Yes. Are you alone?"

"No. I have my wife and daughter with me."

The man relayed this to the other two men in his native language and listened as one of them replied.

He turned back to Nabi.

"How old is your daughter?"

"She is two."

"Then you must look after her well. It will be crowded on the boat and it is windy tonight so the crossing will be rough and dangerous."

"Crowded? But I was told there will be a lot of room."

"These people smugglers lie, my friend. It will be packed, believe me."

Nabi was about to reply when he heard a scraping noise. They all turned and the man with the phone pointed it in the direction of the sound to reveal four men pulling a large dinghy onto the beach.

He was relieved to see its size. There should be plenty of room given there were only eight people, ten including Jamila and Bibi.

The three Asians ran to help the others pull the boat towards the sea.

"Do not leave without us," Nabi called as he turned to fetch his wife and daughter, but his words were lost in the wind.

He ran back down the beach to the point where he had left Jamila, but there was no sign of her.

"Jamila!"

No answer.

He raised his voice and shouted her name as loudly as he could.

"JAMILA!"

Again there was no response.

Had he returned to the wrong place?

He ran to the edge of the shrubs and bent down low beside the dune. Sure enough, he could feel lines in the sand where his wife had been lying.

He stood up again, turned in every direction and shouted her name again.

"JAMILA!"

Chapter 28

"OVER HERE!" Jamila shouted.

Thanks be to Allah, Nabi thought.

He ran around the dune to find his wife lying on the other side and realised he was breathing heavily, though it was more with worry than anything else.

"Why did you move, Jamila?"

"It is more sheltered here. Bibi was shivering."

"Come. The boat is on the beach. We need to go."

He lifted his daughter into his arms and helped his wife to her feet.

"This way. We must be quick."

They raced back down the beach.

His daughter was awake now, but she remained mercifully silent. He didn't think he could bear it if she started to cry. He was putting his family through this and hoped he had done the right thing and that all would end well.

After a hundred paces, he was beginning to fear that the boat had gone without them. Surely he hadn't walked this far the first time.

A few seconds later he heard voices and heaved a sigh of relief.

"They're ahead, Jamila. Not far now."

When the dinghy came into view he saw that it was lying on the very edge of the water and that two men were fitting an outboard motor to the stern. As they approached he recognised one of them as the man from the Toyota.

Nabi was shocked to see that there were many more people around the inflatable than when he had left. There had to be at least fifty and possibly sixty or more. Most were men, but there were a few women and he saw two children aged perhaps eight or nine.

He spotted the Asian man he had seen earlier and led his wife over.

"There are a lot of people. Is there another boat?"

The man grimaced. "No."

The man from the Toyota stood up. "The motor is fitted. Who will hold the tiller?"

No one answered and it was clear that the majority didn't understand what he was saying.

"Someone has to steer. Who is it going to be?"

"I will do it," Nabi said.

He had no experience of boats but he wanted to guarantee that they would be allowed on board.

The man nodded. "You sit here then."

Nabi walked over.

"What do I do?"

The man sneered. "You need to steer, idiot." He looked at another man, who Nabi presumed was the driver of the Toyota, with an expression that said 'what a fool this is'.

Then he turned and raised his voice so that everyone could hear.

"Do not move!"

He raised his arms and held his hands up, palms forward, so that it was clear that everyone should stay where they were.

"You climb in when the boat is in the water. I will give the word." He pointed to a mound of orange buoyancy aids some twenty yards inland. "Put those on."

Nabi walked over with the others, found two adult jackets and a small one for Bibi then returned.

He held them up. "These look flimsy."

The man shrugged. "They're all we've got. It's up to you."

Nabi helped his wife and daughter put theirs on and then fastened his own around his waist.

The man from the Toyota gestured to the men nearest

to him. "Now pull it into the water." They shrugged, not understanding, and he pushed one of them down so that his hands were on the rope around the top of the boat and indicated for him to pull.

This seemed to do the trick and he stood back and watched as they dragged the dinghy into the sea. He waited until most of the boat was in the water then began gesticulating with his hands, ushering everyone towards the dinghy.

"IN! IN!"

There was a rush, but not a stampede, and as people boarded they automatically formed into three rows.

Nabi helped his wife climb on and passed Bibi to her.

"Sit there, Jamila," he said, pointing to the back of the middle row. The men in front shuffled forward to enable her to squeeze in.

She was now directly in front of the engine with men squeezed against her on either side and Bibi on her lap. This would hopefully minimise the chances of them falling overboard if the sea became choppy, and it also meant that they were near enough for him to keep an eye on them.

Nabi squeezed himself into the rear of the left-hand row so that he was able to grasp the tiller with his right hand.

"Turn it to go faster," the man from the Toyota said before adding, "Move aside, fool," as he lifted first one, and then a second, large blue plastic jerrycan over Nabi's shoulder and onto the floor between the rows.

"What are they?" Nabi asked.

"Spare fuel." He grinned. "You don't want to run out half-way across, do you?" He bent down to start the engine.

Everyone was now on board, the majority with buoyancy aids on, although a few hadn't bothered. Nabi wasn't surprised at this. They looked like they were good for a swimming pool, but as lifejackets they would afford little protection.

While the man was starting the engine, his colleague passed two cylindrical pumps to a man in the middle of the right-hand row.

"Use these if water gets on board," he said.

Nabi would have laughed if the situation hadn't been so terrifying. As with the flimsy jacket around his waist, these bright orange devices would surely be of little use if the sea became stormy and waves started to throw water into the dinghy.

Once the engine was started the two people smugglers pushed the side of the boat the few inches necessary for the dinghy to float.

Nabi didn't need to be told what to do next and rotated the throttle, causing the dinghy to surge forwards with more impetus than he had intended. He released pressure slightly, pulled the handle towards him until the boat was facing away from the beach, and then accelerated again.

As he did so he felt something wet on his forehead. A few drops at first but within seconds the clouds had opened and icy rain was battering down on his head and running down the sides of his face.

He glanced at his wife.

All he could see was her outline, but it was clear that she was bent forward over Bibi trying to shelter her from the worst of the rainfall.

Nabi swallowed, returned his attention to the front and accelerated to full power.

Chapter 29

Sam sat in the Orange Grove room staring out of the window and tapped her fingers on the desk as she thought through how to play the meeting.

What if Andy Collins was as much of a dunderhead as his boss? Glen had made him his number two which could mean he was a mirror image.

Then she remembered that Luke had said he had a lot of time for the Deputy Head of Security. His opinion meant a lot, so with any luck…

Her thoughts were interrupted as the door opened and a man a few years older than her walked in. He was much the same height as his boss but there the similarity ended. Andy was lean, almost lanky, and had a neatly-combed head of blonde hair rather than anything resembling a buzz cut. He also had an air of intelligence that had never been evident when she'd been with Glen Baxter.

"Hi, Sam," he said, offering his hand as he walked over.

"Hi, Andy." She shook his hand. "Thanks for agreeing to see me."

He sat down on the opposite side of the table and smiled.

"You said on the phone that you wanted help with something?"

"Yes, Glen and I are presenting to the Board and…"

He held his hand up and snorted out a laugh. "You're not seriously saying that Glen is going to be up in front of Filchers' Board of Directors?"

"Yes. Why?"

"Glen would struggle to go down well if he was presenting to a Skateboard let alone a Company Board."

Sam grimaced. "I was kind of afraid of that."

"Is there any way out of it?"

"Not really."

"It's a case of minimising the damage then. What's the topic?"

"Your department. Ambrose Filcher wants the Directors to understand more about the different sections in Internal Affairs."

"And why are you involved?"

Sam thought about this for a moment. Luke was presenting with Maj and Helen, and had said that given there were three of them 'it would be unfair to ask Glen to stand up on his own'.

Luke wasn't stupid. He knew how Glen would perform if left to his own devices. That was why he'd asked Sam to co-present. He wanted her to rescue the situation.

Crafty bugger. She'd give him a good talking to when they got home.

"I think Luke knows how Glen will perform if he does it on his own."

"Mmm. I don't envy you." He paused. "The trick is to minimise Glen's contribution and make sure he sticks to areas he understands."

"Which are?"

"That's the problem." He hesitated. "Don't get me wrong. He's a great boss."

"He is?"

He smiled again. "Well, no. If I'm honest, he's a crap boss."

"How do you cope?"

"It's not too difficult. He regards letting me run the department as terrific delegation on his part, so I manage the teams, organise rotas, manage staff recruitment and development, select security products, and so on."

"So what does Glen do?"

"He goes to Edward Filcher's weekly meetings, fiddles with his Newton's Cradle, which has him completely bamboozled by the way, and… well, that's about it."

"And areas he understands?"

"Why don't we plan the presentation first and come back to that testing little question later? How long is your slot?"

"Ten to 15 minutes."

"Not too long. That's good. I suggest you start with our three main functions which are to safeguard Filchers' assets, employees and sensitive information. In terms of assets, this involves…"

Sam took notes as Andy ran her through what the teams did.

"That sounds good," she said when they'd finished. She looked through her notes. "I think you're right. Three or four slides should do it. But that brings us back to the thorny subject of Glen's contribution."

Andy thought about this. "There is one subject he knows a fair bit about."

"Go on."

"Dogs."

"Dogs?"

He nodded. "Glen was a dog-handler in his early days at Avon and Somerset Police."

"Is that relevant at Filchers?"

"No." He paused. "However, I know that a couple of the Board are keen on dogs so if we can find a way of mentioning them it might work."

"Which Board members are those?"

"Gillian Ley, our Finance Director, and the Dame. I forget her name."

"Sarah Chittock?"

"That's the one."

"Do we use dogs at all?"

He shook his head. "No, but they've been a consideration. We were thinking of using them to secure the grounds at night but decided it was too expensive."

Sam smiled. "Great. Let's give him one slide on that. We can use it to emphasise how cost-conscious the Security department is."

They spent the next twenty minutes sketching out the slides.

"Thanks, Andy," Sam said when they'd finished. "That third slide is very technical and I'm going to struggle if they ask detailed questions. Would you mind co-presenting?"

"Not at all."

"Thanks." She paused. "Going back to Gillian Ley and Sarah Chittock, you said they're keen on dogs. How do you know?"

"I had to join Glen in a meeting with Gillian about our budget for next year." He grinned. "No way could he have coped without me. Anyway, she had photos of two black labs on her desk and I asked her about them. She told me she's always loved labradors and that they're great guard dogs. Wouldn't hurt a fly, but very vocal when anyone comes near the house, that's what she said."

"And Dame Chittock?"

"She's got five toy poodles."

"Five!"

"Loves them and calls them her bunny bears. She's a real contrast that one."

"How do you mean?"

"She's softly spoken and very Barbara Cartland in many ways. She loves pink, adores her poodles and has a very chintzy taste in soft furnishings. But there's definitely another side to her."

"How do you know all this?"

"Ambrose asked me to help her out as a favour. She wanted a better security system at home and he asked me if I could look at what she's currently got and offer some advice. I was happy to, but I didn't realise she lived in a stately home."

"A stately home?"

Andy nodded. "She told me her grandfather bought it half a century ago. Believe me when I say it's massive. Eighteen bedrooms, would you believe. Took me the best part of two days to review her security system."

"What did you think of her?"

"She's lovely. I was even treated to a posh afternoon tea in her drawing room." He laughed. "I've never heard of anyone outside a Jane Austen novel having a drawing room."

Sam's thoughts immediately went to Luke. Not only did his family home have a drawing room, it also had a billiards room and a library.

"She also had a billiards room and a library," Andy went on and Sam concealed a smile.

"You said there's another side to her. What do you mean?"

"She had a meeting with the senior team of the charity she founded while I was there. I overheard snippets as I was going in and out of rooms checking out the security system and I was amazed at how tenacious she was. She never raised her voice but boy is she good at getting her message heard."

Chapter 30

Sam felt slightly on edge as she emerged from the lift on the Executive Floor, nodded hello to Ellie and walked past her and around the corner. She had never met Gillian Ley and was worried about trying to suss the woman out under the pretence of discussing budget forecasts.

"Hi," she said to the woman seated outside the Finance Director's Office. She was about her own age, but pale-skinned and nervy-looking. "Am I in the right place? I'm here to see Gillian."

"Sam Chambers?" The woman smiled, but it was somewhat hesitant, and then checked her diary. "From the Ethics Team?"

"That's right."

"Yes, you're in the right place. I'm Mollie, Gillian's PA. She's seeing someone at the moment, but hopefully they'll be finished soon. Are you okay to wait?"

"Yes, that's fine."

Mollie returned her attention to her computer and Sam sat down on one of two chairs set against the wall.

It dawned on her that this was an opportunity to see what the PA thought about her boss.

"It must be hard, working for such a busy person, Mollie. How long have you had the job?"

Mollie looked up from her keyboard. "Almost two years."

"I considered being a PA once," Sam lied, "but what worried me was how difficult senior people can be. Power can go to their heads sometimes."

Mollie smiled, again tentatively. "That's true."

Sam lowered her voice conspiratorially and nodded her head to the door of the office. "Is she challenging?"

"No more than any of them. Except for Ambrose. He's a darling."

"I bet she puts demands on you though."

"The hours can be rough. Gillian is an incredibly hard worker, and it's not unusual for it to be gone seven before I leave for home." She shook her head. "You wouldn't believe how many reports she has to produce, and the fact that I'm dyslexic doesn't help. I don't know how I'd cope if MS Word didn't point out my spelling errors."

"Yes, that must make it hard."

Mollie opened her desk and pulled out a dictionary. "I use this for emails when I have to send them on her behalf, but fortunately she writes most of them herself."

This was not the avenue Sam wanted the conversation to go down. She thought for a second about how to find out anything useful and decided a direct approach was her best bet.

"I imagine Gillian has considerable business interests outside of Filchers. That must add to your workload." She paused. "Especially if those interests are overseas."

Mollie furrowed her brows. "That seems an odd question. What makes you think she might have overseas interests?"

"Overseas interests?"

Sam turned when she heard this and immediately recognised the Chief Financial Officer from her photo on the whiteboard.

She stood up.

"Hi, Gillian. I'm Sam Chambers."

Gillian shook her hand but looked distinctly unhappy.

"Let's talk in my office."

Sam followed her into a room that was almost completely characterless. It had none of the stuffiness of Edward Filcher's office, but neither did it have the comfortable relaxed feel of the CEO's enclave. The desk, table, chairs, and even the sofa, spoke of Scandinavian design but in a bland, IKEA fashion. There were a couple of framed certificates on the wall but no family photos, nor even images of Bath, to brighten up the space.

Gillian gestured to the oval meeting table in the centre of the room. "Please take a seat."

Sam sat down and the CFO took the chair opposite.

"You asked to see me to discuss the Ethics Team's forecast for the next financial year?"

"That's right. I'd appreciate your advice in a couple of areas."

"Why are you here and not Luke?"

Sam smiled but it wasn't returned.

"He's the first to admit he's not brilliant as far as budgeting is concerned and asked if I could take the lead."

"And you *are* brilliant?"

"Not at all, but I'm an accountant and know my way around spreadsheets."

"Do you indeed?"

"I like to think so."

"And yet now you work in the Ethics Team. That seems a bit of a leap."

"It's fascinating work."

"Mmm."

Gillian sat back in her chair and looked Sam in the eyes. It was a few seconds before she spoke again.

"Do you personally play a role in your team's investigations?"

"Sometimes."

"Is that why you were asking Mollie about my outside interests?"

Sam swallowed. This was not going the way she had intended, not in the slightest.

"No. Not at all. I was making conversation, that's all."

"Because my commercial interests outside Filchers are none of your business. Is that clear?"

"Absolutely, Gillian. Sorry. I didn't mean to pry."

"You used to work for Elizabeth in the Government sector, didn't you?"

Sam closed her eyes for a split-second. Yes, she had worked for Elizabeth Rogers, the Government Sector Head of Finance, but it was not a topic she wanted to discuss.

"A while ago, yes."

"I seem to recall that she moved you on because you were causing difficulties in her department." Gillian paused. "Wasn't there an issue with your attitude towards the male contingent?"

Sam sighed inwardly. Elizabeth was batshit-crazy and had wrongly accused her of dressing inappropriately and flirting, but relaying her side of the story was not going to get her anywhere.

"There were a number of areas where Elizabeth and I didn't see eye to eye, but I like to think of it as a clash of personalities, that's all. I've moved on and hopefully she has as well."

"Mmm."

This 'Mmm' from Gillian, as with the first, presaged another pause in the conversation as she again stared into Sam's eyes.

After a few seconds, Gillian seemed to come to a decision and gestured to Sam's pad.

"How can I help?"

Sam opened her notebook.

"The first area is capital budgets…"

Twenty minutes later, Sam closed her notebook and stood up.

"Thanks, Gillian. That's been very helpful."

"Good." She looked Sam in the eyes, her tone flat but somehow menacing. "I suggest you watch your step, Sam, and keep your nose out of other people's business. You don't want to do anything that might bring trouble on yourself, or for that matter on those you care about."

It was said lightly, but Sam couldn't help sensing the

threat in her words. She opened the door and turned to say goodbye, but Gillian was already at her desk and focused on her laptop.

Sam walked out, closed the door behind her and leaned back against it.

Mollie looked over.

"Is everything okay?"

Sam smiled as best she could, but everything felt far from okay.

"Fine, thanks. Gillian was very helpful."

She walked to the lift thinking that she might have just messed up the whole investigation if the Chief Financial Officer was indeed the person behind whatever was going on at Tease. To ask her PA about her foreign business interests, and assume Gillian was in her office, was a rookie error. And then there was the lightly veiled threat in the woman's final words.

She also had the beginnings of a splitting headache.

All in all, it hadn't been the best of afternoons.

Chapter 31

Sam was relieved to find Luke in the Ethics Room when she returned.

He was looking at his phone and shaking his head.

"That's awful."

"What is?"

He looked up, put his mobile down on the desk so that it was facing her, and tapped the screen.

"The BBC are reporting another tragedy in the English Channel. A boat carrying dozens of migrants sank off the coast. They managed to rescue 49 people but three people died including a small child."

"How horrendous."

"Yes. I wish they could find a solution to the problem." He sighed. "Anyway, how did you get on with Gillian?"

"Not very well. I kind of cocked up."

She explained what had happened.

"I wouldn't worry too much," he said when she'd finished. "Gillian's got a reputation as a cold fish and she'll have been testing you out."

"But what if she's the person behind Tease? She overheard me asking her PA about her overseas interests."

"I don't think it'll do any harm. It's not as if she told you anything."

"I suppose not."

He looked at her properly for the first time. "Are you feeling okay, Sam? You look as white as a sheet."

"I'm feeling rough, to be honest. My head's throbbing and I'm worried I might have come down with something."

"Why don't you head home?"

"I can't do that. It's not even four."

"Don't be silly. You were in early and you could do with

resting. Take a couple of paracetamol and make yourself comfortable on the sofa. I'll try to get away by six and I'll come straight to yours."

"Okay. I think I'll take you up on it."

She said goodbye to the others, grabbed her coat and bag and headed home.

By the time she was on the bus she was shivering and pulled the lapels of her coat tightly up to her neck. It wasn't much above freezing, and at first she thought the problem was the weather, but her palms felt damp and she could feel a pinkness to her cheeks that was more than just a reaction to the icy conditions.

The idea of curling up on the sofa with a cup of hot chocolate was massively appealing. She'd change into the pink onesie Luke had given her for Christmas and watch Bridgerton.

Yes, that would make her feel a ton better.

She reached the door to her apartment, felt around in her bag for her keys, pulled them out and then hesitated as she realised that the door wasn't properly closed.

It had looked fastened at first sight but there was definitely a small gap.

She pushed on the door and heard a tiny click as it started to open.

This didn't make sense. She was sure she had locked the flat when she'd left in the morning.

Unless…

She smiled.

That was it. It had to be.

Her mother had a key and must have come around for some reason. Perhaps she had some news. A new beau perhaps?

The trouble was that she didn't feel well enough to see anyone, even her mother. On the other hand, the idea of regressing to childhood, and have her Mum make her up a bed in the lounge, did have a degree of appeal.

"Mum!" she called. "I'm home!"

She pushed the door wide open and put her bag down beneath the hall mirror.

"Mum?" she called again as she started to unbutton her coat.

Still no response.

Perhaps she was in the bathroom.

It was then that she heard the slightest of noises from the lounge. It wasn't much, almost a shuffling, but it couldn't be her mother who would have answered her call.

She felt a lump in her throat.

"Who's there?"

It had to be a burglar.

Her heart was pumping in her chest.

Whoever it was knew she was there and any moment now they would appear. This was their only route out.

What if the thief was armed?

She had to act quickly and looked around for anything that she could use to defend herself.

The only object to hand was her briefcase.

That would have to do.

She leaned down to grab the handle and something, or more accurately someone, barrelled into her. She was thrown against the open door, her temple banging hard into the sharp edge.

Sam was already losing consciousness as her assailant pulled her to the ground, opened the door wide and fled.

Chapter 32

Luke was pleased that he'd managed to leave the office before 5:30.

Poor Sam. She'd looked rough and it seemed likely that she was coming down with a virus.

As he walked out to the car he called her on his mobile. It rang several times and then went to voicemail.

"This is Sam. You know what to do when it beeps."

"Sam, I'm on my way. Ring or message me if there's anything you want from the shops."

He decided that her not answering meant she'd fallen asleep which had to be a good thing. It also gave him time to buy her flowers. Normally, he'd be thinking chocolates as well, but she probably wasn't up to eating anything.

Forty minutes later he was smiling to himself as he mounted the stairs to Sam's apartment. He had a big bunch of red roses in one hand, which she was going to love, and he had every intention of spoiling her throughout the evening.

Three things happened in quick succession when he reached the upstairs landing.

First, he saw that the door to Sam's apartment was wide open.

Then he spotted dark red smears on her hall carpet.

One pace further and strands of her hair became visible on the ground.

He dropped the flowers to the floor and raced forward.

"Sam," he said as he bent to his knees.

He put his fingers to her neck.

She was breathing, thank god.

He reached for his phone and rang 999.

Chapter 33

Nabi was exhausted.

He had remained on the tiller throughout the crossing, not trusting anyone else with the responsibility.

Sleep had not been an option. The lives of his wife and daughter depended on him. He owed it to them to bring them to safety.

And, although his eyes were gritty and he was physically wrecked, they had managed to reach the United Kingdom.

Almost.

He looked over to his wife who continued to cradle Bibi in her arms. The little girl had been scared when she'd been awake, but mercifully had fallen asleep again.

The others in the boat looked universally frozen and miserable. There had been a period soon after they had left the French coast when someone had started singing, but it had been in a language he didn't know, and it soon fizzled out.

He couldn't believe how long the journey had taken and almost laughed when he recalled being told it would take no more than five or six hours.

Nabi tapped the shoulder of the Asian man he had spoken to before they left.

"How long have we been travelling?"

The man looked at his watch. "Nearly fifteen hours, my friend."

"Not far now. Perhaps an hour, maybe more."

"Let us hope that is the case."

"I do not even know your name."

"I am Giang and I am from Vietnam. You?"

"Nabi. I am Afghan."

"I hope all goes well for you and your wife and

daughter."

"And for you, Giang."

The driving rain had stopped and there was now only an icy-cold drizzle falling on the boat and its occupants. Daylight had come and gone, but Nabi had been able to see the white cliffs of England intermittently for the past hour or more under the moonlight. It continued to draw closer, albeit inexorably slowly.

They had been fortunate with the weather. There had been squalls, and water had been driven into the boat on occasions by waves, but it had not caused undue problems. The boat had stayed afloat and everyone had remained squeezed into their original positions, only moving to the edges of the dinghy if they needed to urinate over the side.

He had counted and there were sixty-two people on board including his daughter and the two other small children.

Sixty-two!

He wondered whether the other passengers were as fortunate as he was in having employment and accommodation waiting for them, or whether they would be forced to beg or worse.

There was still the possibility that the authorities would be there when they landed. If that was the case would they be immediately deported and sent back to France, or worse to Afghanistan, or might they find themselves in a detention centre while their asylum applications were processed?

Surely they would regard his family favourably given he and his wife had a small child and he had been forced to leave his country of birth to avoid almost certain capture, imprisonment and death.

He sighed as he recalled what had got them to this position. All that he and Lodhi had done was to speak up for women in a meeting, saying that they should have the right to full education and to employment. But the next day armed men had dragged his beloved brother from his home and twenty-four hours later his body had been found on the edge of an industrial estate.

Nabi had no proof that the men who abducted, tortured and killed Lodhi were agents of the Taliban, but he was certain that they had been.

He had been left with no option other than to take his family and leave Kandahar. Luckily, he had had some savings and, coupled with the sale of his wife's jewellery, this had enabled him to pay for their passage to the UK.

After another forty or fifty minutes one of the passengers shouted out and pointed to the shore. Nabi could not understand what the man was saying but soon another joined in and he saw that there was a light shining on the beach.

No, two lights, their spacing suggesting it was a vehicle.

The beams were aiming directly out to sea.

This had to be for them.

But was it friendly or hostile? Was his employer out there, or were they to be greeted by faceless officers who would bundle them into vans and take them to a prison.

Nabi turned the tiller slightly to steer the dinghy towards the vehicle.

As they neared the shore another pair of lights turned on and then a third. He saw at least five figures standing beside the vehicles.

After another hundred metres it became clear that the men on the beach wore coats, and in some cases warm hats, but no uniforms. Relief surged over him. This was it, safety from persecution, a home for his wife and daughter.

He slowed the dinghy as it came within a boat's length of the sand. Men started climbing out and the others onshore joined them as they helped to drag the dinghy forwards onto the beach.

Nabi felt the pressure on his legs release as the people in front of him started to move away. He turned to his wife.

"We are here, Jamila. We are in the United Kingdom."

A wan smile appeared on her face and he held out his hands for her to pass Bibi over.

He cradled his daughter in his left arm and held out his right hand to help his wife to her feet.

"Come," he said. "Let us find our employer."

Giang turned to them.

"Before we part, Nabi, may I offer you some advice?"

"Of course."

"I recommend you conceal your knowledge of English, at least initially."

"But why?"

"You saw how the men in France were. They are ruthless men, bad men. There is no reason to believe your employer will be any different. You need to be very careful." He held out his hand and shook Nabi's. "Farewell, my friend. Perhaps we will meet again."

"Goodbye, Giang, and thank you."

Chapter 34

Connor climbed into the van's driving seat, pulled out his phone and called Lewis's number.

While he was waiting for an answer he peered through the window at the foreigners standing a few yards from the vehicle. They looked wretched and cold but so what? They'd spent the best part of the day on open waters so he was sure they could handle a few more minutes in the rain.

Not that he gave a shit either way.

There was a click and Lewis came on the line.

"Hi. Everything okay?"

"Not really."

Connor wound the window down and glared at the small group. The man was cradling the infant in his arms and towered over his partner.

"The woman's tiny. Can't be much more than five foot. I can't see her pulling her weight."

Lewis grunted. "She'll have to. What about the man?"

Connor looked the Afghan up and down and sniffed.

"He seems strong enough. Doesn't speak a word of English though and neither does she. I tried asking their ages and all I got was blank looks. Fuck knows how we're going to show them what needs doing."

"How old do you reckon they are?"

"Twenty-five perhaps. Summat like that." He paused. "There's a bigger problem. Did you know they had a daughter?"

"What do you mean?"

"They've got a girl with them, must be only one or two."

Lewis sighed. "That sod Henri didn't mention any child."

"Want me to see if I can get one of the other illegals to take her?"

"Nah, can't see that happening."

"What about the boss? Won't she be annoyed?"

"There's no reason for her to know. This is my side of the business and we can ensure the child stays out of view. Remember, all the boss cares about is cheap labour." He chuckled. "It's a double whammy for her. She gets a cut of the money they've paid for the journey, plus she saves on maintenance costs for the estate.

"Yeah, I guess."

"Don't forget to check for passports. I don't suppose they'll have any, but best to be sure."

"Right."

Connor ended the call, climbed down out of the van and stood in front of the man.

"You're lucky." He pointed at the child. "My boss says you can bring her."

The man's eyes widened but he didn't say anything.

"You got passports?"

Again no reaction.

"Fuck's sake."

He decided to change tack and raised his voice.

"MY... NAME... IS... CONNOR."

There was no answer.

"CONNOR," he repeated, indicating himself with his thumb.

The man pointed at him. "Connor."

"Now we're fucking getting somewhere." He jabbed the man in the chest. "You?"

"Nabi."

"Nabi! What kind of a name is that?" He indicated the woman with a nod of his head. "What about her?"

"Jamila."

Connor shook his head. "Stupid fucking names."

The man indicated the child in his arms. "Bibi."

"What, like a hornet?" He chuckled at his own joke then raised his voice again.

"HAVE... YOU... GOT... PASSPORTS?"

The man shrugged.

"DOC... U... MENTS?"

He mimed leafing through a passport.

"Ah," the man said and nodded. "Gozarnameh."

"Eh?'

"Gozarnameh. Passport." He mimicked Connor's impression of turning the pages of a passport and shook his head. "No gozarnameh. No passport."

"Right. Well, I don't necessarily believe you, do I? Come here and hold your arms up to the side."

He held his own arms up to show what he meant and Nabi passed the child to Jamila, stepped forward and followed suit.

Connor frisked him and found nothing. He indicated for Nabi to move back, then moved in front of Jamila and indicated for her to step forward and do the same.

"NO!" Nabi exclaimed.

Connor grinned. "You think I'm gonna cop a feel?"

"NO!" Nabi said again and moved sideways to stand between Connor and his wife.

Connor grunted. "Okay."

Nabi stood back and Connor looked Jamila up and down. "Nowhere to hide anything anyway. Right, get in the van."

He moved to the back of the vehicle, opened the door, gestured for them to climb in and watched as Nabi helped his wife up onto the bare metal floor before passing the child to her and stepping up to join them.

Connor closed the door, walked to the side of the van then stopped, returned to the rear, inserted his key in the lock and turned it.

No point in taking any risks.

He returned to the driver's seat, started the engine and

began the long drive back to Somerset.

Chapter 35

Luke held Sam's hand as the needle was pushed in and out of the cut on the side of her head.

"You were lucky that door didn't cause more damage," the nurse said.

Sam tried to smile, but it was a weak attempt. "I don't feel very lucky. How many stitches?"

"Six. I've done as neat a job as I can but I'm afraid you'll have a scar. Your hair should cover it though." She tied the last one, stood back to check her handiwork and nodded. "I think you're good to go."

Sam stood up and Luke steadied her as she wavered and almost flopped back down into the seat again.

"Sorry," she said. "I came over all faint for a second."

The nurse looked over at Luke. "What your wife needs is rest."

"She's not…" he started to say then decided not to bother correcting her. "Don't worry, I'll make sure she takes it easy."

When they returned to Sam's flat she insisted on sitting on the sofa rather than going straight to bed.

"I don't think I could sleep anyway. It's not a nice feeling knowing your home has been broken into."

"Well at least lie down. Do you want your pyjamas? Or that onesie I bought you?"

Sam smiled and it was more genuine this time.

"Stop fussing. I'd rather sit. Those strong painkillers the nurse gave me are starting to cut in and I'm feeling a heap better. You could make us some hot chocolate though, if you don't mind."

Luke made their drinks, put Sam's mug into her hands and then sat on the armchair opposite.

"That was nice of that PC," he said, looking over at the window sill.

"What was?"

He indicated the vase of roses.

"She rescued the flowers I bought. When we left here in the ambulance they were scattered all over the landing."

"They're lovely. Thanks, Luke." She took a sip of her chocolate. "Do you think they'll catch her?"

He sat up. "Her? Did you see the burglar?"

Sam hesitated. "No, but I got a real sense that it was a woman. I'm not sure why though. It might be because at first I thought it was my mother."

"Can you try to think back so that you can work out why you think it was a woman who broke in?"

She smiled again. "Is this a formal police interview, DCI Sackville?"

He returned her smile. "You *are* feeling better, aren't you?"

"A little." She sighed. "I don't know, there was something…"

"Did you get any sense of size?"

"I certainly got a sense of power when she shoved me into the edge of the door." She thought for a few seconds. "There was something before that though. A noise, or was it…" She shook her head. "I can't remember."

"Don't worry for now. Hopefully, it'll come back to you." He looked around the room. "Is there anything missing?"

She sat forward and turned to look at the bookcase and shelves. "Not that I can see but given I interrupted her I guess that's not surprising." She sat back, took another sip of her hot chocolate and then furrowed her brows and looked back at the shelves next to the fireplace.

"What is it?"

"Have you moved the photo?"

"What photo?"

"The photo of you and me that Mark took at Christmas." She pointed to the middle shelf. "It was over there."

"Are you sure you haven't moved it?"

"I'm certain. It's not something a burglar would take though, is it?"

"Where's your rubbish bin?"

"The only bin I've got is the one in the kitchen."

He went into the kitchen and returned a moment or two later.

"It's empty."

"Empty?"

"Yes."

"Completely empty?"

"Yes. Why?"

"I threw a load of stuff away before I left for work this morning."

"What kind of stuff?"

"Flyers that had come in the post and all my Christmas cards."

"Anything like bank statements?"

"There was a utility bill."

"Mmm. It could be identity theft. That's the kind of thing they do, rifle through bins in the hope of finding account details and so on."

"It doesn't explain the missing photo though."

"No, you're right. It doesn't."

Chapter 36

Josh was surprised to see Carys on reception when he and Leanne arrived at Filchers.

"Morning, Carys," he said. "I thought you were on the late shift."

"I was."

He looked at his watch. "It's 8:30. That's not late, that's early. Not ultra-early like 4 am would be, but not late, not a late shift."

"Well spotted. I was on the late shift but now I'm in early."

"Exactly." He paused. "Wowza! Have you been in all night?"

"That's right. They make a bed up for me in the ladies' loo and order a hamper from Fortnum and Mason for my supper."

"Eh?"

Leanne had been smiling at this exchange but decided now was the time to rescue her boyfriend.

"Stop teasing him, Carys. Has Harriet called in sick again?"

Carys nodded. "Yes. I was called at six to cover until you come in."

"Ah!" Josh said, and pointed a finger gun at her. "Gotcha."

"So I bet you two are excited to be jetting off to Cambodia," Carys went on. "Have you got your travel pillows?"

Josh smiled. "Definito."

He nodded at his girlfriend as if to say *'I've got this'*.

"We've both got our travel pillows at the ready, haven't we, Leanne?"

She sighed. "Yes, Joshy."

"They're very important because we're travelling in economy without lie-flat seats or champagne or amenity kits from the White Company."

"Or candles," Carys suggested.

"Candles?"

She nodded. "Some airlines put out battery-powered candles when they serve your posh business class meal."

"Some airlines?"

"Emirates, I think."

"British Airways?"

"I'm not sure. Why? Are you hoping for an upgrade?"

"From BA to Emirates?"

"No, from economy to business class."

"Ah… Right. No."

"You don't want an upgrade?"

"Shannon."

Carys furrowed her brows, confused by this random reply. "Pardon."

Josh turned to Leanne. "Over there. Look." He pointed at one of the floor-to-ceiling windows to the right of the entrance door. "She's there, standing outside the building."

"Who is?"

"Shannon. You must remember Shannon?"

"Environmentalist Shannon? With the lip rings and goth clothes?"

He nodded. "Uh-huh. That's her. I wonder what she's doing here."

"Why don't you go and ask? I need to take over on reception so that Carys can go home."

"Right, yeah. Good idea." He hesitated. "But what if she remembers George Bailey?"

"Who's George Bailey?" Carys asked.

"Me. Well I'm not, but I was. Temporarily."

He felt a shove in his back.

"Go and speak to her, Joshy," Leanne said, widening

her eyes in a way that suggested she'd fry him alive if he said anything else.

"Right. Yes." He swallowed, looked at Carys and then back at his girlfriend. "I'll go and speak to her."

"Now."

"Yes. Ah… Now."

He walked to the entrance, trying to work out how to explain why he was there and indeed who he was. The last time they had met he'd been undercover. She knew him only as George so it was going to be a big shock when she…

"Hi, Josh,' she said as he approached.

"Eh?"

She smiled and he could immediately see that this was a much-transformed Shannon. Yes, she still had the piercings and the all-black clothes, but she seemed more relaxed, more comfortable in her own skin.

"Are you wondering how I know your name?"

He stared at her open-mouthed. Her fake cockney accent had gone too. Boy had she changed. It made her much more attractive.

No, not more attractive.

He mustn't think that.

He jerked around to check that Leanne wasn't watching. She could read his mind and if she knew he thought Shannon was attractive he was going to be in big trouble.

He swallowed.

"Are you going to speak?"

"What? Yes. You look att…"

He swallowed again, though it was more of a gulp this time.

"Go on. What do I look like?"

"Att… Ah…. At… peace with yourself. That's it. You look at peace with yourself. Not att… Ah… Not at all black."

"I'm not black."

"There you go then."

"I came here specifically to see you."

"You did?"

She nodded. "I wondered if you could help me."

"I'd be happy to, but how did you know where I worked? How do you know my real name for that matter?"

"Bob Matthews told me. We were talking about what a wonderful job your team did, and he told me about his relationship with Helen and how you'd been working undercover."

"Was this at an environmental action meeting?"

"No. I've moved on from that. I volunteer for Migrant Plus now and so does Bob."

"Migrant Plus?"

"It's a charity providing support to refugees and to victims of modern-day slavery and human trafficking."

"Gucci! Is that what you want help with?"

She smiled. "No. The reason I'm now more, as you put it, at peace with myself...."

"Rather than attractive."

"What?"

"Sorry, I meant... I mean, you are, uh..." He gulped, looked back through the window to check that Leanne wasn't giving him the evil eye, and then turned back to Shannon.

"Carry on."

"As I was saying, the reason I'm feeling better about myself is because I've been having counselling. Real counselling."

"What do you mean, 'real counselling'?"

"Have you ever heard of Beacon?"

Josh shook his head. "I can't say I have, no."

"Beacon is a so-called 'mentoring group'. They profess to help people who are struggling with mental health and other problems. That was me about 18 months ago and they sucked me in. Sucked a load of money out of me too before I managed to escape."

"Escape? What do you mean 'escape'?"

"Believe me, once they've brainwashed you it's as if you're their prisoner. Anyway, a journalist tracked me down and I'm helping her to do an exposé. I wondered if you could... Fuck!"

Shannon was now staring through the window into the reception area and her face had gone deadly pale.

Josh put his hand on her shoulder. "What's wrong, Shannon?"

She gasped and seemed to be struggling for breath.

"Erebus," she hissed. "It's Erebus."

"What's Erebus?'

"She is. I've got to go, Josh. I'll be in touch."

She turned and ran away from the building.

Josh looked through the window. The only people in view were Leanne at the reception desk and Ambrose Filcher who seemed to be holding court, explaining something to a group of five or six individuals.

It took him a second or two to realise that Ambrose was with the Board of Directors who he recognised from their photos on the whiteboard. He couldn't see Francois Lausanne or Alistair Ritchie, but the nearest person to Ambrose was Janice Martin, and standing next to her was Gillian Ley, Filchers' Chief Financial Officer. Slightly to one side were Dame Sarah Chittock, Meredith Holcroft and David Parsons.

Which meant one of the women in the group had to be Erebus.

Whoever Erebus was.

Chapter 37

"My main issue is with Cuthberts' drafting of the social responsibility clause," Helen said. "I don't think section 4.1.2 is comprehensive enough."

She passed the contract to Luke and he read through the paragraph in question.

"I see what you mean. What about stealing the clause we proposed in the Supracom renewal? That was well-received."

"Good idea. Thanks, Luke."

They both looked up as Josh bounded into the Ethics Room.

"Guv, guv, you'll never believe it." He was panting and swallowed as he continued. "Beacon... Erebus... Shannon...'

Luke held his hand up. "Woah, son. Calm down."

Helen stood up, helped Josh out of his coat and then wheeled up another chair beside hers and Luke's.

"Sit down here," she said, tapping the seat. "Were those crossword puzzle clues you were quoting?"

"No, I... Erebus... Beacon..."

She tapped the seat again, harder this time.

"SIT!"

He flopped into the chair obediently.

"Explain yourself, Josh," Luke said, "and try to calm down. You're talking gibberish."

"Gotcha, guv." Josh took a deep breath in an attempt to control himself. After a few seconds he felt ready to continue. "You remember Shannon from Earth Conflict?"

"The woman with the piercings and mockney accent?"

"That's her. Well, she appeared outside reception when Leanne and I were talking to Carys. I went outside and she asked for my help. She's working with a journalist researching an organisation she used to be a member of. It's called Beacon and the way she described it made it sound like a cult."

"A religious cult?"

Josh shook his head. "No. They provide mentoring services and Shannon joined about 18 months ago because she was suffering from mental health problems and thought they'd be able to help. However, once she was in their clutches it seems that they brainwashed her into doing anything they said. She told me that she was lucky to escape. That was her word for it. Escape."

"Ach, that sounds awful," Helen said.

"I assume they took money from her," Luke said.

Josh nodded. "Lots by all accounts."

"It's what's called a therapy cult. I came across one a few years ago when I was at Avon and Somerset. They're evil, and prey on the weakest in society, but they're very hard to bring to book."

"You also said 'Erebus' when you came in," Helen said. "What's an 'Erebus'?"

"It's not a what, it's a person, more specifically a woman. Shannon was explaining what she wanted me to do when she saw Ambrose and some of the Directors through the window, swore, said 'She's Erebus' and then ran off."

"Shannon definitely said 'she'?" Luke asked.

"Definito." He swivelled around and looked across at the whiteboard. "All four of our suspects for Project What were there. This has to be connected, doesn't it, guv?"

"Did Shannon say that Erebus was part of Beacon?"

Josh shook his head. "No, but I guess she has to be. I mean, the way Shannon ran off like that. She seemed genuinely frightened."

"Mmm." Luke rubbed at the bristles on his chin. "We've got an unknown whistleblower telling us one of the female Non-Execs is up to no-good in Cambodia, and now we've got Shannon suggesting that one of them is part of a therapy cult. They don't seem connected but I can't believe we've got two rogue directors on the board."

"Which means one of those women," Helen said, "is a sleekit old bint."

Luke smiled. "I couldn't have put it better myself, Helen."

"Why 'Erebus' though?" Josh wondered. "I guess it's in part to keep her identity a secret, but why such a wacky name?"

Helen turned to her laptop and googled it.

"According to Wikipedia," she said, "Erebus is a character in Greek Mythology. The God of Darkness no less."

Josh shivered. "That's not nice."

"The good news," Luke began, "is that if the person behind Beacon is also the person behind Tease we now know someone who can identify her. Do you know Shannon's address, Josh?"

"No, but I know where her mum works. She was behind the bar when I met Shannon and the others in the Centurion Inn in Twerton."

"Great. I've got a hunch we need to move quickly. Can you ring the pub now?"

"Will do."

Helen searched on Google and read the phone number out to Josh. He typed it in, hit the green button and waited.

After six or seven rings it went to voicemail.

"Hi. This is Josh Ogden. I need to speak to Shannon Wilson urgently but I don't have her address and I believe her mother works at the pub. Could someone ring me back as soon as possible please?" He gave his number, added "Thanks" and then hung up.

"It says here," Helen said, pointing at her screen, "that they open at noon. That's over three hours away."

"I suggest we give it an hour," Luke said, "and if they

haven't rung back by then someone ought to head to the pub."

Josh put his hand up. "I could go."

"You haven't got time, son. You've got a plane to catch, remember." He looked at Helen. "And you're on a deadline with the Cuthberts contract. Maybe Maj would be best."

"Or Sam?" Josh suggested.

Luke shook his head. "She's come down with a virus, plus yesterday…"

He stopped as his phone rang. He looked down at the screen. "It's Pete. Excuse me a second." He accepted the call.

"Hi, Pete. Can I ring you back?"

"We need to speak now. There's been a development."

"Okay. Just a second." He turned to Helen. "Helen, please can you explain to Josh what happened at Sam's flat yesterday, and also, when Maj gets in, can you prepare him for a trip to Twerton?"

"Aye, I can do that."

Luke stepped away. "What's happened?"

"We've found something on the CCTV footage. It shows a man wheeling the suitcase into the Lost Property room at Bath Spa."

"One of the station staff?"

"Could be, but he's casually dressed. I think we should get Simpson back in to look at it, but the footage is very grainy. In all likelihood, it can be enhanced but I can't find anyone who's up to the job. That's the main reason I called. Would it be possible for Maj to have a stab at it?"

"Of course. Would he have to come to Portishead?"

"No. Redbridge House has everything he'd need."

"Okay. Maj isn't in yet and he's going to Twerton later this morning. I could ask him to go into Bath afterwards."

"Great. Thanks."

"Any progress identifying the body?"

"Not as yet. DS Hewitt and I visited those Syrian

refugees who settled in Bath but they weren't aware of anyone going missing. One of them had heard of the slogan 'Idlib is my Freedom' though. He said it was used by the Syrian Liberal Front which was an anti-Assad political group."

"You said 'was'?"

"He said that the SLF was part of the new administration after Assad was ousted, but a rival group killed the leader and his deputy and other members were forced to flee. It was big news in Syria apparently."

"Mmm. Is it possible that he fled to the UK but was tracked down?"

"That was my first thought, but there are two reasons why I don't think that's the case."

"Go on."

"First, the man wheeling the suitcase into Lost Property doesn't look in the slightest bit Syrian. You'll see for yourself when you view the footage. And secondly, Sally found amphetamines in his system but no traces of poison or anything else that might point to him being murdered. If you remember, she believes that he most likely died from a heart attack."

"But if he died of natural causes why would anyone squeeze him into a suitcase and take him to a train station? This is an odd one, Pete. A very odd one." He looked up. "Ah, Maj has just walked in. I'll have a word with him and get back to you."

"Thanks, Luke."

"What happened with that woman found under Churchill Bridge?"

"It looks like suicide, and it's not the first time someone's chosen that spot to end their life."

"Has she been ID'd yet?"

"Yes. Her name was Anna Grayling and she was well-known to the police, although she'd gone off the radar in the last few years."

"Why was she well-known?"

"She ran a brothel in Pear Street and received a twelve month custodial sentence in 2021. However, once she got out of HMP Downview she went off the radar."

"Sounds like she was an almost unique example of a prison successfully rehabilitating someone. Although it doesn't seem to have done her much good in the end."

Luke hung up and his phone immediately rang again. This time it was Ambrose's PA.

"Hi, Ellie."

"Ambrose needs to see you, Luke. Could you come straight up please?"

"Of course."

Chapter 38

"You can go straight in," Ellie said.

Luke walked into the CEO's office to find Ambrose on the further sofa and Edward Filcher on the front edge of the nearer one, looking for all the world as though he had been summoned to the Headmaster's office for being a very naughty boy.

"Ah, Luke," Ambrose said. "Thank you for coming up. We have a problem." He turned to his nephew. "Tell him, Edward."

"Gillian," Filcher said, shaking his head and frowning. "Not happy."

"Gillian Ley?" Luke asked.

"Indeed. Not at all happy. Displeased. And peeved. Very peeved."

Ambrose sighed. "For heaven's sake, Edward, get to the point."

"I was, Uncle. As I said, she's very…"

"Unhappy. I know. You said as much. Five times."

"Wasn't it four times?"

Ambrose ignored him and addressed his next comment to Luke.

"Edward found himself in the lift with Gillian a few minutes ago and she complained to him about one of the staff in his department."

"Was that me?" Luke ventured.

"No. It was Sam." Ambrose held his hand up. "Before you say anything, Luke, please be assured that I do not think for one moment that she has done anything wrong."

"Needs disciplining though," Filcher said.

"Why?" Ambrose asked.

"Upsetting our CFO. Shouldn't be done. Not cricket."

"What exactly did she say?"

"I wasn't there."

"No, Edward." Ambrose shook his head. "You are beginning to try my patience. I know you weren't there when Sam supposedly upset Gillian. What I meant was, what did Gillian say to you?"

"Ah… Right… Gillian. What she said. Ah… that she was unhappy. Very unhappy. Not happy at all."

"I gathered that, but why?"

"Sam was prying. That was what Gillian said. Prying."

Ambrose waited, but it took a few seconds for his nephew to realise he was expected to continue.

"Gillian overheard Sam. Asking her PA questions. Not on. About outside interests. Inappropriate." He shook his head. "Most inappropriate."

"Gillian thought it was inappropriate?"

"As do I. Poking her nose in. Shouldn't be done. She's our CFO. Very senior. Deserves better."

"What did you say to Gillian?"

"I told her I would deal with Sam. Leave it to me, I said." He lowered his voice to a whisper, seeming to sense that his next words wouldn't be well received. "Suspension."

"What was that, Edward?"

He raised his voice a notch. "I said I'd suspend her."

"You said what!"

Filcher gulped. "Surely, it's not a problem, Uncle. She's not senior. Woman too. Won't be missed. Important I suspend her. Shows respect for our CFO."

"Shows you toady up to her more like."

Filcher had the good sense not to respond to this.

"You are not suspending Sam Chambers, Edward."

"I'm not?"

"No. You're not."

"Even though…"

"Watch my lips, Edward. You… are… not…

suspending… Sam. Understand?"

Filcher nodded but didn't say anything.

Ambrose turned back to Luke. "I think we need to tell Edward about Project What."

"What?" Filcher said.

Ambrose glared at his nephew but ignored the question.

"Luke and I are going to let you into our confidence about a secret project we are working on."

Filcher started to speak but Ambrose continued glaring and he closed his mouth again.

"I don't care what you think about us missing you out, Edward. The reason we didn't involve you is because there was no benefit in doing so. However, I now believe that you need to know. Over to you, Luke."

Luke explained about the whistleblower's emails.

"As a result," he said when he'd finished, "we believe that one of the four female Board Directors is involved in something immoral and possibly illegal."

"The reason I wanted to tell you now," Ambrose said, "is because you can help."

"Of course, Uncle. At your service. Anything you say."

"Stop fawning, Edward."

"Absolutely. Anything you say."

"I believe that you know Meredith."

"Indeed."

"In the biblical sense."

Filcher's chin seemed to visibly recede from his face and his lips started vibrating against each other as small noises issued from them.

It was as if he was trying to blow a raspberry but didn't quite have the energy.

He looked wide-eyed at his uncle, then at Luke and then back at his uncle.

"B… b… b…"

A smile came over Ambrose's face.

"Suddenly, I'm rather enjoying this meeting."

He turned to Luke.

"This will be news to you, Luke, but last year my nephew and Meredith Holcroft developed what I will euphemistically call a close bond."

"B… b… b…"

Ambrose grinned. "It was, shall we say, a very up-and-down relationship." He turned to face his nephew again. "You didn't think anyone knew about it, did you, Edward? However, Ellie spotted some diary clashes that, well, they gave the game away."

"F… f…" Filcher began and for a moment Luke thought a profanity was going to be the next thing from his lips.

Filcher swallowed and managed to force a full word out.

"Finished."

"No, Edward, you're not finished."

"No… I… Of course not… But we're… She and I… We're, ah… Finished."

"So I believe. But you remain on good speaking terms, do you not?"

"We do."

"Albeit without the rumpy-pumpy."

Hearing this expression come from the CEO's mouth made Luke snort and he put his hand over his mouth to avoid the risk of a full-on belly-laugh escaping.

"You don't have to answer that, Edward," Ambrose continued. "I'm having my bit of fun, that's all." He paused. "Rest assured that the only people who know about your affair are Ellie, Luke and me and we won't tell another soul."

"Thank you, Uncle."

"Now, as Luke has told you, Meredith is one of our suspects. What are your thoughts? After all, you know her rather better than we do."

"Good sort. Trust her. Tough though."

"Tough? In what way?"

"Harsh. Strong views. Not to be trifled with."

"Can you expand on that?"

"Her ex-husband is Ralph Holcroft. Works for Bannermans."

"I've seen his name," Luke said. "Wasn't he involved in the Netso deal?"

"Yes he was," Ambrose said. "He runs their media sector and led their successful bid against us. Very good negotiator."

"Merry can't tolerate him," Filcher said, then added hastily, "I mean Meredith."

Ambrose's smile returned.

"Was Merry your pet name for her when you were together, Edward?" He didn't wait for an answer, merely chuckled before continuing. "Did she call you Teddy or was it Eddie?"

Filcher mumbled something under his breath.

"Sorry, Edward. I didn't catch that."

Filcher swallowed. "Filly," he whispered.

"I beg your pardon."

"She called me Filly. Short for Filcher. Ah… she likes to ride horses."

A picture formed in Luke's mind that made him feel distinctly nauseous. He decided to return to the key issue.

"In what way was Meredith tough with her husband, Mr Filcher?"

"Told him what was what. He threatened to share details. Of her first business. On the borders apparently."

"On the borders?"

"Of legality. She admitted as much. It worried her but she gave Ralph what for. Made him go quiet. Threatened to expose his predilections."

Ambrose's eyebrows went up.

"His predilections?"

"He liked to wear…"

"It's okay, Edward. That is a detail we don't need to know."

"Do you know anything more about this first business of hers?" Luke asked. "Did she tell you why it straddled the line between being legal and illegal?"

"Ladies' underwear."

"I told you we don't want to know the details regarding her husband," Ambrose said.

"No, Uncle. That was her first business. Ladies underwear. You know…" He pointed to his groin and then to his chest.

"I know what ladies' underwear is, Edward." He turned to Luke. "Are you thinking what I'm thinking, Luke?"

Luke nodded. "Tease manufactures women's clothes."

There was a knock and Ellie's head appeared as the door opened.

"Meredith Holcroft is here to see you, Ambrose."

"Ah, excellent."

Filcher looked at Ellie then turned to his uncle and opened his mouth though no words came out.

"Don't worry, Edward, I'm not going to embarrass you in front of…" His smile returned. "…Merry." He paused for a second to let this sink in. "I invited her up so that Luke can meet her and form his own opinions. You may leave."

"Oh, thank you, Uncle. Ah…" he pointed to the door. "But she… Ah…"

"Yes, she's outside but all you have to do is say hello on your way past. You did say that you remain on good terms."

"Indeed. Yes. Not a problem." He bent forward in a mini-bow then backed to the door and left.

A few seconds later Luke heard him say, in a voice that was noticeably deeper than normal, "Good morning, Meredith."

Chapter 39

"Ah, Meredith," Ambrose said as she walked into the room. "Thank you for sparing some of your valuable time. This is Luke Sackville, our Head of Ethics."

She walked forward and shook Luke's hand, her grip strong and her eyes focused on his.

"It's good to meet you at last, Luke. I've heard a lot about you."

"Good things, I hope."

She laughed. "Mixed, I'm afraid. However, the bad things came from my ex-husband and to be honest, his opinion is meaningless. He believes Filchers made a mistake recruiting you, but then he *is* employed by our competitor Bannermans so anything he says has to be taken with a pinch of salt."

"Please take a seat, both of you," Ambrose said. "As I said on the phone, Meredith, I wanted you to meet Luke and his co-presenters before they stand up in front of the Board next week. It's your chance to clarify the areas you'd like them to cover."

There was a knock on the door and Ellie appeared.

"Maj and Helen are here."

"Ah good," Ambrose said. "Please ask them to join us."

A few seconds later they entered, Helen looking at ease while Maj seemed distinctly on edge.

Ambrose gestured to the sofa Luke was on.

"Shuffle along and make room, Luke. I'll sit here beside Meredith."

He waited until they were all seated before continuing.

"Maj, Helen, thanks for joining us. I was saying before you arrived that this is Meredith's opportunity to spell out what she would like you to cover when you present next week. Meredith, over to you."

"Thanks, Ambrose." She turned her attention to the three members of the Ethics Team. "You will not be aware of my past, but I grew up in abject poverty, left school at sixteen and was a millionaire before I was twenty-three. I'm not saying this to boast but because, in my entire career, which now spans three decades, I have never seen the need for an ethics adviser, let alone an expensive team."

She was smiling as she said this but Luke could immediately see why Edward Filcher had said she was tough. She had concerns and she was making them crystal clear.

Whether this was because she genuinely doubted the need for an ethics team, or because she didn't want them prying into her business dealings, remained to be seen.

"What I require," she went on, "and I'm sure this goes for my fellow Board members as well, is full and proper justification for your existence."

Luke returned her smile.

"Thank you for being so frank, Meredith."

She continued smiling as she pushed the knife a little deeper.

"A number of your investigations have involved working alongside the police, and it appears to me that you are acting as if you are still a DI rather than in the interests of Filchers. These cases are at a tangent to what we are about which, as the three of you well know, is business outsourcing." She paused for her words to sink in. "For example, when you exposed the goings-on at GNE, can you seriously claim that doing so was of value to our company? I'm sure the police appreciated your help, and your personal profile certainly went up afterwards Luke, but how did we benefit?"

There was a lot to take in. Luke was sure that she had deliberately referred to him as having been a DI rather than a DCI to wind him up. Her insinuation that he worked on cases to further his personal profile was intentional too.

However, there was no way he was going to rise to the bait. He decided to turn the conversation on its head so that he could find out more about her.

"I can understand your concerns, Meredith, but I assure you that every case we work on is for Filchers' benefit. Perhaps I can illustrate this by referencing your own experience. You said you had success in your early twenties?"

"That's correct."

"May I ask what business you were in?"

"I started a chain of underwear shops which I later sold."

"Manufacturing as well as retail?"

"No, just retail. I employed a team of buyers as the business grew."

"Wasn't it difficult to straddle the line between legality and illegality, morality and immorality? After all, the clothes industry has been beset by problems."

"Only when manufacturing is overseas. All our underwear was made in Britain."

"But what about that scandal in 2020 when the BBC uncovered poor working conditions in a Leicester garment factory? Didn't they find that the online retailer Boohoo had pressured suppliers to lower prices?"

"It was the exception that proves the rule."

"My point is that a check and balance is needed, Meredith, and that's what our Ethics Team provides. I assume that your buyers were incentivised to keep costs to a minimum?"

"Of course. It's standard practice in our industry."

"And were their activities checked by anyone to ensure they always acted ethically and didn't cut corners?"

"I recruited them personally and trusted them implicitly. Their work didn't need checking."

Luke smiled. "That's what senior management said at

Boohoo, but their business has been beset by problems since that BBC investigation. If I remember rightly, they cut 1,000 jobs and declared a loss of £160 million. I guarantee that they wouldn't be in that position if they had employed the services of an ethics expert."

Meredith didn't comment and instead turned her attention to Maj.

"Maj, what ethics experience and expertise do you bring to the team?"

Maj hesitated, but only for a second.

"I've worked in technology and security for my entire career, Meredith," he said, "and both areas are critical in ensuring that Filchers' activities are ethically sound."

She turned to Helen. "And you, Helen?"

"I've been a paralegal for over thirty years." She laughed. "In fact, you were probably still in primary school when I first started. My job is to ensure that Filchers' contracts are comprehensive in ensuring we meet our social and corporate responsibilities."

Meredith sat back in the sofa.

"You and your team are beginning to sway me, Luke, but only beginning to. When you are in front of the Board next week, I suggest you run through an investigation, past or present, and summarise the benefits. I appreciate that most of those will be intangible, but the company's bottom line is what the Board cares most about so try to show quantifiable savings from your team's activities."

"Thanks, Meredith. That's good advice."

Ambrose stood up.

"I hope the meeting was useful, Luke, and gave you the information you needed."

"It did indeed, Ambrose. Very much so." He turned to Meredith. "Good to meet you, Meredith."

"And you too, Luke."

Luke, Maj and Helen walked back to the Ethics Room and Luke walked straight to Josh's desk.

"Has anyone called back?"

Josh shook his head. "I left another message a few minutes ago." He looked at his watch. "It's been three-quarters of an hour. Do you think…"

"Yes, I do." He turned to Maj. "I need you to do two things for me please, Maj."

"I told him about Shannon identifying Erebus when he got in, guv."

"Good. So first, Maj, I want you to visit the Centurion Inn in Twerton and find out where Shannon's mother lives. Take photos of the female board directors with you then when you catch up with Shannon she'll be able to tell us who Erebus is. Keep us in touch with progress."

"Do you think Shannon's in danger?"

"She could be. My suspicion is that the woman calling herself Erebus is central to Beacon, the therapy cult that drew Shannon in. If that's the case she won't want her real name revealed. I don't want to risk her getting to Shannon before we do."

"And the second thing?"

"DI Gilmore's asked for your help with some CCTV footage. He's going to be in Redbridge House in Bath so please can you go there as soon as you've finished with Shannon?"

"Will do."

Maj entered the address and postcode into his phone, put his coat on and headed off.

Chapter 40

Erebus stood at the window looking out at Filchers' car park. There was no sign of Fern, but that wasn't a surprise. The wretched girl would be long gone by now.

She walked to the office door, checked it was locked and then sat at the table and called Skylar.

"Hello."

"Hello, Skylar. How did it go with Wynna?"

"It was as easy as pie. We met again for her to continue bleating out her concerns and I persuaded her to go for a walk with me so that we could talk things through." He laughed. "Unfortunately, when we reached Churchill Bridge she decided to take her own life."

"And no one saw you with her?"

"I was very careful."

"Good. What is happening with her replacement?"

"She's already on board. Do you want to meet her?"

"At some point. Give it a few weeks though to make sure she's completely up to speed. What's her background?"

"She's a GP or, more accurately, an ex-GP. She was struck off the register two years ago for selling prescription drugs over the internet. I've been courting her for several months with a view to her working in one of our East Anglia operations but, given this vacancy has arisen, it seemed sensible to allocate her to Bath."

"And you have complete confidence in her?"

"Definitely. She's very personable, which helps to attract new clients, but absolutely and totally motivated by money. She's both immoral and amoral, I'd say."

"Excellent."

"I also have evidence that she's been supplying recreational drugs to people in high circles, including one of the local MPs and a rock star. I haven't told her I have it though. It's there as a back-up should we ever need to exert pressure."

"Has she been allocated a name?"

"Brell."

"Mmm. That sounds good. What's her real name?"

"Candice Harrison." He paused. "There's good news with Valmoria too."

"You've persuaded her to sell her apartment?"

"Yes, I have. She was very keen when I said it would help to sanctify her aura and improve her chances of achieving Level Rising Sun. It should go on the market next week and I'm authorised to act as her agent."

"I'm pleased all is going well with Brell and Valmoria because we have a problem. That's the real reason for my call."

"Really? What kind of a problem?"

"You remember Wynna telling us that she'd seen Fern, who's very much alive and now a goth?"

"Of course."

"I saw her this morning."

"Where?"

"In the offices of a company I'm visiting. She saw me too, and I'm convinced she recognised me because she turned and fled as soon as our eyes met." She sighed. "If she tells anyone it won't be good for me, or for Beacon and you either. The whole venture could blow up in our faces."

"Do you want me to deal with her?"

"Yes, but you need to move quickly."

"It should be straightforward. Her mother posted about her suicide on Facebook so I should be able to track her down from that. If I remember correctly, Fern's original name was Shannon Wilson and her mother's name is Yvonne."

"Make it clean, but don't make it Churchill Bridge again. Two we can get away with, but a third may raise suspicions."

"I'll get on the case."

"Good. I need reassurance that you have made the issue disappear. Make this your top priority."

Chapter 41

Maj pulled up outside the Centurion Inn.

For some reason, perhaps the suggestion of age in the pub's name, he'd expected an old building, possibly Victorian. However, it was clearly post-war, built in Bath Stone and full of sharp angles, the picture-windowed first floor suspended on pillars above the entrance.

As expected, given it was still only 10 am, the front door was locked. He pressed the button on the side panel and a man's voice answered almost immediately.

"Hello."

"Hi, My name's Maj Osman. I'm looking for Shannon Wilson."

"She's not here. Are you a friend of hers?"

"No, but…" Maj hesitated as he decided how best to gain entry. "Does the name Erebus mean anything to you?"

There was a short pause then the man said, "Come up," and there was a click as the door was unlocked.

Maj walked inside, up the stairs and through an open door into the main bar area.

As soon as he appeared a man in his mid-forties marched towards him, his chest puffed out and a scowl on his face.

He came to within a couple of paces of Maj and waved his finger in his face.

"I don't want your sort coming here."

For a split-second, Maj wondered if this was blatant racism, but the man's next words confirmed why he was angry.

"How did you track my daughter down? Your cult almost killed her, you bastard."

Maj held his hand up and backed away a pace. "I'm not

from Beacon, Mr Wilson."

The man looked doubtful. "Who are you then? How do you know about Erebus?"

"Has Shannon mentioned Josh Ogden?"

"No. Is he one of them?"

"What about George, George Bailey?"

Wilson shook his head.

"Is your wife here? Perhaps Shannon told her about George. He's my colleague and she came to see him this morning. We're worried she might be in danger."

"Just a second."

He turned, walked to the far end of the room, opened a door and called out. "Yvonne! Please can you come down."

A few seconds later his wife appeared. She was wearing an apron and carrying a duster and a tin of Pledge.

"What is it, Patrick?" She spotted Maj. "Oh."

"This is…" Patrick began. "Sorry, I forgot your name."

"Maj."

"Maj asked if we know a George Bailey."

Yvonne nodded. "George was in that environmental lobbying group with Shannon. I met him when he came to the pub for one of their meetings. Why?"

"Can we sit down?" Maj asked. "This may take a bit of explaining."

'Sure," Patrick said and gestured to the nearest table.

Maj waited until they were all seated before beginning.

"My colleague's real name is Josh Ogden. He was going under the name George Bailey because he was working undercover."

"Are you in the police then?" Yvonne asked.

"No, but we were working alongside them."

"Private detectives," Patrick said, nodding his head.

Maj decided to let this pass. Saying they worked for a private sector business outsourcing company was not going to help convince them he was telling the truth.

"Shannon came to see Josh at our offices this morning.

While they were talking she spotted someone she knew through a window. She told Josh her name was Erebus and then ran away."

Yvonne put her hand to her mouth.

"Did Erebus see her?" Patrick asked.

"Josh thinks she might have done, yes. Do you know who Erebus is?"

Yvonne sighed. "We don't know her real name, but she was the person at the top of that evil organisation."

"Beacon?"

She nodded.

"When did this happen?" Patrick asked.

"About 8:30 this morning. We rang you soon afterwards and left a voicemail."

Patrick turned to look at the top of the counter.

"The bloody phone system's temperamental. I'll have to get an engineer out."

"Do either of you know where Shannon is?" They both shook their heads. "Please can you give it some thought?"

The phone rang.

"Excuse me," Patrick said.

He stood up, walked to the bar and picked the handset up.

"Hello, Centurion Inn. How can I help?"

He listened for a few seconds, then turned to Maj and gestured for him to come over. As he did so Patrick pressed the speaker button.

"...need to speak to her as soon as possible." It was a man's voice and he had an Australian accent.

"Are you a friend of hers?" Patrick asked.

"Oh yes." The man laughed. "We go way back."

"She hasn't mentioned you. Did you say your name was Silas?"

"That's right."

Patrick looked at his wife. "Do you know a Silas, Yvonne?"

She shook her head. "No."

Maj caught Patricks's attention and mouthed '*ask how he knows her*'.

"How do you know Shannon, Silas?"

"We met a couple of years ago. Look, I really need to speak to her as a matter of urgency."

"Why? What's happened?"

"A mutual friend of ours is in difficulties and I know she'd like to help her."

'*Ask him to come here,*' Maj mouthed. '*At lunchtime*'.

"Oh dear," Patrick said. "How awful. We're expecting Shannon back between one and two this afternoon. Do you want to come over then?"

"Yes, I'll do that."

"Okay. We'll see you later. Goodbye, Silas, and I'm sorry to hear about your friend."

"Yes, it's tragic."

There was a click and the line went dead.

Patrick put the handset back on its cradle and turned to Maj. "Are you thinking what I'm thinking?"

Maj nodded. "That man's working for Erebus. He wants to persuade Shannon to keep quiet."

"Should we call the police?"

"Possibly. Can you try Shannon's phone first?"

Patrick rang but it went straight to voicemail. He waited for the bleep after her message before speaking. "Shannon, it's Dad. Please give me a ring as soon as you get this."

"Okay," Maj said. "Give me a moment while I speak to my boss."

Maj moved to the end of the room, called Luke and ran through everything that had happened.

"I'm sure you're right that he's been sent by Erebus," Luke said when he'd finished, "which means he'll arrive before noon. He won't want to risk Shannon telling her parents she's never heard of anyone called Silas."

"Patrick suggested calling the police."

"There's no point. They might send someone around to speak to her parents but it'll be a pop-in visit, no more than that. They need someone with them. We don't know if this Silas is intent on more than just persuasion."

"Shall I stay here then?"

"Yes, but I need you to help with that CCTV footage so I'll head down there now to relieve you so you can go into Bath."

Chapter 42

Maj introduced Luke to Shannon's parents and then drove into the centre of Bath, parked in Southgate car park and walked the short distance to Redbridge House.

The door was opened by a uniformed constable.

"Hi," she said. "Are you here about Dave?"

"I don't think so. I'm here to see DI Gilmore."

She smiled. "Ah, right. Sorry. Are you Maj Osman?"

"That's me."

"Come on in. I'm PC Warwick. He told me to expect you."

She opened the door wide and gestured to an office at the back of the room.

"He's in there. Can I get you a coffee?"

"I'd love one thanks. White, no sugar."

Pete looked up when he walked in and they shook hands.

"Thanks for coming in, Maj. My guys have tried to get to grips with the software but they've got nowhere and our technical department is busy as hell."

"No problem. I'll give it my best shot. What exactly is the issue?"

Pete gestured for Maj to take the seat next to him and then clicked on the keyboard a couple of times. He pointed to the image frozen on the screen.

"I'm sure this is grainier than it should be. It's our best shot and we can see the guy wheeling the suitcase is big but that's about it. His features are all fuzzy."

Maj pointed to the keyboard.

"Do you mind?"

"Help yourself."

Maj clicked on the menu, then went down a level to

tools, clicked a few times so that a series of complex button-filled boxes appeared on the screen and then pointed to one of them.

"There's your problem."

Pete looked at the screen and shrugged. "Where?"

Maj smiled and indicated one of the slider buttons on the screen. "Someone's turned rasterisation on."

"Rasterisation?"

Maj nodded. "It's a computer graphics technique that converts vector-based images into pixel-based representations."

"And that's bad?"

"It's not needed. Rasterisation projects geometry onto the screen and determines if pixels fall within 2D triangles. It's the primary rendering technique used by GPUs to generate images of 3D objects."

"You do know you've completely lost me, don't you?"

Maj laughed. "The point is that you don't need it for CCTV footage."

"Can you turn it off?"

"I'm not sure. It's been hard set." He put his hand to his forehead and thought for a few seconds. "If I..." he began, talking under his breath. "Yes, that should work."

"What are you going to do?"

"I'm going to disable rasterisation. If I tell the pipeline there's no pixel shader and if I also disable depth and stencil testing, then with any luck…"

He continued clicking as PC Warwick appeared with two coffees.

"Are you getting anywhere?" she asked as she placed the drinks down in front of them.

"He's removing shading from the pixies," Pete said and shrugged. "Something like that, anyway."

"Done!" Maj exclaimed.

He clicked a few more times and the image of the man with a suitcase appeared again and it was much clearer.

Pete moved closer to the screen.

"It might be only a side-on view but it's a pretty good picture."

PC Warwick bent down between them and pointed at the man's neck. "Is that a tattoo?"

Maj zoomed in on the image. It was a side-on image of a rat with its mouth open and teeth bared.

Pete wrinkled his nose. "Not the most pleasant of images."

"Are those letters above it?" PC Warwick asked.

"Just a second." Maj pressed a few more buttons and the image became even sharper. "RRMC. I haven't the faintest what that means. Any idea?"

They both shook their heads.

"It's a shame the camera hasn't caught him full on," Pete said. "but it might be enough for our man Simpson to recognise him. PC Warwick, please can you try to get him in for another interview?"

"Will do, sir."

Maj pointed at the man on the screen. "Is he suspected of committing a crime?"

"He certainly is. Over a week after that footage was taken one of the Bath Spa staff noticed a smell in the Lost Property office. He realised it was coming from the suitcase and opened it to find a curled-up body inside."

"Nasty." Maj paused. "When I get back to the office I can try to find out what RRMC might stand for, if that would help."

"That would be great, and thanks for your help with the, ah… rasters."

Maj smiled. "No problem, Pete. Any time."

Chapter 43

Luke was shocked to hear the full details of Shannon's seduction into the therapy cult.

"And it was eighteen months ago that you managed to persuade her to leave?"

Yvonne nodded. "She was a complete mess at first, hardly eating, awake most of the night and full of guilt about betraying Beacon, almost as if she'd left a religion rather than a mentoring group."

"It must have been hard for you to see her like that."

"It was horrendous. The worst year of our lives. Becoming an environmental activist helped to take her mind off things, but it's only since she started counselling with a friend of ours that she's returned to her old self."

"Has she spotted anyone else from Beacon since she left?"

"No. She went to Glastonbury a couple of weeks ago with a friend, but fortunately she didn't come across that dreadful woman Wynna who recruited her."

"They have a kind of Druid thing going on," Patrick added, "which I guess appeals to some of the crazies in the town."

Luke raised an eyebrow. "What do you mean?"

"All the recruits were given new names. Shannon became Fern and the women she shared a dormitory with were called Celestina, Valmoria and Brenonna. I looked the names up and they're all connected to Druidry."

"Did she find out the other women's real names?"

Patrick looked at his wife. "Didn't she say that Celestina's real name was Marie?"

Yvonne nodded. "Marie Cotton. She was the one they moved on from Glastonbury because she'd been elevated to the next level. The Level of Rising Sun they called it."

"Have you got the address of the building Shannon was staying in when she was with Beacon?"

Patrick read out the address and Luke added it to his contacts.

He walked to the window, looked up and down the street and then peered more closely at one of the parked cars. He called Patrick and Yvonne over and pointed to the vehicle, which was parked fifty yards or so along the road on the opposite side from the pub.

"Do either of you recognise that blue Kia?"

Yvonne shook her head.

"Never seen it before," Patrick said. "Why?"

"From this angle it's impossible to see if anyone's inside, but I'm sure I saw movement a few seconds ago." Luke hesitated. "I'm going to go down and check."

"Do you think it might be the man who rang earlier?"

"I'll soon find out."

He headed downstairs, exited the pub and walked towards the Kia. As he approached he saw the reflection of a man's face in the wing mirror and heard the noise of the gently purring engine.

Luke upped his pace, bent down to the driver's window, smiled and indicated for it to be lowered.

The man lowered the window about a third of the way and attempted to return his smile but Luke could see he was on edge.

"Hi," the man said. "How can I help?"

Luke didn't believe in coincidences and this man's Australian accent told him everything he needed to know.

He continued smiling.

"Are you waiting for Shannon?"

The man hesitated before replying.

"That's right. I thought I'd wait outside until she gets back. Was it you I spoke to on the phone earlier?"

Luke ignored the question.

"Why don't you come inside and wait? You'll be much more comfortable."

"Thanks for the offer, but I'm fine here."

"You said on the phone that you've got a mutual friend who's in difficulties. I'm sorry to hear that."

"Yes. It's not good."

It was then that Luke noticed a tea towel on the passenger seat. It was folded over in a way that suggested there was an object inside it, something long and thin.

It could be something innocent.

But then again…

"Would you mind lowering the window completely? It's difficult talking like this."

The man responded by putting his hand to the toggle switch on the door, but instead of the window descending it started to rise.

"I'll wait and talk to Shannon when she gets here," he said just before it closed completely.

Luke stood back, trying to decide what to do for the best.

It was clear that he wasn't going to be able to entice the man out of the car, but there was no way he was letting him wait outside the pub ready to confront Shannon, or possibly her parents, and use the weapon concealed in the tea towel.

No, it would be better to scare him off and track him down afterwards.

He banged his fist on the window, glared at the man and raised his voice.

"Shannon knows you're here Silas, and she won't be returning. Erebus sent you, didn't she?"

The man's eyes widened as he heard this. His left hand went to the gear stick and there was a crunch as he pushed it forward into first.

Luke banged on the window again but the car was already starting to move away. He stepped back as it careered down the road and rounded the corner at the end with a screeching of tyres.

He took a note of the registration number, returned to Shannon's parents and explained what had happened, leaving out his suspicion that the man had a knife.

"Do you think he'll come back?" Yvonne asked, a note of desperation in her voice.

"No, I'm confident he won't. He knows we're onto him and believes we've told your daughter not to return here. You'll be fine, but please let Maj or me know if Shannon calls or turns up, or if he rings you again."

"Will do."

"Please excuse me a moment. I need to talk to a colleague of mine and call in a favour."

Pete answered on the first ring.

"Hi, Luke. Thanks for sending Maj over. He found our problem and we've now got a great image of the guy who dumped the suitcase. PC Warwick's managed to cajole Barry Simpson into coming in at four. Are you okay to come over?"

Luke looked at his watch. "Yes, that'll be fine. I need to go back to the office first though." He paused. "Do you think you could do me a favour?"

"Sure. What?"

"Could you trace the owner of a car for me? It's a sky blue Kia Sportage, registration number CU70 ADF. The driver threatened a friend of Josh's and I want to have a word with him. He gave his name as Silas."

"Anything the police should be involved with?"

"Not at present."

"I'll get on it."

"Thanks. I'll see you later."

Chapter 44

Luke asked Helen and Maj to join him at the team's table when he returned to the Ethics Room.

He pointed to the whiteboard.

"We now know that one of those Board members is involved with, if not at the head of, a therapy cult. What that tells me is that the whistleblower's emails about immoral activities in Tease are genuine, and that the same woman is almost certainly making money from both Tease and Beacon. And if she's making money from those two wildly diverse operations, what's to say she's not involved in other dodgy dealings." He paused. "The problem is that we have absolutely nothing to pinpoint the culprit. We've spent time with each of them, but aside from gaining an insight into their characters I'm not sure we've learnt very much."

"Perhaps we should concentrate on their personalities then," Helen suggested. "Details such as whether they've ever been married are irrelevant."

Luke was tempted to add '*Or whether they've ever played 'Please be my filly and let me ride you' with Edward Filcher*' but he'd been sworn to secrecy on that front.

"You're right Helen," he said. "Perhaps you could simplify the board and add our opinion as to their characters. It's going to be highly subjective but it's all we've got."

They spent the next few minutes discussing the four directors, with Luke inputting everything that Sam had learned from her meeting with Gillian Ley. When they'd finished Helen wiped the board clear and started again.

Gillian Ley (48)

- Finance Director
- troublemaker, secretive

Meredith Holcroft (49)
- underwear entrepreneur
- challenging, very direct

Dame Sarah Chittock (69)
- Inherited money, charities
- charismatic, warm

Janice Martin (56)
- neurosurgeon
- Confrontational
- dislikes Ethics Team

Luke sighed. "There's not a lot to go on there. Sarah Chittock is the only one who didn't directly challenge our team's existence, but that doesn't mean she's innocent. Our best chance is that Shannon turns up. Failing that, we're reliant on Josh and Leanne turning something up in Cambodia, or our whistleblower contacting us with a name."

"What about that guy Silas who phoned The Centurion?" Maj asked.

"Yes, there's a possibility he might lead us to Erebus. He turned up at the pub and I made it clear Shannon wasn't returning and he drove off. DI Gilmore's doing a trace on the number plate for me."

"I've had a wee idea," Helen mused. "Given our villain is involved in at least two shady businesses, could we lay a trap for her?"

Luke was intrigued. "Go on."

"We haven't talked about our presentation next week. What if we describe a failed investigation into an invented organisation? One that appeals to whichever of those four…" She gestured to the whiteboard. "…is our baddie."

"Mmm." Luke rubbed his chin. "Meredith Holcroft suggested we run through an investigation so it fits. She also asked us to summarise the benefits though, and that'll be difficult if we say we failed."

"Ach, I'm sure we can spin it. Do you want me to work on it?"

"Yes, please. Let's talk about it tomorrow."

"Before you go, Luke," Maj said, "I said I'd look into a tattoo for you and Pete."

"You did?"

"Sorry, I haven't had time to tell you. Once we obtained a clear image of the man who wheeled that suitcase into Lost Property we saw that he had a tattoo on his neck. It was an image of a rat with the letters RRMC above. I told Pete I'd try to find out what it represents."

He was smiling and Luke could tell he was pleased with himself.

"Rolls-Royce Motor Cars?"

It was Maj's turn to smile.

"You couldn't be further from the truth. RRMC stands for Road Rats Motorcycle Club. It evolved from a London street gang sixty years ago and has been in trouble with the law on numerous occasions. Think the most violent of Hells Angels' chapters and you wouldn't be much off the mark."

Luke's phone rang.

"Guv… Guv…" Josh sounded breathless.

"What is it, Josh? Have you seen Shannon again?"

"No… Running out of time." He took a deep breath. "Are there two or three? Straight or circular prongy-thingios?"

"What?"

Josh's voice faded slightly as he turned away from the phone. "He doesn't know what I mean."

Then Luke heard Leanne's voice. "How could he, Joshy? You haven't even mentioned plugs."

"Oh." His voice became louder again. "Do you know which plugs they use in Cambodia, guv?" He paused. "Not for sinks. I guess they use round ones like we do. No, for…"

"Whoa, son. Why don't you look on the internet?"

"Eh? Oh… Yes… Gotcha."

The line went dead.

"Has the wee boy got a problem?" Helen asked.

"He certainly has, Helen, but I'm sure he'll improve as he grows older."

Helen grinned. "Aye, we can always hope."

Chapter 45

Josh wasn't pulling his weight. He knew that.

But Cambodia!

Siem Reap!

Wowza!

He was excited and keeping up with Leanne's demands was a struggle. She kept asking him to find clothes or hair driers or whatever, but it was difficult when his mind was on their mission.

He'd been undercover before, but never as part of a couple. They'd be like Bonnie and Clyde, but without the ambush at the end. Dying in a hail of bullets wasn't on the agenda either.

Nor would they be outlaws.

Not like Bonnie and Clyde at all in fact.

More like Mr and Mrs Smith.

Yes, that was them. Leanne was Angelina Jolie and he was Brad Pitt.

Only much younger.

…and with better hair.

"Do you want to take your slippers?"

"Eh?"

He was confused as his mind was dragged painfully back to reality.

"Slippers, Joshy?"

"Oh… right. Yes, please."

"Have you found out what type of adaptors we need?"

"Ah… I'm on it."

He tapped on his phone a few times, looked sheepishly across at his girlfriend who was busy loading clothes into one of the cases, and then started reading an outline of the film.

He shook his head, disappointed. Mr and Mrs Smith weren't spies at all. They were assassins.

Hang on! What was that?

Angelina Jolie had starred in a film made in Cambodia.

He read on.

Of course.

Lara Croft: Tomb Raider.

He'd loved it. Lara Croft had been like Indiana Jones but in temples dealing out ju-jitsu kicks to all and sundry. She'd been a one-woman army.

He'd be just like that.

Only not a woman.

He crouched down, flattened his hands, then leapt into the air, landing with his knees bent and his arms thrust forward.

"HI-YAH!"

Leanne stood up from the suitcase, glared at him and put her hands on his hips.

"What on earth are you doing?"

He grinned.

"I'm not Brad Pitt."

"I can see that."

"I'm Angelina Jolie."

"You're Angelina Jolie?"

"Uh-huh."

"And has Angelina Jolie found out what adaptors we need?"

"Ah…"

"Don't bother. We'll look at the airport. I'm sure they'll sell the right one in Boots. Can you close this suitcase for me, please?"

"Sure."

He closed it and the doorbell went.

"That'll be our taxi," Leanne said. "Thanks for your help."

"No problemo. Did you pack my hair gel?"

She gave him a withering look as she grabbed the smaller of the two suitcases and led them out of the apartment to the waiting cab.

Chapter 46

"He arrived early," PC Warwick said as she opened the door.

Luke walked in and hung his coat up.

"Is he with DI Gilmore?"

"Yes, sir… I mean, Luke." Her cheeks turned a subtle shade of beetroot. "Strong, black coffee?"

"Yes, please."

He opened the door of the interview room to find Pete sitting with his back to the door opposite a scowling Barry Simpson.

"Dave's working again," Pete said, pointing to the interview recording system. "It's a bit iffy though so I've already started recording." He cleared his throat. "Luke Sackville has entered the room."

"About time," Simpson said. "I left work early for this."

"Is your boss a hard taskmaster then?" Luke asked as he dropped into the chair next to Pete.

Simpson sniffed. "He's okay."

"I hope you won't get into trouble."

"He's not around much."

"That must be convenient."

"What do you mean?"

"I suppose it means that if you need to leave early, or even take the whole day off, you can do it without him knowing. "

"What are you insinuating?"

Luke narrowed his eyebrows and leaned forward over the table.

"Where were you on Sunday the 5th of January, the week before you found the body?"

Simpson sat back in his chair, looked at Pete and then

back at Luke. "I told you last time. I was at work."

Luke turned to Pete. "Have you told him about the CCTV, DI Gilmore?"

"Not yet."

Luke returned his attention to Simpson.

"We took up your suggestion of looking at the CCTV, Mr Simpson, and we managed to find footage of a man placing the suitcase in Bath Spa's Lost Property office."

"That's good then, isn't it?"

"It was date and time-stamped," Pete said. "Thursday the 2nd at 7 pm."

Luke remained leaning forward and stared into Simpson's eyes. "You lied to us. You didn't go into work at all that day, did you?"

Simpson looked away to one side, then briefly back at Luke and then down at the table.

"I didn't want to get into no trouble."

Luke slammed his fist down on the table and Simpson jumped a foot in the air and squealed like a stuck pig.

"This is a murder investigation! Lying about your whereabouts has severely held us back."

"I'm sorry. I…"

"How long could he be looking at, DI Gilmore?"

Pete was quick to pick up the hint.

"Someone who's found guilty of accessory after the fact is treated as if he committed the actual offence, which in the case of murder is life imprisonment."

"What! I wasn't no accessory. I found the body, that's all. Rang it in, didn't I?"

Luke sat back.

"We're going to show you the CCTV footage now, Mr Simpson."

"Yes." He gulped. "Fine. I…"

Luke held his hand up.

"But first, you had better heed my warning. If you lie to us again we *will* bring charges. Do you understand?"

Simpson nodded several times, his chins struggling to keep up with the rest of his face.

There was a light knock at the door and PC Warwick walked in with a tray of coffees.

"Thanks," Pete said as she handed them out and then left.

He raised the screen of his laptop, keyed in his password and turned the computer to one side so that they could all see the screen. The film was paused with only the front of the suitcase in view.

"There's the timestamp," he said, pointing to the bottom right of the screen.

"Right."

"I want you to watch carefully."

Simpson looked at him, then at Luke and then back at the screen.

"Right," he said again.

Pete hit play and they watched as first the suitcase appeared and then the man pushing it. He was in his late thirties, Luke judged, strongly built and ridiculously underdressed for the time of year in dark grey shorts and a black t-shirt. Only the side of his face was visible, insufficient for a photofit but enough that anyone who knew him would recognise him.

The man pushed the suitcase from left to right, then disappeared from view.

Simpson started to speak but Pete held his hand up to stop him.

After another minute the man reappeared and walked quickly to the left and out of sight.

Pete hit stop.

"Do you recognise him, Mr Simpson?" Luke asked.

To his surprise, Simpson nodded his head.

"For the recording, please," Pete said.

"Yes, I recognise him. Don't surprise me none. Got a violent streak, that one. Took an instant dislike to him."

"What's his name?" Luke asked.

Simpson gestured to the laptop. "That's Connor, that is. Connor Iverson."

"How do you know him?"

"He had my job before me. Showed me the ropes before he left."

"How do you know he's got a violent streak?"

"He was boasting about a bust-up he and his biker mates had with a rival outfit. Knives and all according to Connor."

"Did he tell you why he was leaving?"

"He said he'd be making loads more money working on a farm and would have a bunch of foreigners working for him. I didn't probe cos, well, cos he's not the sort of guy you want to find out more about."

"Any idea where this farm is?"

"He didn't say, but I got the impression it wasn't far from Bath."

Chapter 47

Sam had alternated ibuprofen and paracetamol all day to keep her temperature in check but it didn't keep her from aching all over. Her headache hadn't completely disappeared either.

Even the idea of watching Bridgerton didn't appeal, proof positive that she wasn't at her best.

She stood up from the sofa, determined to stop feeling sorry for herself. She needed to do something, anything, to shake herself out of her stupor.

What about chocolate? Chocolate always helped. She could wrap up, walk to the local shop, grab a bar of Cadbury's Dairy Milk and be back inside ten minutes.

She sat back down again.

Come on, you lazy…

She forced herself to her feet, retrieved her coat and put it on quickly, before she thought too deeply about going out into the cold January air, and wrapped a scarf around her neck.

Two minutes later she was standing outside and already regretting leaving the warmth of the flat.

The mini-supermarket was only a few hundred yards away. She pulled the scarf tight, then heard the sound of a WhatsApp message arriving.

Normally, she'd pull her phone out and check straight away, but it was too cold for that so she upped her pace, paused while the traffic passed and then crossed the road and walked into Sainsbury's Local. Turning right towards the confectionery aisle, she stood to one side and retrieved her phone, hoping it was Luke saying he had left or was leaving soon.

She gasped when she saw what had been sent.

It was the photo taken of her and Luke at Christmas, the one that had been stolen from her apartment, but it had been edited so that Luke's eyes were blacked out.

She almost dropped the phone when it pinged again and a message came through.

You brought this on yourself…

She stared at the screen, unsure what to make of it. It had to be the person who had broken into her apartment which meant…

A second message appeared.

…and on those you care about

She put her hand to her mouth.

Did this mean Luke was in danger?

"Are you all right?"

She looked up to see an elderly woman standing a couple of feet away, concern etched on her face.

"You look very pale, dear."

Sam tried to smile. "No, I'm okay." She lifted her mobile. "I need to phone someone, that's all."

The woman stepped away and Sam called Luke's number and waited.

It started ringing.

Please be there.

It rang three more times.

Answer, damn you.

He was normally quick to…

"Hi, Sam. I'm hoping I can…"

She didn't let him finish.

"Luke, thank goodness." She was trying to control her breathing. The elderly woman stepped forward again but she waved her away. "I'm fine, honestly."

Not that she felt in the slightest bit fine.

"Who was that?"

She ignored his question.

"I received another message, Luke. And it was threatening this time."

"From Ollie?"

"I… I don't know. The sender sent the photo taken from my apartment, but the eyes, your eyes, had been blacked out."

"What did the message say?"

"Just a second." She read from the screen "*You brought this on yourself and on those you care about.* I'm worried he might hurt you, that he might…"

She stopped talking as a thought occurred to her.

"What is it, Sam?"

"Those words… I thought it was a woman in my apartment… It could be her…"

"Sam, you're not making sense."

She swallowed.

"Gillian Ley used words like that when she told me off in her office."

"Can you remember exactly what she said?"

"No, not exactly. She told me to keep my nose out, I remember that. But she also said something about bringing trouble on those I care about. I'm sure she did."

"Where are you now?"

"I'm in Sainsbury's Local. The one near my apartment." She suddenly felt guilty for having gone out. "I wanted some chocolate."

"Could you have been followed?"

Sam hesitated before replying.

Cogs were spinning in her head, connections being made.

Late hours, that was it.

"Sam! Could you have been followed?"

"Sorry. I was remembering something else. Mollie said she works long hours."

"Gillian's PA?"

"Yes. She said Gillian rarely leaves before seven. Can you check if she's still there?"

"I'll go up there now, then I'm heading straight over. I'll ring you once I've checked."

"Thanks, Luke. Take care."

"And you, Sam." He hesitated. "I…" There was another pause. "I'll speak to you in a minute."

The line went dead and she stared at the phone.

Had he been about to say that he…

Surely not.

They'd only been going out for a few weeks.

But they'd known each other and been close for almost a year, so it was possible.

"Is everything sorted, dear?"

She looked up from her phone and her smile was genuine this time.

"Yes," she said, "I think it might be."

Chapter 48

Luke took the stairs three at a time.

A thought occurred to him as he emerged onto the Executive Floor.

He'd said he'd be straight over, but he hadn't told Sam to stay in the supermarket. With luck, she'd realise that her apartment was the last place she should go to, given it had already been broken into once.

Gillian's PA was sitting at her desk, staring at her screen and tutting to herself.

"Hi, Mollie."

"Hi," she said absentmindedly and tapped the screen. "Sep-a-rate." She shook her head. "You'd think I'd know how to spell it by now but my brain can't seem to learn."

She looked up for the first time and saw the concerned look on his face.

"Sorry, Luke. I was distracted by this report. Is there a problem? I'm afraid you won't be able to see Gillian."

"Isn't she in her office?"

"I'm afraid not. Do you want me to make an appointment?"

"Where is she?"

"She's in a meeting with the company accountants. It started a couple of hours ago so she should be back soon."

"In Bath?"

"First your deputy and now you?"

Luke turned to see a scowling Gillian walking towards them.

"This prying has to stop."

"Where have you been, Gillian?"

"I've been with our accountants in Ambrose's office, not that it's any of your business."

He turned and sprinted back towards the stairs.

"We need to talk about your team's nosiness," she shouted after him, but he had already disappeared from view and was bounding down the stairs.

He called Sam's number as he ran to the BMW.

It went straight to voicemail.

"This is Sam. You know what to do when it beeps."

Bugger!

"Sam, ring me."

He climbed into the BMW, started the engine and screeched out of the car park, hoping against hope that there weren't any holdups.

Or police cars.

He tried her again.

Again it went straight to voicemail.

He swore and pressed his foot hard on the accelerator pedal.

If it wasn't Gillian then the person sending the messages had to be Ollie. However, the problem with that theory was that Sam had seemed certain it was a woman who had forced entry into her apartment.

Hang on a minute.

There hadn't been any signs of forced entry.

Sam had said that the door was slightly open leading her to assume the person inside was her mother.

Which meant a key had been used.

She hadn't given Ollie a key, but he would have had plenty of opportunity to make a copy.

So if it was him, was there any danger in his threats?

Most definitely, as far as Luke was concerned. He'd seen instances in his time at Avon and Somerset Police where inappropriate messaging had rapidly evolved into full-on stalking and in a few cases to extreme violence.

He called again.

Yet again it went straight to voicemail.

He banged his hand on the steering wheel.

Chapter 49

The older woman meant well, Sam knew that, but the way she continued to stare was unnerving.

She decided to buy the bar of chocolate and return to the apartment. It was nice and warm in there and she'd be away from the woman's gaze while she waited for Luke to arrive.

Hopefully, he'd ring at any moment to let her know whether or not Gillian Ley was in her office and that he was on his way.

She hadn't heard any pings, but turned her phone on in case any additional messages had arrived that she'd somehow not heard. The screen came on, faded out after a few seconds and a picture of an empty battery appeared.

She tapped on the screen and the battery disappeared completely.

"FUCK!"

"Oh!" the woman watching her exclaimed. She turned and left the supermarket, tutting under her breath.

Sam shook her head in annoyance. Of all times to run out of power it had to be now. She didn't have cash or credit cards with her either, so she couldn't even buy the Dairy Milk she'd been eagerly anticipating.

She shoved her phone into her coat pocket, pulled the scarf tight and headed out of the shop.

As soon as she was outside she wished she'd brought gloves. She'd only been in the supermarket a few minutes but it seemed even colder outside than she remembered. She dug her hands as deep into the pockets of her coat as she could and walked towards the crossing.

At least the senior citizen had disappeared, no doubt completely shocked and traumatised by the Anglo-Saxon expletive.

She was half smiling to herself as she crossed the road and headed towards her flat.

After a few steps she was conscious of someone behind her. She spun around and a middle-aged man leapt back several paces before looking at her oddly and then stepping quickly past her and on up the hill.

She was being stupid.

She continued for a hundred yards or so, heard more footsteps, thought about turning and decided just to up her pace. The sooner she was in the safety of her apartment the better.

The person behind sped up as well.

Sam started jogging.

Her follower started jogging.

Sam upped her speed to a sprint.

The person behind started running.

"Wait!"

It was a woman's voice.

Sam stopped and turned around, ready to defend herself if need be.

"Jazelle?"

A woman was bent over, panting for breath.

After a couple of seconds she looked up, her hands still on her thighs as she tried to gain control of her breathing.

"Who the fuck is Jazelle?"

Chapter 50

Luke went to Sainsbury's Local first, dashed through the aisles to check Sam wasn't there, and then climbed back into the BMW and drove the short distance to her flat.

He bounded up the stairs to find the door wide open.

Not again.

Please let her be okay.

He pushed the door open, ready to confront anyone who might try to jump him.

"Luke, we're in here."

He walked into the lounge to find Sam on the sofa being passed a mug by a woman he didn't recognise. She looked to be forty or so but her stand-out feature was her size. She had to be two or three inches over six feet and bulky with it. Not overweight, but sturdily built.

"This is Misty," Sam said. "She made me a hot chocolate."

"Fucking hell, you're big," Misty said as she shook his hand.

"It was Misty who broke into my apartment," Sam went on, seemingly unfazed by her presence.

"Yeah, not my best moment. Six stitches, eh?" She shook her head. "Fuck, that's not good."

Luke looked at Misty and then back at Sam.

"Would you mind explaining what's going on?"

"Do you want a hot chocolate?" Misty asked.

He glared at her.

She held her hands up in submission. "Fair enough. Only trying to be nice."

"Only…"

"Luke," Sam said, "sit down and I'll explain."

He descended into the armchair.

"Thank fuck for that," Misty said as she sat on the other end of the sofa from Sam. "I don't like it when someone's bigger than me, and you, you're like King Kong on steroids. Less hairy mind, but I mean. How tall are you?"

He turned to Sam.

"Sam?"

"6 foot 6."

"No, I meant…"

Sam smiled. "I know what you meant, Luke. Misty is a private investigator."

"Here," Misty said, leaning forward to pass him a business card.

Luke read what was written on the card.

"Misty Mitchell?"

"That's me. Wouldn't be my choice. I mean Misty. What kind of a name is that? I guess my parents chose it because it goes with Mitchell, but look." She laughed and gestured at the outline of her body. "I'm hardly fucking ethereal, am I? Better if my parents called me something like Stormy, mind you that's got associations hasn't it, especially now the orange-faced man is back in power."

"It was Ollie," Sam said. "He sent the photo and those messages."

"I thought he was genuine," Misty said. "He told me you two had been having an affair and that his wife abused him."

Luke was confused. "His wife?"

Misty nodded. "He told me Sam was his wife and that he was subjected to domestic abuse. Said she'd regularly come home drunk and lay into him with a rolling pin. He was convincing too, only it turns out he was fucking lying through his teeth."

"He paid you to break into her apartment?"

"Yes, but he said it was jointly-owned by Sam and him. Told me he wanted a divorce and needed proof of her infidelity."

"So what happened tonight?"

"I smelt a rat. There's something slimy about him."

"I'll second that," Sam said.

"So I spoke to Alison and she told me Sam was single. That was proof enough for me."

Sam raised an eyebrow. "Alison Billings?"

"That's right."

"Who's she?' Luke asked.

"She's a friend from school." Sam turned back to Misty. "How do you know Alison?"

"She's moved house and put her new name and number on the Christmas card she sent you. Oh, yes. That's another thing. When I handed over the photo and the contents of your bin, that wanker got really excited about the Christmas card from Luke. 'Proves it' he said, because Luke had written how much he cared about you."

"The question now," Luke said, "is what we do next."

"Beat the shit out of him," Misty suggested.

Luke smiled. "Much as that appeals, there's got to be a better way." He thought for a few seconds. "I take it he still thinks you're on his side, Misty?"

"Abso-fucking-lutely."

"Mmm. Perhaps we can turn that to our advantage. Misty, this is what I want you to do…"

Chapter 51

"Are you sure you're up to coming to mine?" Luke asked.

Sam smiled. "I'm feeling a lot better this morning and besides, it'll be nice to see Chloe and meet her new man."

"I hope he's good enough for her."

"Stop fussing, Luke. I'm sure he's lovely. You can introduce him and me to that pub you're so fond of. The one with no bar. What's it called?"

"Tucker's Grave. Are you sure you're up to walking there? It's forecast to snow this evening."

"Honestly, Luke. If I'm not up to it I'll say."

It was just gone ten when they arrived in Norton St Philip. Sam put the kettle on while Luke walked the short distance to Marjorie's house.

"How's he been?" he asked when she answered the door.

There was a noise behind her and the next thing he knew Wilkins was leaping up and down at his thighs, his tongue flopping to one side in his excitement.

"I think he's pleased to see you," Marjorie said.

"Thanks again."

"Any time. He's easy as pie and great company."

He walked the spaniel back to the farmhouse where he appeared to be just as excited to see Sam when she emerged from the kitchen.

She retrieved a dog treat from the cupboard, made him sit and then fed it to him. Half a second later it was gone and he looked up at her appealingly.

"Go on then," she said as she passed him a second biscuit.

Luke laughed. "No wonder he likes you. You spoil him rotten."

He heard the noise of an engine, swivelled around to look at the front door and then returned his attention to Sam.

"They're here. I wasn't expecting them until later. I, ah…" He took a deep breath.

Sam laughed.

"Relax, won't you? He won't bite. Come on, let's say hello."

"In your bed," Luke said to the cocker. "You can see them when they've settled in."

Once the crate door was latched shut, Sam opened the door and gestured for Luke to go first.

Chloe was already out of the car, a metallic red, two-seater convertible.

Luke frowned.

It was the sort of car that Lotharios used to seduce young women. Fast and trendy. Was that what this guy Denver was like?

"Dad!" Chloe said, holding her arms out for a hug.

He enfolded his arms around her.

"Sorry, Darling. I was miles away."

"This is Denver."

He released his daughter and looked over to the man who had emerged from the driver's side. He was tall, perhaps six foot two, with neat blonde hair and a youthful appearance.

Very youthful.

If Luke hadn't known better he would have put him in his early twenties rather than twenty-nine.

He walked over and they shook hands.

"Hi, Denver. It's great to meet you."

"Hi, Mr Sackville."

"Luke, please."

He backed away as Sam kissed first Chloe and then Denver on the cheek.

"Come on in out of the cold," she said.

Chloe grabbed her boyfriend's hand.

"Come on, Den. Meet Wilkins."

He smiled as she half-dragged him to the house.

A couple of hours later, the four of them were sitting in the kitchen chatting while Luke and Sam prepared lunch.

Chloe and Denver were clearly very fond of each other and hadn't stopped holding hands since they'd arrived. What was more, and much to his surprise and relief, Luke found himself warming to her new boyfriend who was telling them the story behind his unusual christian name.

"The truth is that my parents beat David and Victoria to it by four years," Denver said with a chuckle. "Mum and Dad were on a skiing trip to Colorado when I was conceived."

Luke almost caught his finger on the cheese grater when he heard this.

"You mean you're only four years older than Brooklyn Beckham?"

"Just under four years actually."

Luke shook his head in astonishment. "It seems like yesterday that his father was playing for England."

"I watched every game when Beckham was in the team," Sam said. "I hate to admit it, but I had a real crush on him. I remember I cried when he played his last international game." She smiled. "Mind you, I was only fifteen."

"Between the two of you, you're making me feel really old."

"You are old, Dad," Chloe said.

"Thanks, Darling."

He finished grating the cheese and looked over at Denver.

"This issue you want to talk about. Is now a good time?"

Denver suddenly looked on edge. "Sure. Can we talk in the lounge?" He turned to Chloe. "Why don't you stay here? You've heard it before so there's no sense in you having to go through it all again."

Luke immediately sensed the lie behind this. Denver had information he wanted to impart to Luke that Chloe wasn't aware of.

Was he married?
Did he have a criminal past?
Had he been inside?

He led the way into the lounge and dropped into what the children called his 'Dad chair'.

Denver sat on the sofa, but on the front edge, almost as if he was ready for a rapid exit.

"This is difficult," he said.

Luke didn't say anything. It was clear that he was ready to admit to whatever he'd been hiding. He'd come out with it in his own time.

"I haven't told Chloe everything about me."

He'd been right.
He was married.
He probably had children as well.
Bastard.

Luke shaped his face into what he hoped was a semblance of a smile and waited.

"The truth is…"

Denver stopped abruptly, stood up and walked to the window. He stared out for a few seconds then seemed to come to a decision and turned to face Luke.

"You're married," Luke suggested.

Denver pulled his chin in and furrowed his brows.

"What? No. Whatever gave you that idea?"

At least that was one potential issue ticked off the list.

"You seem nervous, son. It has to be something significant."

Denver swallowed.

"Before I went into lecturing, I was…"

Here it comes.

He was a drug dealer.
Imprisoned for several years probably.
"…in the police."
Luke involuntarily twitched his head.
"What did you say?"
"I was in the police."
"You were in the police?"
Denver nodded. "Not for long though, and over a decade ago. I was 18 when I joined and five days from my 19th birthday when they sacked me."
"Sacked you?"
"Uh-huh. For misconduct. It's an embarrassing episode in my life and I haven't had the courage to tell Chloe."
"What had you done?"
"Nothing." Denver paused. "I know everyone accused of something says that but it's true. I swear it's true."
"What was the charge?"
Denver returned to the sofa and sat down again, but resumed his perching position on the front edge.
"'Deliberate indifference to serious medical needs'. Those were the exact words. My partner and I arrested a drug dealer who claimed he was a diabetic and needed insulin. He didn't receive any and died in his cell." He hesitated. "The thing is, I wanted to give it to him but my fellow officer, who was very much my senior in experience as well as age, insisted he was faking it. I tried to challenge him but he pulled rank and I'm ashamed to say I gave way."
"Was your partner sacked as well?"
"No. He claimed it was the other way around. That I'd been the one who refused to believe the man who died. It was his word against mine and they believed him."
Luke thought about this for a second.
"This isn't just about telling Chloe, is it? There's something else going on."
Denver tried to smile but it was half-hearted at best.
"I can see why you were a good detective."

Chapter 52

Luke sat back and waited.

After a minute or so, Denver started talking and it all came out in a rush. It was clear that he was carrying a heavy weight on his shoulders and was desperate to unburden himself.

"Gerry Saunders is my boss. He's a professor and heads up the School of Humanities, but only took up the post about three months ago. When he joined the Dean had a drinks party to welcome him. All the Humanities lecturers and staff were invited. The following week Gerry's secretary scheduled a meeting for me to have a 1:1 with him. I thought it was routine, that he was having a similar session with my colleagues, but I was wrong. That was when it all started."

"When what started?"

"I guess you'd call it bullying, but it feels like more than that." He sighed. "Gerry pulled a printout out of his desk drawer and passed it to me. It was my CV, the one I used when I applied for the position of lecturer three years earlier. He told me I'd obtained the job under false pretences. I didn't know what he was talking about and he grinned and said, 'You don't remember me, *ex-PC* Bailey, do you?'. I knew something bad was coming the way he said 'ex-PC', but I still couldn't place him."

Denver swallowed and took a deep breath before continuing.

"He told me that he was on the panel that sacked me. That's how he remembered me."

"Is he an ex-policeman?"

"He must be I guess, but there were six of them there when I was dismissed including the chief constable and he was the one I was focused on. Gerry told me I'd lied about the reason I'd left Wessex Police. That wasn't true. I'd provided the dates I'd been with them but that was all. He insisted it was a lie of omission and he was very convincing. He told me that I'd be dismissed instantly if he told the Dean I'd been responsible for a man's death."

"Did he ask you for money?"

"He said that he'd be willing to overlook it, but that I'd need to earn his trust by taking on more responsibility." Denver laughed, but it was a shallow, brittle thing. "Chloe thinks my hours are ridiculous and I should push back but I haven't any choice. I'm providing one-to-one mentoring for 10 students on top of my normal workload, and each of them takes two or three hours a week."

"How's Gerry Saunders benefitting?"

"They're allocated to him, and as far as the powers-that-be are concerned they're receiving the individual support they need and that's all they care about. I do up to thirty hours extra each week and he does thirty hours less. I've seen him leave as early as two in the afternoon."

"You're right, he's bullying you, but I'd put it stronger than that. You're being blackmailed."

"I don't know what to do, Luke. I can't go to anyone, least of all over Gerry's head to the Dean. It'll be the same story as at Wessex Police. My word against the professor's and they'll believe him because he's more senior."

"What about the students? They'll say it's you providing the mentoring."

"Gerry's answer to that would be that I asked for the additional workload to enhance my career prospects."

The lounge door opened and Chloe popped her head in.

"Are you two okay in here?" She laughed. "Not too heavy a conversation I hope."

Denver was sitting with his back to her and didn't turn around.

"We're fine," Luke said. "A few minutes more and we'll be done."

"Good timing. Lunch should be ready in ten minutes or so."

She disappeared back into the kitchen, but without closing the door.

Luke stood up, closed the door and then returned to his chair.

"Try not to worry, Denver. There are a couple of ways I think I might be able to help."

"Really? If you could do anything, anything at all, it would be fantastic."

Luke pulled his phone out of his pocket.

"I'll make a note of some of the key names. You said your boss's name is Gerry Saunders?"

"That's right. Professor Gerald Saunders."

"And the Dean?"

"Professor Randolph Foster. His formal title is Executive Dean for the Faculty of Humanities and Social Sciences."

"And who does he report to?"

"Sir Howard Carter, the Chancellor."

"That's enough to be getting on with. I'll let you know if I need the names and contact details for one or more of the students."

"What are you going to do?"

"In the first instance make a few phone calls. It'll have to be Monday though."

"That's fine." Denver paused. "Ah… what about Chloe? I don't like keeping secrets from her but…"

"Son, you have absolutely nothing to be either embarrassed or ashamed of, and I know my daughter will be nothing but supportive."

"Would you mind me telling her while you're there?"

"Of course not. Let's do it after lunch."

This time it was Sam's head that appeared at the door.

"Come on, boys. Lunch is served."

Chapter 53

After two flights, and a journey that had taken twenty hours, Josh and Leanne emerged into the arrivals hall at Siem Reap International Airport.

It wasn't what Josh had expected. Somehow, he'd thought it would be small, old and, well, Cambodian, whatever that meant. In reality, it was super-duper-plush and cavernous too. They could have been in any country in the world were it not for the seven-metre-high intricately designed copper statue in the central atrium.

"It's got four faces," he said as they walked past.

"It's Brahma, one of the Buddhist gods," Leanne said. She was holding their travel guide in her hand. "I read about it in here. The faces represent the four sublime states: compassion, kindness, sympathy and equanimity."

"Gucci!"

Josh was shattered and buzzing at the same time. They were in an exotic country and travelling business class had been fantastico!

Watching films while having the seat in full lie-flat mode hadn't been easy, and the stewardess had given him an odd look when he'd asked for a candle with his meal, but the whole experience had blown him away.

Leanne had enjoyed it too, revelling in the food that had been dished up, and even watching *Lara Croft: Tomb Raider* on the entertainment system to find out what on earth he'd been talking about before they left.

She'd also managed to grab several hours of sleep whereas he'd been awake throughout.

"What time is it?" he asked, trying to stifle a yawn.

"Ten past eleven."

"Right. And we're seven hours ahead?"

"Got it."

"So in our heads it's four in the afternoon and we're still at work, but we're not, we're at the end of the evening."

"Correct."

He grinned. "Only we are."

"Are what?"

"At work. We need to be on our guard. Aware of everything around us." He lowered his voice. "Take that woman over there."

He pointed to a woman in her mid-thirties staring into the window of a gift shop.

"What about her?"

"She might be following us." He tapped his nose. "I've done this before."

They both watched the woman turn and smile as a two-year-old girl jumped into her arms. Behind the girl stood an older couple, evidently her grandparents.

"She's got a good cover," Leanne said.

Josh nodded. "They'll go to any extreme to catch us. We're Mr and Mrs Smith, remember. Undercover couple extraordinaire." He paused. "Hey, are we booked in as Mr and Mrs Smith, because that would be cool?"

"No, we're booked in as Josh Ogden and Leanne Kemp. Come on, let's grab a taxi."

"What's the name of our hotel?"

"The Elephant."

"Gotcha. Leave it to me."

They went outside, joined the queue of people waiting for a cab and after a few minutes found it was their turn.

The driver climbed out, put his hands together as if he was about to pray, and bowed slightly.

"Ah…Su-os-tei," Josh said, pronouncing the word slowly and deliberately.

The man smiled. "Suostei."

Josh had to admit the man's delivery was smoother, but the syllables were similar so he was pleased with his performance thus far. He turned to Leanne, a grin across his face.

"It means 'hello' in Khmer."

"Very clever. Can you tell him where we're going?"

He returned his attention to the driver and again spoke slowly and deliberately.

"Yeung chng dek cheamuoy damri."

The man shook his head and held his hands out, making it clear that he hadn't understood.

"Yeung chng dek cheamuoy damri," Josh repeated, saying it a little louder this time and trying to emulate the man's smooth delivery.

The man laughed, walked to the cab behind, turned to point at Josh and said something in Khmer. The second driver chuckled and they exchanged a few more words before he retraced his steps.

This time it was Leanne he addressed his words to.

"Which hotel do you want me to take you to?" he asked with only the slightest trace of an accent.

"The Elephant, please."

"I see. That makes sense."

He opened the boot and loaded their suitcases, then gestured to the rear door.

"Please make yourselves comfortable. There's fresh water in the seatback compartments if you'd like some."

"Thank you," Leanne said as she waited while Josh clambered in and slid across to the far side. "Tell me, did my boyfriend's words make sense?"

The driver chuckled. "In a way, yes," the driver said. "He told me you want to sleep with the elephants."

She shook her head and smiled. "Did he indeed?"

Leanne slid into the back seat, put on her seatbelt and turned to Josh to find his head flopped against the side window. Stretching forward, she saw that his eyes were closed and small bubbles were issuing from between his lips.

She poked him in the side and he sat up straight.

"Sorry, Mr Ferguson."

He shook his head as he realised where he was.

"Have I been asleep for long?"

"About a minute, although you seemed to find time for a dream. Who's Mr Ferguson?"

"My old Geography teacher. Why?"

"Never mind." She paused. "I think we should go straight to bed when we get to our room. You're shattered and it'll be gone midnight."

"Or five in the afternoon if we were at home."

"Which we're not."

"I guess." He yawned, and it lasted for several seconds. "Perhaps you're right. We can go for cocktails tomorrow evening."

He put his head back against the window and was asleep again within seconds.

Chapter 54

Connor sat back in the director's chair, pulled his beanie down over his ears and watched as the three men trimmed the grapevines.

This was the fourth time he'd been down to check on them since they'd started work at eight that morning. He liked to surprise them rather than appear at regular intervals. That way he could be sure they weren't slacking.

He waited until Nabi started a new vine and then looked at his watch and took a mental note of the time. After he'd finished pruning five of them he saw that it had taken him three minutes. It wasn't as fast as he'd like, but it was certainly better than the two Eritreans who were taking around a minute for each one.

It was clear that meeting Lewis's target of completing the vineyard in less than two weeks wasn't going to be achievable.

The problem was that Connor's methods of persuasion were limited to violence or the threat of violence. A few slaps on the head the day before had had some effect but not enough. Sure they sped up if he hit them, or even if he just raised his hand in a threatening gesture, but their improvement only lasted for a few minutes and then they were back to their painfully slow tempo.

He'd threatened them verbally, told them they'd be given up to the authorities if they didn't pull their weight, but none of the three spoke English so that hadn't got him very far.

Mind you, he had wondered a couple of times if the Afghan understood more than he was letting on. It wasn't anything specific, but occasionally he would react to something that was said and there'd be an awareness in his face. He needed to test him, find out once and for all if he was trying to pull a fast one. If he was lying about his language skills he might be lying about other things too. He'd vehemently denied having a passport and Connor hadn't searched his wife. That was a stupid mistake, but it was too late now. If they had any documents they'd have found a hidey-hole for them somewhere on the estate.

He grinned as it dawned on him that the most likely place was their shed. Yes, if they had anything it would be there and it wouldn't take him long to search it.

He stood up from the chair and walked back towards the woods where the two sheds had been erected back in the summer.

As he approached another thought occurred to him. If he put the woman to work as well they stood a chance of meeting Lewis's deadline. She was tiny, but it wasn't as if it was heavy work.

The issue was what to do with her child if she was out in the vineyard.

The brat could walk, and she'd want to be with her mother, but he could lock her in the shed. She was far enough away that no one would hear her if she started crying and there was a small paraffin heater in there so she wouldn't freeze.

It wasn't as if he was a monster.

Chapter 55

Nabi watched in horror as Connor headed towards the woods.

He had to be making for one or other of the makeshift buildings erected for the five of them to live in. But if that was the case, what was his reason? It was clear he was frustrated at their lack of progress in the vineyard. Was he intending to use Jamila or Bibi to make them speed up?

If so, how?

What did he intend to do to them?

He dropped his secateurs and started down the slope.

"Where are you going?" Hene called after him. His English was nowhere as good as Nabi's but he understood the basics.

"I have to help my wife and daughter."

"We will come."

Hene turned to his younger brother and spoke quickly to him in their native language. Idris nodded and both men dropped their tools and ran after Nabi.

Connor was now approaching the buildings and, as Nabi had feared, veered off towards the shed that Jamila and Bibi were in. He swung the door open and thrust his head inside.

"Put her down and come outside!"

There was no response

"If you don't come here now I'll…"

Nabi upped his pace and charged into the man's back. Connor stumbled forward against the wall of the shed and immediately turned around, glared at the much smaller man and swung the palm of his hand across Nabi's left cheek.

His head cocked to one side as the blow connected.

Connor pulled his arm back to swing again and two

more bodies ploughed into him.

This time the force was too great and he fell to his back on the floor.

"Leave my family alone!" Nabi shouted.

Connor laughed up at him.

"So you do speak English?"

He tried to get up but Hene raised his foot and held it over his face.

Connor pushed it away dismissively and clambered to his feet.

"I wasn't going to harm them, but you three are too slow." He gestured to the shed. "She needs to work as well."

"That is not possible," Nabi said. "We cannot leave Bibi on her own. She's only two years old."

"We will work harder," Hene said.

Connor grunted. "You're all excellent English speakers all of a sudden. What else have you been lying about?" He glared at Idris. "What about you? How good is your English?"

Idris shook his head. "No."

Connor laughed again. "Is that it?"

He addressed his next words to all three men, wagging his index finger at them as he spoke.

"You need to get it in your thick skulls how important it is that you do what I ask. If the authorities found you you'd be back in your shitty countries in an instant. I'm your saviour, that's what I am, but you can only stay if you pull your weight."

He glanced back at the shed.

"I'll leave her here for the time being, but you three have got to work a lot faster otherwise she'll be joining you. If necessary the brat can work on the vines as well."

Chapter 56

Nabi's hands were sore from hour upon hour of squeezing the handle of the secateurs, and the growing darkness was making it increasingly difficult to see the branches.

He was relieved when he saw the silhouette of Connor coming down the slope towards them from the direction of the big house on the hill.

"Okay, you lot. Come over here."

Connor waited until they were in front of him before continuing.

"It's too dark to carry on. You've done better this afternoon but it's still not good enough. Here's your dinner." He handed two bags over to Nabi and Hene. "There's a flask of soup and some sandwiches. I'll be back for you at first light, and you'll need to work even more quickly tomorrow."

He turned and went back up the hill.

The three men walked slowly down towards the sheds.

"We have to escape," Nabi said, a desperate tone in his voice. "I cannot keep my family here."

"We have no choice," Hene said. "It is only while they process our visas."

Nabi stopped in his tracks and put his hand on the man's shoulder.

"Do you truly believe him, Hene? What if he claims delays? How long would you stay? Three months? Six months?"

"There is no choice," Hene repeated.

Idris said something in Tagrinya and there was a short exchange between the two brothers. The tone of their conversation suggested they were disagreeing about something.

"What did he say?" Nabi asked.

"He is also concerned. He saw what happened before."

"What do you mean? What was it that happened before."

"I did not like to tell you. You have enough worries."

"You have to tell me.'

Hene took a deep breath. "We were brought here four weeks ago. Latif was already here."

"Latif?"

"Yes. He was living in the building you are now in. I do not know how long he had been here. He was from Syria and had very little English. We worked with him erecting fencing but only for a week."

Nabi's hopes lifted for a second, though his gut told him the story wasn't going to end happily.

"Did Latif receive his visa?"

Hene shook his head.

"One day we heard him yell out. He was clutching his chest and he staggered backwards and fell down. My brother and I tried to help him. We pushed down on his chest for twenty minutes, perhaps longer, then Connor arrived. He pulled us off, listened to Latif's chest and then flung him over his shoulder and carried him away. Connor seemed to be in a panic and was cursing to himself as he mounted the hill."

"What did he say when he returned?"

"That it was unfortunate but that accidents happen. Those were his very words: 'accidents happen'."

Chapter 57

Josh wasn't sure what he'd done to infuriate Mr Ferguson.

It had to be a problem with his essay on the animals of the Far East. He'd written about elephants sleeping in hotels. Or was it hotels sleeping on elephants? No, that couldn't be right...

Mr Ferguson's voice was raised but it was more high-pitched than he remembered.

Almost feminine.

"Joshy, wake up!"

He turned over and pulled the duvet tight over his head.

It was promptly pulled down again.

"It's gone ten!"

His brain tried to process this. Was this his score? Had he aced the essay after all?

"Ten out of ten?" he half-whispered, half-mumbled, his eyes still closed.

"Ten in the morning!"

"What!"

He shot up, looked around the room and then turned in the direction of his girlfriend.

"Where's Mr... Ah..." He hesitated as reality hit him. "Leanne?" he squealed.

"You've been dreaming, Joshy."

"Eh?"

He rubbed his eyes.

"Come on, up you get."

She pulled the duvet off him.

"You've got fifteen minutes to shower and dress otherwise we're going to miss breakfast."

"Ah... Gotcha."

He shifted his body ninety degrees, rose gingerly to his

feet and headed towards the bathroom. He opened the door and was about to go in when a thought occurred to him. He turned back to face Leanne.

"Are we in Cambodia?"

"Yes, Joshy, we're in Cambodia. Now get a move on."

He grinned as everything came back to him.

"Gucci!"

An hour later, having finished freshening up after breakfast, they left their room to head down to the hotel's reception.

Josh was feeling replete after a full English, Cambodian style, which was pretty bang on as far as he was concerned. Okay, the bacon was a tad over-crisped in the way people from the United States liked it, but that was a minor thing. The fact that they'd given him two extra sausages when he'd asked for them had been brillianto!

And now he and Leanne were setting off on an adventure. Not the undercover-spy-couple-find-the-baddies adventure he was eagerly anticipating. That was tomorrow. No, today they were going on a temple tour, courtesy of Ellie. Well, courtesy of Ambrose Filcher, but it had been Ellie who'd arranged it.

She'd booked the services of a driver and guide to take them to view the temples and Apopo. Josh assumed Apopo was another city taken over by the rainforest, along the lines of Angkor Wat, but when he'd suggested this to Leanne she'd just smiled and said, 'Wait and See'.

Their guide was waiting for them when they arrived downstairs. He stood up from his chair and smiled.

"Josh and Leanne?"

"That's us," Josh said.

"Lovely to meet you. My name is Sol and I will be your guide today. Please, follow me."

He led them outside and gestured to a second man.

"This is my friend, Poly," Sol said. "He will be our driver."

They shook Poly's hand, then Josh spotted the vehicle behind him. "Is that a tuk-tuk?"

A concerned look appeared on Sol's face. "Is this a problem?"

Josh grinned. "Not at all."

He waited while Leanne climbed in, then sat beside her while Sol sat opposite and Poly climbed into the driver's seat.

"This is what I plan for today…" Sol began.

They started with some of the minor temples in the Angkor Wat complex, then spent the last hour of the morning at the largest, an immense structure with five central towers.

They returned to the tuk-tuk, blown away by what they had seen, and Poly drove on a couple of miles before turning into the car park of a restaurant.

"This is the PalmBoo," Sol said. "They serve excellent food and I am sure you will enjoy your lunch." He smiled. "Please take your time and be sure to try some of our local delicacies. We will be waiting here."

Josh and Leanne made their way inside where a waiter showed them to a table and handed out menus.

Josh looked at the front cover and immediately called the waiter back.

"I'll have a Palm Gaga Shake," he said, gesturing to the photo on the front cover.

"Certainly. Excellent choice, sir." He turned to Leanne. "Madam?"

"Diet Coke, please."

"Of course."

"Coward," Josh said after the waiter had left. He puffed his chest out. "I'm going to follow Sol's advice and try the local delicacies."

He turned the page, starting reading the menu items, then stopped and furrowed his brows.

"Does that really say 'tasty fried crickets'?"

Leanne nodded. "And it says 'local delicacy' underneath so you had better go for it."

"You've got to be joking. Crickets! They're like small locusts. Yuk. I'm not going near it."

"Who's the coward now?"

Josh decided on a Beef Lok Lak while Leanne chose the Fish Amok.

"We need to give some thought to our visit to Tease tomorrow," he said when they'd placed their orders. "What time are we expected?"

"11 am. We're meeting the Operations Manager. Her name's Claire Gibson."

"It doesn't sound like she's Cambodian."

"Well spotted."

Josh grinned and tapped his nose. "I'm not just a pretty face." He paused. "When she agreed to our visit did she say anything about what we'd see?"

"Not really. In my email, I told her I was a big fan and that I'd love to see how they made the outfits, so they're bound to show us the factory floor, but we may be able to see other areas.." Leanne smiled. "Did you notice that pale green summer dress I packed? The one with the tiny flowers and the thin shoulder straps."

"Ah…"

"It doesn't matter. What's important is that it's one of Tease's. I'm planning to wear it tomorrow to support my claim that I'm a fan."

"Good idea."

He looked up to see the waiter arriving with their drinks, Leanne's a tumbler of Diet Coke and his an oversized martini glass filled with a thick white liquid and topped with two cocktail umbrellas.

Josh took a hesitant sip.

"How is it, Joshy?"

"It's nice." He took a bigger slurp. "Very nice. Surprisingly nice."

"No crickets in it then?"

He grinned, took a third even bigger slurp and put his glass down.

"I may be able to slope off while you're looking around the main building. I can act bored…"

"…which you probably will be."

"True. I could say I need the loo and then have a nosey."

"Good idea. I guess what's most important is that we find evidence to show the whistleblower's telling the truth."

"Yes, although I'm hoping there might also be some clue as to who our offender is. We know it's one of Gillian Ley, Dame Sarah Chittock, Janice Martin or Meredith Holcroft so we need to look out for one of those names." He looked up. "Ah, here's our food."

Chapter 58

The next morning, after another breakfast that he had deemed 'delicioso', Josh was sitting on the bed waiting for Leanne who was applying the last of her make-up.

"We ought to be leaving, Leanne. It's 10:30 and we're expected at 11."

She stepped away from the mirror, clicked the top onto her mascara, smiled at him and spun around on the spot.

"Do you like it?"

"Lovely. Is it more curly than usual?"

"Not my hair, Joshy, the dress. I'm wearing the one I bought from Tease."

"Oh, right."

He looked her up and down.

"It's nice. Are you ready?"

"Just about."

He called up the Grab app on his phone and entered Tease's address.

"It's offering me a tuk-tuk," he said. "Shall I go for it?"

He looked over at Leanne who didn't seem to have heard him. She had put the mascara away and was smiling down at the screen of her mobile.

"I think I'll send it to Luke and the others," she said almost under her breath. She clicked twice.

"Send what?"

She looked up. "The photo of you at Apopo."

"No, you can't. Don't, Leanne…"

He reached forward but wasn't quick enough. There was a whooshing sound as the message disappeared on the airwaves.

She chuckled. "They're going to wet themselves when they see it."

"I was scared, that's all, and it's hardly surprising. I thought Apopo was going to be a hidden city, not a breeding ground for rats the size of mastiffs."

"They were lovely."

"And making me hold one of them…" He shuddered and gestured to her phone. "It's no wonder I look scared. That monster could have taken my nose off."

"They're tame and they do a great job."

"Yeah. A great job of scaring the living daylights out of people."

"They breed them to clear landmines."

"I know, but still…" he sighed. "First, tasty fried crickets, then humungous South American rats, and the icing on the cake last night, those fried… those fried…"

"You can't bring yourselves to say it, can you?"

"I thought they were twiglets. All it said on the menu was bar snacks. That's what it said. Bar snacks."

"I tried to warn you, but you'd had one too many frozen margaritas."

"You said they might be different to the snacks we get at home, not that they'd be…" He gulped as the memory came back to him.

Leanne laughed. "You'd had four before you realised. I could see what you were eating, because its body was on the other end of the plate, but you were too busy crunching the legs between your teeth and saying how delicious they were."

"Stop it, Leanne." Josh put his hand to his mouth. "Who in their right mind eats fried tarantula?"

"You, apparently."

"Well, never again." He put his index finger in his mouth. "I'm sure there are still bits of it in my teeth."

"Probably the eggs."

"Eh?" This came out as a squeak. "Tell me you're joking."

"Of course I'm joking. Come on, book this Grab or

we'll be late."

Twenty minutes later a tuk-tuk dropped them off at the gates to Tease's complex some four or five miles to the west of Siem Reap. As they approached an armed security guard gestured for them to come over to his cabin.

He was in his late-twenties, Josh judged, and wore his peaked hat low over his forehead. He tutted to himself as they walked over, as if their arrival had completely ruined his day.

"Names?"

"Leanne Kemp and Josh Ogden," Leanne said. "We're here to see Claire Gibson."

He didn't say anything, but glared at Josh while picking up his phone and dialling a number.

"Your visitors are here, Miss Gibson," he said after a few seconds and then hung up, his unblinking eyes still focused on Josh.

They waited for him to say something else, but he merely continued staring.

For half a second Josh considered trying out his latest Khmer phrases, but the look on the guard's face made it clear that it wouldn't go down well.

He plumped for, "Nice weather today."

The man's scowl seemed to double in intensity.

"What do you expect? It is the hot season."

"Is it?"

This was good. He was striking up a conversation, putting the man at his ease.

"Ah… How many seasons do you have?"

"One."

Josh nodded. "Uh-huh." He swallowed. "So, is it always hot here?"

"Yes. It is the hot season. It is always the hot season."

Josh was stuck. He'd done the weather. What else could they talk about?

"Do you enjoy being a security guard?"

"In this heat?"

"I forgot. It's the hot season." He tried to laugh. "Still, at least you have a gun. That must be fun."

Why had he said that? What if the man turned on him, pulled out his pistol and…

"It can be fun," the guard said and his mouth distorted into a Joker-like smile as he bent down beneath his counter.

A second or two later he reappeared.

"Take this!" he said.

Josh was ready to pounce on Leanne, throw her to the ground, protect her with his body.

Then he saw what the man was holding.

"Your visitor's badges," he said as he passed them over.

"Ah…"

"Thanks," Leanne said as she took the badges from the guard, put one around her neck and passed the other one to Josh.

Two minutes of uncomfortable silence followed.

"There she is," Josh said, after what seemed like an eternity, as a woman emerged from one of the buildings and started walking towards them.

Chapter 59

Claire Gibson smiled as she shook their hands. She was a slight woman, perhaps forty years old, with thick glasses and an earnest air.

"We don't have many visitors, but since you're such big fans of our clothing line…"

"Fan," Josh said.

"Pardon."

"Fan singular. Leanne's the fan. I'm more of a Maze man myself."

"That's understandable given we only manufacture women's clothes."

He fired a finger gun at her.

"Gotcha."

She led them away from the security guard, much to Josh's relief, and towards three buildings, each of them similar to warehouses he'd seen in England. They were single-storey and uniformly dull grey in colour. There were no windows, but each had a single entrance door.

"We'll start in the administrative area," Claire said, gesturing to the central, smaller building. "I'll give you some background to our operation but I'll keep it brief so that we can move on to the more exciting bit."

She gestured to the building on the left.

"After that, I'll lead you through the factory floor to see our employees in action. You'll have the chance to talk to some of our staff, Leanne, if you'd like that."

Leanne smiled enthusiastically. "That would be great, Claire. Thanks."

"We're very proud of them. They've got a wide range of skills and talents."

"Are they all women?" Josh asked.

"Mostly women, but we have a few men."

Josh pointed to the warehouse on the right.

"Will we be looking in there too?"

Claire laughed. "No, there wouldn't be much point. Building C is our standby facility. We recently upgraded our equipment and keep the older machines in there in case the main building becomes unusable."

"If there was a fire," Leanne suggested.

"Exactly. Or some kind of natural disaster. It's standard practice in our industry."

She opened the door to the central building and led them down a gap between two banks of eight desks, occupied by sixteen men and women who wore headsets and were watching their screens while talking to callers.

"These are our call centre staff. We're very proud of our response rates."

There was a low partition before they reached the next area, where six people sat at individual desks. The nearest woman looked up and nodded hello.

"This is where we handle accounts, personnel issues, security and so on," Claire went on.

At the back of the building was a glass-lined office with a young woman sitting directly outside.

"Kanya, could we have some coffees please?"

Kanya smiled and stood up. "Of course, Claire."

Claire led them into her office and gestured to a small meeting table around which were four chairs.

"Please take a seat." She pulled a screen down from the ceiling, picked up a remote control and clicked. A slide appeared saying 'Welcome to Tease'.

"And don't worry." She smiled again. "I won't bore you for too long."

She'd been lying, was Josh's thought twenty minutes later as he drained his mug and looked idly around the room. Claire had moved from loom design to structured performance incentives, whatever they were, and there was no indication that the end was in sight.

It wasn't as if there was even anything decorative on the walls to distract him while she blabbered on. There were a few certificates and graphs but nothing that in his view brightened the room.

He looked through the window at the staff seated outside. The woman who had nodded hello looked up at him, smiled, then faked a yawn.

He nodded unobtrusively in acknowledgement. Clearly, this wasn't the first time Claire had bored people half to death.

Having struck up some kind of rapport with the woman outside, Josh decided to try to create an opportunity to speak to her.

"Claire," he said, when she paused her monologue for a few seconds to change slides.

"Yes, Josh."

"Could you tell me where the bathroom is?"

She pointed through the window. "It's the door in the far corner, behind the right-hand bank of call centre staff."

"Thanks."

He stood up.

"Do you want me to pause my presentation while you're gone?"

"No," he snapped, then realised he'd sounded abrupt and smiled apologetically. "Don't wait. Leanne can update me later."

He wandered slowly towards the loo, trying but failing to read what was written on the various printouts and notes on people's desks.

After a perfunctory wash of his hands, he returned via the woman who had mock-yawned.

"Hi, I'm Josh."

She looked up.

"Nice to meet you, Josh. I'm Sonisay." She glanced over at Claire who was still talking, her attention focused on

Leanne who was trying her hardest to look interested. "I'm afraid that Claire can go on a bit."

He smiled in silent agreement.

"What do you do, Sonisay?"

"I handle complex queries, ones that require time to be answered."

"Such as?"

He was looking at her desk as he asked this, keen to see if there was something, anything, that might indicate untoward goings-on.

On the right was a single out-tray, while a bank of four in-trays rested on the back left. They were labelled 'sales', 'refunds', 'staff' and 'operations' and each one contained several printouts.

She saw him looking at them.

"We have a computerised system," she said, "but I have to admit I'm old-fashioned and like to print everything. That way it's easier for me to see how much progress I'm making."

He nodded. "I understand. What are you working on now?"

She tapped the piece of paper in front of her.

"It's a non-delivery. What happened was…"

She continued to talk but Josh was only half-listening. He was trying to read upside-down and it was proving difficult.

The top sheet on the sales in-tray was something about postage costs. He moved onto the refunds stack. Import tax it said, again not of interest.

The top sheet on the staff in-tray was about graduate opportunities, while the email he could see relating to operations was even more irrelevant, something about…

He stopped as he realised Sonisay had gone quiet.

"It sounds challenging," he said, in the hope this would reflect whatever it was she'd just told him.

"It is," she said and he heaved a mental sigh of relief.

"Some more than others. Take this one for example."

She reached for the top sheet of the staff in-tray.

"This one's from someone who graduated in textile design. They want to know…"

Josh's eyes widened as he read the name on what was now the top sheet in the staff in-tray.

Wowza!

"Are you rejoining us, Josh?"

"Eh?"

He turned around to see Claire poking her head out of her office.

"Sure," he said. He looked down at Sonisay. "Thanks, Sonisay. That was very illuminating."

No problem.

He returned to sit beside Leanne as Claire pointed to the third of eight bullet points on the screen.

"We have two cutting machines," she began. "One is German and…"

Leanne turned to Josh and mouthed, "Is everything okay?"

He grinned, winked, gave a thumbs-up and whispered, "I know who the villain is. I'll tell you later."

Chapter 60

Fifteen minutes later, Claire finally finished her presentation.

"And there you have it," she said as she clicked the screen off. "Any questions?"

Josh could think of plenty, but none that she'd be happy to answer.

"I've got one," Leanne said, and Josh had to admire her feigned enthusiasm. "Why have you only got one fabric-spreading machine?"

"That's a good question, and the answer is very interesting."

Interesting it most certainly was not, as they found out when Claire spent the next few minutes running through the benefits of interchangeable cradles.

"Anything else you'd like me to clarify?" she asked when she'd finished.

Josh kicked Leanne under the table.

She gave a small squeal of pain, sat bolt upright and gave him a stare that said clearly 'you'll pay for that later' before replying.

"No. That was very thorough. Thanks, Claire."

"Good." She reached for her desk phone. "I'll check we're okay to go into Building A."

She rang a number, said, "Is it all right if I bring our visitors in now?" listened to the answer and then hung up.

"All clear." She laughed. "Sometimes they have fire drills, and I wanted to check they weren't in the middle of one."

This seemed a touch spurious to Josh, but he let it pass and they followed Claire as she led them out of Building B and around to the front of the manufacturing facility. She opened the door and they were immediately hit with the sound of multiple machines as textiles were spun, weaved, sewed and otherwise assembled into women's clothes.

She began by taking them to a machine that had to be at least thirty feet long. It was operated by two women and a man, and comprised a series of wires, tubes and who knows what with fibres and yarn shooting up, down and sideways.

"This is a Rieter 38," Claire said proudly. "It was installed last month and incorporates a new doffing system with a cycle time of less than 30 seconds."

Josh nodded as if this was excellent news.

"I know," Claire said, a broad grin across her face. "Plus, and you're not going to believe this, it has a new short-balloon setting for balanced yarn tension peaks which reduces the ends down rate by up to fifty per cent."

"Very impressive," Josh said. "Ah… that coffee's gone straight through me. Do you mind if I pop back to the bathroom?"

"Of course not," Claire said absent-mindedly. She was in full flow again and enjoying every moment.

She addressed her next comment to Leanne.

"As you'll appreciate, Leanne, the limiting factors in ring production are yarn tension peaks and the interaction with the ring and traveller."

Leanne appreciated nothing of the sort, but smiled and nodded as if this was exactly the information she'd been seeking.

Once he was outside, Josh realised that he did indeed need the loo. He glanced over to the security cabin and was horrified to find peaked-hat-man glaring straight back at him.

"Bathroom," he mouthed, then pointed down to his groin. "I need the toilet."

The guard didn't move a muscle, and Josh made his way to the admin building, all the while conscious that a pair of vivid blue eyes were burning into his back.

Once he'd been to the bathroom, he came out of Building B and was surprised and relieved to see that the security cabin was now deserted.

This was his chance.

He turned towards Building C but after a few paces heard a soft scuffling sound behind him. He turned, ready to defend himself should the guard jump him, and then squealed, and leapt a foot in the air, when a large brown lizard appeared around the corner and started wandering in his direction.

"Shoo!" he said, his voice an octave higher than normal. He wasn't fond of lizards, never had been. "Go away." He waved his hand. "Shoo! Shoo!"

It didn't even bother to look at him, its eyes fixed on a fly that had settled on the gravel. As Josh watched the reptile shot out a ridiculously long tongue and the fly was dragged back into its mouth.

Josh watched as the lizard turned and retreated, then, with another glance at the deserted cabin, he walked to the door of the standby building and opened it to reveal something that wasn't in the slightest what he had expected.

There was the noise for a start. It wasn't the smooth humming and regular rattling of the machines in Building A. No, these were irregular clicking noises.

However, what was even more astonishing, and made it apparent that this wasn't, in any sense, a standby building, was that the warehouse was full of people, the clicking coming from their sewing machines. There were four lines of tables stretching to the back of the building, each one occupied so that there had to be upwards of eighty people, perhaps as many as a hundred.

Josh stepped forward to the first table and watched as the needle hummed and fingers flew backwards and forwards. The operator was making pockets for denim jeans, stitching piles of cloth together at amazing speed.

"That's amazing," he said, then looked up from the sewing machine to the woman operating it.

She stopped what she was doing, returned his gaze and his mouth opened wide.

He continued staring for a moment, then looked past her to the next operator and on to the one after that.

They were all the same, every single one of them.

He was about to say something when he noticed someone bending over one of the tables at the far end. Not just anyone either, it was the dreaded security guard.

"Buggery-boo-boo," he said under his breath, then looked at the sewing machine operator again, held his hand up and mouthed, "Sorry."

He turned and speed-walked back to the door, half expecting to hear a shout of 'halt', or a hand on his shoulder, at any moment.

When he emerged into the fresh air he took a deep breath and practically ran back to Building A.

Chapter 61

"What time do you have to be there?" Luke asked as he and Denver carried the cases to the car.

"By nine."

Luke looked at his watch.

"It's only just gone seven so you should be fine."

"Thanks for saying you'll help me out with Gerry Saunders, Luke. I really appreciate it."

Luke smiled. "I can't promise anything, but I'll do the best I can."

He turned to see Sam and Chloe emerging from the farmhouse. They embraced, then Chloe walked over and he put his arms around her.

"Thanks for a lovely weekend, Dad."

"Any time, Darling."

She climbed into the car and Luke and Sam waved them off before walking back into the house.

"I'll put the kettle on," Sam said when they got to the kitchen. She turned to face him. "Well? What do you think of Denver?"

Luke didn't appear to have taken in what she said. He was looking down at his phone and smiling.

"What's so amusing?"

"Have you seen the photo of Josh that Leanne sent?"

"No."

"Have a look."

She pulled her phone out, clicked on her messages and started to laugh.

"It's hilarious. He looks very scared and no wonder. Look at the size of that rat."

"Gillian Ley," Luke said. "Who'd have believed it?'

She looked over at him. "What do you mean?"

He looked up.

"I've had another message, but this one's from Josh. He saw a letter marked 'from the office of Gillian Ley' in Tease's admin building."

"What did it say?"

"He hasn't said."

He looked down again, and swiped up on his phone.

"Is there something else?"

"There certainly is. He's found out what Tease are up to. Read this."

He passed his mobile over and Sam read Josh's message.

I now know what the whistleblower meant by saying Tease's operations are immoral and exploitative. Between 80 and 100 children are working in a building they tried to conceal from Leanne and me. None were over fifteen and some looked to be as young as nine or ten.

Sam shook her head as she reread the message. "That's horrific." She turned to Luke. "I didn't take to Gillian, but to think she's involved in child labour and presumably making money from it."

"We don't know that she *is* involved."

"What do you mean? Josh saw her name and he's seen the children. What more evidence do we need?"

"We haven't got proof. It could be a different Gillian Ley, or it could be that she's written to them on a completely different matter."

"Come on, Luke. I thought you didn't believe in coincidences."

"I don't, and I'm sure you're right, but the fact is that we haven't got any evidence. We need to know what was in that letter."

"How are we going to do that?"

"I'm going to ring Josh and see if he can return to

Tease."

"Mightn't that be dangerous?"

"I don't know. I'll speak to him and see what he thinks."

He retrieved Josh's number and was about to call it when a series of dots connected in his mind.

"Hang on a minute."

"What is it?"

"Maybe it's not Gillian Ley at all."

Sam furrowed her brows. "What are you talking about?"

"Something Josh said in his message." He passed his mobile to her. "Read what he said about Tease's operations."

She looked down at the screen. "That there are between 80 and 100 children."

"No, the first sentence."

"That their operations are immoral and exploitative."

"And how did he spell 'exploitative'?"

"E-x-p-l-o-i-t-a-t-i-v-e. That's correct, isn't it?"

"Exactly. There are two 'I's not three. It all makes sense now. Damn, I should have seen the link earlier."

"I don't get it."

He shook his head. "I've been so stupid. I need to speak to her as soon as possible. Do you mind if we finish getting ready and head straight into the office?"

"Sure."

"I'll explain everything on the way in."

Chapter 62

When they arrived at Filchers, Sam headed for the Ethics Room while Luke bounded up the stairs to the Executive Floor.

There was no sign of activity at Gillian Ley's office. He walked further down the corridor to find Ellie in the process of firing up her laptop.

She looked up and smiled.

"Good morning, Luke."

"Is Ambrose in?"

Ellie smiled. "He's been in a while. Six is his normal starting time."

"Could I have a word with him?"

She picked up her phone.

"Ambrose, Luke wants to see you." She listened and then hung up. "He says to go on in."

"Thanks. I think you should come in as well. You need to hear this."

Ambrose was at his desk when they entered.

"Please take a seat, Luke."

"Would you mind if Ellie joins us?"

"Of course. Ellie…" He gestured to one of the sofas.

Ambrose walked to the other sofa, sat down and looked at Luke.

"I take it Josh has made some progress."

"He has indeed."

Luke told them about the children working at Tease, and the name Josh had seen on a printout in an in-tray.

Ambrose shook his head. "That's awful, but I sense that you don't believe Gillian's our culprit."

"She could be, but not necessarily."

"What do you mean?"

"Did you know that Mollie, Gillian's PA, is dyslexic?"

"No."

"Of course," Ellie said. "It all makes sense now."

Ambrose chuckled. "You two seem to be well ahead of me. Please can you explain?"

"It's the spelling errors," Ellie said. "Several words were misspelt on the whistleblower's emails. 'Separate' was one. Also 'emperor'."

Ambrose was quick to put two and two together.

"Are you saying Mollie is the whistleblower?"

"Almost certainly," Luke said. "However, it doesn't follow that Gillian's involved. It could be that Mollie was simply using her name when she contacted Tease in the hope that her seniority might encourage them to answer."

He turned to Ellie.

"Do you know what time Mollie gets in?"

"Usually around 8:15."

"And Gillian?"

"About the same time."

"Mmm. I need to speak to Mollie but I don't want to risk Gillian seeing me. She's already suspicious of the Ethics Team."

Ambrose smiled. "Ellie, I need an urgent meeting with Gillian to discuss the government sector's revised forecasts. Could you set it up for 8:30?"

"Of course."

He turned to Luke.

"How long do you think my discussion with Gillian will take, Luke?"

"Twenty minutes should do it."

"Let's make it half an hour to be on the safe side."

"I'll give you a call when the meeting starts, Luke," Ellie said.

"Thanks."

He left Ambrose's office and made his way to the Ethics Room where Helen and Maj were huddled together at the meeting table, both focused intently on a laptop screen.

"Working on our presentation?" Luke suggested.

They looked up.

"Aye, got it in one," Helen said. "Sam's working on hers with Andy Collins in the Orange Grove Room."

"Okay. Let's run through ours this afternoon."

"Sam told us what Josh and Leanne discovered," Maj said. "It sounds like the children working there are Sabrina's age and some even younger. It needs to be stopped."

"You're right, but the first thing is to find out who's behind it."

Luke walked to his desk, intent on finding something, anything, that might help Denver. He turned his laptop on and searched first for Professor Gerard Saunders, then for Saunders's boss, Randolph Foster, and finally for Sir Howard Carter, Chancellor of Portsmouth University.

Google returned numerous photos, mainly of the Chancellor, but little else. He tried Facebook, but other than revealing that Saunders was married it wasn't much use either.

He hit paydirt with LinkedIn. Saunders's entry included a summary of his career and confirmed Denver's belief that he had worked for Wessex Police. However, he hadn't been a serving police officer but the Head of Personnel, reporting directly to the Chief Constable.

Saunders had left in 2019 which gave him an idea. With any luck there was an overlap with Craig Reynolds who had joined Wessex Police as Chief Constable around that time.

Luke made some notes, then spent a few minutes looking into the backgrounds of the Dean and Chancellor. Nothing of interest turned up for the Dean, but he was intrigued to find that Sir Howard Carter had studied at Merton College, Oxford.

This gave him another idea, but first he needed to speak to Craig. Luckily he had his personal mobile number from when they'd worked together a few months earlier, which meant he didn't need to go through the pain of speaking to his secretary and booking an appointment.

Craig picked up after only a couple of rings.

"Good morning."

"Good morning, Chief. It's Luke Sackville. Have you got time to talk? It's a personal matter."

"Of course. And please, Luke, call me Craig. How can I help?"

"Was it 2019 that you became Chief Constable?"

"That's right. Why?"

"I don't suppose you remember Gerard Saunders, do you?"

"No, I don't... Hang on, yes I do. How could I forget? He was Head of Personnel."

"That's him."

"Oh, yes, I remember Gerry all right. It was my first disciplinary panel after I joined. A painful but clear-cut decision and a unanimous vote."

To find that Craig had been the one who had dismissed Denver came as a shock. Luke had assumed it was his predecessor who'd chaired the panel.

"When you say clear-cut, Craig, wasn't it Denver Bailey's word against his partner's?"

There was silence for a couple of seconds before Craig responded.

"You've lost me, Luke. Who's Denver Bailey?"

"Denver's my daughter's boyfriend and was the man sacked by the panel. A diabetic drug dealer died in custody and he was found guilty of misconduct by ignoring his medical needs."

"I'm sorry, but that must have been before I joined. I'd recall the name if it had been me chairing. Denver's not a name I'd forget."

"I see. Sorry for the confusion. It was worth a try."

"Any time, Luke. I'm sorry I couldn't help." He paused.

"I must admit I'd put Gerry Saunders to the very back of my mind. That panel was one of the most painful I've ever had to chair."

"Why was that? Was it difficult to come to a decision?"

"Not at all. As I said, it was cut and dried. No, it was the fact that the accused had been leaning on so many members of the force, using information he'd unearthed to coerce them into turning a blind eye. We had several officers come forward to testify, but no proof that he was receiving money from criminals for what he was doing. I was disappointed that all we could do was sack him, when what he really deserved was his day in court and a prison sentence."

"Was the accused senior then?"

"As Head of Personnel, he reported directly to me."

It took a moment for this to sink in.

Luke's phone pinged and he looked down to see that Ellie was trying to ring.

"This is incredibly useful, Craig. Could I ring you later for more details?"

"Of course. Goodbye, Luke."

"Goodbye, Craig."

He switched to the other call.

"Luke, it's Ellie. Gillian's in with Ambrose."

Chapter 63

For the second time that morning, Luke took the stairs three at a time.

"Good morning, Luke," Mollie said as he approached. "I'm sorry, but Gillian's just gone into a meeting with Ambrose."

He smiled in an attempt to put her at ease. What he was about to say was going to both surprise and shock her.

"It's you I want to speak to, Mollie."

She reached for her diary.

"I think she's got some availability later in the week."

"It's nothing to do with Gillian. Can we talk in her office? I don't want anyone overhearing our conversation."

"I suppose so, but she might be back at any moment. What's this about?"

"She'll be at least twenty minutes. Ambrose has asked her to his office to give us the time to talk."

She put her hand to her mouth.

"Oh!" She lowered her voice to a whisper. "It's about my emails, isn't it?"

"Let's talk in there."

He walked to the door to Gillian's office, held it open for Mollie, then followed her in and closed the door behind them.

She walked in a few paces and then turned to face him.

"I thought I was being so careful. How did you find out?"

"Your spelling."

She sighed. "I might have known. I had to send those emails from home and I was in a rush. What's going to happen to me?"

"Nothing's going to happen to you, Mollie. You've

done nothing wrong."

"Do you believe what I said then? Does Ambrose believe me?"

"More than that. We've now got proof that Tease is using child labour in its factory in Cambodia."

He ran through the details of Josh and Leanne's visit to the warehouse.

"And they were there today?"

He nodded. "A few hours ago."

"I didn't think I'd be taken seriously. You hear about companies ignoring whistleblowers, don't you? And sometimes they're treated badly as if they're the ones in the wrong. I read about people being dismissed for it."

"Ambrose isn't like that."

"I know. That's why I went to him rather than Gillian. I get on okay with her, don't get me wrong, but, well…"

"You don't completely trust her?"

She half-smiled. "Not completely, no."

"What first put you on to what was going on?"

"It was a sheet of paper left in the printer tray, the one at the end of the corridor on this floor. I found it after a Board meeting, and read it to try to identify who'd left it behind. Filchers' directors are the only ones who can use that printer so I knew it had to be one of them." She swallowed. "I could immediately tell it was the second page of an email printout and what I read made my blood turn cold."

"Have you still got it?"

"I've locked it in a drawer at home, but I took a photo."

She clicked on her phone a couple of times and then passed it over for Luke to have a look.

and use Tease's Building C to conceal the additional prohibited staff from the police and authorities. Your suggestion will reduce our outgoings significantly.

I confirm that this will increase the monthly payment

to you by 40% effective from the 1st of next month. I have adjusted the destination account as requested. The payments will no longer be paid into the account in the name of Miss Elizabeth Rebus but into your new offshore account.

Regards

Claire

Luke read it, then passed the phone back.

"Mollie, in your second email to Ambrose you said you'd found additional evidence."

She suddenly looked sheepish.

"It wasn't true. I thought if I said that I might be taken more seriously."

"So you haven't found anything else to confirm that the recipient of this email is a woman?"

"No, but it says 'Miss', doesn't it? I know the name itself has to be fake, but why put 'Miss Elizabeth Rebus' if you're a man?"

He stared at her as her words sunk in.

"What is it, Luke?"

He held his hand out. "Give me your phone again."

She handed it over and he reread the email.

"You're right. It is a woman. It's Erebus."

"Who?"

"Elizabeth Rebus is Erebus."

His phone buzzed. It was a message from Ellie.

They'll be finishing shortly

"We'll have to stop there, Mollie."

"But…"

"That was Ellie. Gillian could be back at any minute. I'll give you a call later."

Chapter 64

Luke passed Gillian on his way back to Ambrose's office.

"Good morning," he said pleasantly, but she didn't respond and looked at him suspiciously.

He heard her ask Mollie for a folder once she'd rounded the corner.

Ellie stood up when he approached and led him into Ambrose's office.

"Well," Ambrose said once the door was closed. "Was it Mollie?"

Luke nodded. "I'm no further forward in knowing who the culprit is, but it's clear that the person making money from what's going on in Siem Reap is also heading up a therapy cult in Glastonbury."

"A what?"

"I think we'd best sit down for this."

"This is becoming more and more sinister by the minute." Ambrose turned to Ellie. "I suggest you return to your desk, Ellie. Please ensure that, short of a nuclear attack, Luke and I are not interrupted."

"Certainly, Ambrose."

She left the room.

Ambrose sighed as he sat on the sofa. "I find it hard enough to believe one of my fellow directors is involved in child labour, let alone in… Did you say a therapy cult?"

Luke lowered himself onto the edge of the other settee.

"A young woman called Shannon, who Josh met during one of our investigations, came to see him last week. She revealed that eighteen months ago she joined a mentoring organisation called Beacon, only to be brainwashed into giving them money."

"And why do you think this is connected?"

"I don't think it's connected, Ambrose, I know it's connected. While Josh and Shannon were talking outside this building, she spotted a woman in reception who she identified as Erebus, the cult's leader. The only people visible at the time, apart from Leanne, were you and several of the Board members. Secondly, and this is what makes it a cast-iron certainty that it's the same person, Mollie found an email printout on the printer used by Board members. It named Miss E Rebus as the person being paid money by Tease."

"Mmm. That does sound conclusive. But what do we do now? We still don't know which of the four directors it is."

"I've been thinking about that. We're presenting tomorrow, and I aim to say things that may induce the culprit into giving themselves away. However, it's a long shot, and we've only got fifteen minutes. I may also ask Josh and Leanne to return to the factory to do some more digging."

Ambrose considered this for a moment.

"There is one way I might be able to get you more time with the directors. The challenge will be setting it up without it being obvious you're spying on them."

"What's that?"

"Sarah Chittock's hosting a party at her house on Saturday. It's a joint celebration for her 70th and Meredith Holcroft's 50th." He paused. "You've got a dog, haven't you?"

"That's right. Wilkins. He's a cocker spaniel."

"I thought so."

Ambrose stood up and walked around to his desk drawer. He pulled out a cream envelope and passed it to Luke.

It was elaborately decorated, with 'Ambrose Filcher' printed on the cover in an extravagantly ornamental font within multiple pink and lilac flowers.

Ambrose smiled. "If you think that's fancy, wait until you see the invitation."

Luke opened the envelope, pulled out the card and returned Ambrose's smile.

He hadn't been joking. The same ornate font was used, but this time the words were surrounded by a circle of pink cartoons of five smiling toy poodles with more pastel flowers between each of them.

> You are invited to join Sarah and Meredith at Rockington Manor on Saturday 25th January to celebrate their birthdays.
>
> Festivities begin at 2 pm and will conclude with fireworks at midnight.
>
> Trixie, Pippa, Roxanna, Tinch and Bonnie will be hosting their own event at 3 pm, so if you own one or more dogs please bring them along.

It had clearly been professionally produced, but Luke had no doubt that Dame Sarah Chittock had provided the design brief.

Ambrose confirmed Luke's thoughts with his next words.

"Between you and me, Luke, Meredith's none too pleased that Sarah has taken the whole thing over. Meredith hasn't got any pets, so this dog event has particularly annoyed her. However, it does give us a potential way in for you."

"How so?"

"Sarah's struggling to get enough people to bring their dogs for this 3 pm event." He paused. "I think they're put off by the pampering element."

"The what?"

"Each dog will be professionally groomed, after which three judges, including yours truly, will select the winner. Knowing Sarah, I'm confident that this will result in seriously coiffured dogs adorned with a variety of pastel-coloured bows, collars and costumes."

"It does seem like an opportunity too good to miss, although pampering is not exactly Wilkins' cup of tea. He has his hair cut every three months and that's about it." He laughed. "Finding dead pigeons in the field behind my house is more his kind of thing."

"I don't suppose anyone else in the Ethics Team have a dog, do they?"

"No."

"Mmm. That's a shame." He stood up. "Good luck with the presentation tomorrow, Luke."

Luke remained seated.

"Before I go, there's something I wanted to ask you."

Ambrose sat down again.

"Fire ahead."

"You went to Merton College, Oxford, didn't you?"

"That's correct."

"I don't suppose you know Howard Carter, who's now Chancellor of Portsmouth University, do you? He was there at around the same time as you."

Ambrose smiled. "Oh, yes, I know Howie very well. Not only were we in the same college, we both read Economics. I still see him from time to time. Why do you ask?"

"I wonder if you could do me a favour?"

"Of course."

"My daughter's boyfriend is a lecturer at Portsmouth

and he's being bullied by Professor Gerry Saunders, who heads up the School of Humanities. He's accused Denver of lying when he applied for the job."

He ran through the details of Denver's sacking by Wessex Police, and how Saunders had said he would expose his lie if he didn't take on extra responsibilities.

"I'm not sure Howie could do much about it," Ambrose said when he'd finished. "It's one man's word against another's."

Luke smiled. "There's more to it. I spoke to Craig this morning…"

"Craig Reynolds, Chief Constable of Wessex Police?"

"Yes, and he told me that back in 2019, shortly after he joined the force, he chaired a disciplinary panel where Gerry Saunders was dismissed. Apparently, several officers testified that Saunders had blackmailed them into turning a blind eye to criminal activities. It couldn't be proven that he'd received money so it didn't go to court."

"But he was sacked?"

"Yes."

"I'd be very surprised if the University would have recruited him had they known."

"My thoughts exactly."

Ambrose stood up again.

"Leave it with me, Luke. I'll see what I can do."

"Thank you, Ambrose."

Chapter 65

Maj called to his wife from the kitchen.

"Do you want any toast, Asha?"

She appeared from the hall, her coat half on and a shoe in each hand.

He laughed. "It looks like you're in a rush."

"I've only just remembered I've got an 8:30 meeting. I'll grab something on the way in."

She bent over to put on first one shoe and then the other, kissed him on the cheek, wrestled the remaining half of her coat on, grabbed her briefcase, turned to leave and then rotated to face him again.

"I nearly forgot. Fatima's Mum texted me to say that she can't take the girls this morning. Are you okay to drop them off at school?"

"I…"

Maj hesitated. He had wanted to get to work early himself, so that he, Helen and Luke could put the finishing touches to their presentation to the Board, but there was no point in arguing.

"Yes, I'll drop them off. Have a good day."

"Bye."

She vanished.

He went to the hall and called up to his daughter.

"Sabrina. Any toast?"

"Two, please."

He put four pieces of bread in the toaster and looked at his watch. It was only 7:45 so he had a while to wait until he could leave.

Ah well, he thought, why not indulge himself with the telly for half an hour?

The toaster pinged. He extracted the four pieces,

buttered them, returned to the hall and called up again.

"Toast's ready."

"Could you bring it up, Dad? I'm in a rush."

He climbed the stairs to find Sabrina standing in her bedroom doorway holding a stud earring on the palm of each hand. They looked identical.

"Which one do you think, Dad?"

"That one," he said, pointing to her left hand.

She thought about this for a second.

"Nah. I think I'll go with the other one."

He passed over her toast and returned downstairs, a broad grin on his face.

What was it with teenagers? Fourteen years old and it took her an hour to get ready for school each morning.

He retrieved his own plate from the kitchen, carried it into the lounge, sat down on the sofa and clicked the TV's remote control.

Two smiling presenters appeared on the screen and he immediately recognised the programme as Good Morning Britain.

"Well, who'd have thought it, Lucy?" the man said.

"Yes, and it's still January, Paul."

They both laughed.

Maj took a bite of his toast and wondered if he could take any more of their inane chatter. He reached for the remote as the man started speaking again, his voice deeper and more intense.

"And now to a shocking story from the West Country."

Maj paused. West Country could mean local, which made it potentially of interest. He decided to give them two minutes more.

Lucy spoke next, her tone also altered from lightly amused to deadly serious.

"A six-month investigation into a mentoring organisation called Beacon has made some startling discoveries."

Maj almost choked on his toast and sat forward on his chair.

The camera panned back to reveal a younger woman seated at the end.

"Please tell us more, Rhianna," Lucy said.

Rhianna smiled as the camera focused on her, a caption at the bottom of the screen saying 'Rhianna Bandicoot - Independent Journalist'.

"I came across this by accident. I was writing a piece about the poor support given to people with mental health issues when I heard the sad story of MC, a social worker who killed herself after a history of depression and anxiety."

"MC?" Lucy asked.

"You'll have to excuse the abbreviation, Lucy. I promised her parents that I wouldn't mention their daughter by name. They're still traumatised by everything that happened to her and told me that, rather than being let down by the government, it was her affiliation with Beacon that drove her to suicide. I was intrigued and started researching them and what I found out was truly shocking. They claim to provide pioneering life coaching to help people find direction. However, in reality, what they're doing is drawing people in and brainwashing them so that they can extract money."

"Those are very strong words," Paul said. "Have you evidence to substantiate your claims?"

"I haven't finished my investigation but I have established that, during the twelve months before her death, MC transferred over £20,000 to Beacon, money she obtained by selling her car and borrowing from her parents." She paused. "I am now convinced that the organisation is a cult in all but name. However, their power over mentees is so strong that I've found it difficult to find anyone to speak against them. It's only in the last few weeks that I was able to track down a woman who had escaped their clutches and was willing to talk."

Lucy spoke next, addressing her comments to camera.

"I interviewed the victim found by Rhianna yesterday and in the clip you are about to see we are using an actor's voice to protect her identity."

The image transitioned to show a woman's silhouette. She had her back to the camera and Lucy could be seen seated a few feet away facing her.

"Thank you for agreeing to talk to me," Lucy said.

"It's important that the truth is out there," the female actor said. "People need to be warned about Beacon so that they're not sucked in like I was."

"What first attracted you to them?"

"I ran into a woman called Wynna in a shop in Glastonbury. I was low at the time and she was very friendly. We went for a coffee and she told me about an organisation that provided free counselling sessions. And that's all they were at first."

"Had Wynna also been seduced by them?"

"No. I later discovered that she was an employee."

"When did you realise that there was more to Beacon than counselling?"

"I didn't, or at least not until I escaped. It changed slowly but gradually. Sessions became longer and longer, and we were told to prepare extensively and make notes throughout. It was exhausting and time-consuming, and I willingly accepted their invitation to move into their house in Glastonbury, where I shared a dormitory with three other women."

"Did the sessions continue to focus on counselling?"

"No, they centred on what Beacon call the four levels of spiritual development. I was told I was in a chaotic, childlike state, and to progress to level two, which they call Level Rising Sun, I needed to invest in myself."

"By which they meant money?"

"Yes. They said it would liberate me and make me feel

better about myself while also being of value in their charitable work. I went along with it because by that time I would more or less do anything they said."

"Why was that? You come across as an intelligent woman. How did they manage to coerce you?"

"They used many tactics. Keeping me busy and tired all the time was one, but they also did everything they could to strip me of my past and muddle my brain. They gave me a new name, tried to drive a wedge between me and my family, changed what I ate on a regular basis, made me feel guilty about the slightest mistake or error of judgement, insisted I seek approval for everything, even going to the toilet. The list goes on and on."

"What would you like to see happen now?"

"Beacon's founder needs to be brought to justice, as do all the evil people she employs to do her dirty work, and I'm hoping that with my help Rhianna can achieve this."

The camera switched back to Paul, Lucy and Rhianna.

"Rhianna," Lucy began, "how confident are you of putting a stop to this organisation?"

"Until this week I wasn't at all confident because of the secrecy surrounding Beacon. However, the woman we just saw being interviewed spotted Erebus this week so I am hopeful."

"Erebus?"

"That's the name Beacon's leader uses, but I am hopeful that we are only days from finding out her real identity."

"Thank you for coming on the programme, Rhianna, and good luck."

"Thank you."

"And now," Paul began, his grin restored as if by magic, "to our reporter in Ipswich who has solved the mystery of the invisible sheep…"

Maj clicked the TV off.

Chapter 66

Erebus clicked the TV off.

She was annoyed that Beacon had been mentioned on national television, but it didn't worry her excessively. This woman Rhianna Bandicoot seemed to be acting on her own, and had so far only managed to pin down one Beacon mentee. What was more, that mentee was almost certainly Shannon Wilson, otherwise known as Fern, who had a history of mental health issues and would be easy to discredit if necessary.

However, Erebus hadn't got to where she was without being cautious, and she knew the value of being ahead of the game. It was important to put a stop to Bandicoot's investigation as soon as possible, just in case she got lucky and pulled together a convincing set of evidence.

Having spent a decade building Beacon up from nothing, she wasn't prepared to afford anyone the chance to destroy what had become a lucrative business.

She decided on a dual strategy.

First, she would try to stop the investigation in its tracks by targeting the journalist herself. Everyone had a weakness. In some instances it was money, while for others it might be a skeleton in the closet, a dark secret they were desperate to keep hidden.

And if neither of those worked out, then Bandicoot was bound to have someone near and dear who she desperately wanted to keep from harm.

Yes, there was always a way.

Second, to be on the safe side, Fern needed to be silenced once and for all. It wasn't as if she had had a happy life, poor thing, what with her background of depression. No, it would be better for everyone if she exited stage left.

She picked up the phone and rang Skylar.

He picked up on the first ring.

"Hello, Erebus."

"Have you located Fern yet?"

"Unfortunately not. She still hasn't surfaced."

"Please can you make it your top priority? She's been contacted by a journalist who's looking into Beacon. Her name's Rhianna Bandicoot and we need to silence her as well."

"In the same way?"

"No. That would be too much of a coincidence. I want you to find out more about her. There may be something in her past that we can use to persuade her to move on to another project."

"And if there isn't?"

"Obtain details of Bandicoot's personal circumstances. It may be necessary to bring home to her the harm that might come to a partner, child, parent or even beloved pet if she proceeds with her investigation."

Erebus hung up, happy with her powers of delegation, and looked at her watch. She had a few minutes to spare and decided to make two more phone calls.

She started with Tease, and was once again pleased when the phone was answered quickly.

"Good morning, Claire. I'm ringing to check everything is okay with our new recruits."

"They're settling in well, Miss Rebus. It's surprising how quickly young ones can learn, even the seven-year-olds."

"Seven-year-olds? I didn't realise any of them were that young. Do they bring value for money?"

"Oh, yes. We have a sliding scale so the children earn more the older they are. The youngest are bargains as we only pay them 12,000 riels for a day's work, and that's ten hours. The adults in Building A receive over triple that amount."

"How much is 12,000 riels in sterling?"

"About £2.50."

"And their parents are happy with that?"

Claire laughed. "Most definitely. One family has four children with us so they're raking it in."

Erebus wasn't sure she'd class £10 a day as 'raking it in', but it was all relative she supposed.

"Is there anything else I should know about?"

"We had a Tease fan come to visit the factory with her boyfriend yesterday. I showed her around and she went away delighted with what she'd seen."

"You didn't take her to Building C, I hope."

"Most definitely not."

"Good. Keep up the good work, Claire."

"I will, Miss Rebus."

Erebus ended the call and retrieved Lewis's number.

"Good morning, Lewis. I wanted to check everything's well on the estate. How are the new staff settling in?"

Lewis hesitated before answering and she could sense something was wrong.

"What's the problem?"

"It's the new Afghan couple. We're having trouble getting the woman to pull her weight."

"Why? Have you set Connor on her?"

"The problem is…" He hesitated again. "I didn't like to tell you this, but they brought a child with them."

"Can't it help out as well?"

"It's a girl and only two years old. The mother's insisting she can't be left alone."

She tutted. "What on earth was Connor thinking allowing them to bring an infant? It was bound to cause problems. You need to bring him into line, Lewis. I want this resolved, whatever it takes, before the end of the week. Either the woman agrees to work, or we remove her child so that I'm no longer having to bear the burden of paying for her food and lodging."

"Remove her? What do you mean, remove her?"

"That's down to you and Connor, but ensure you speak to him this morning and work up a plan between you."

"Very well."

"Good. Keep me updated."

Erebus hung up and grabbed her coat and bag.

She had a Board meeting to go to.

Chapter 67

Luke and Sam were walking from the car park to Filchers when his phone rang.

He looked down at the screen.

"It's Misty."

As he said this, Sam's mobile rang.

"It's Maj," she said and looked across at Luke. "I'd better see what he wants."

She put the phone to her ear and walked towards reception, while Luke stayed beside the car and accepted the call.

"How did you get on?"

Misty chuckled. "He fell for it hook, line and sinker. Told you he was a plonker. I did what you suggested, told him you and Sam were shacked up together, that I'd seen you both at it through a window and got photos. Going at it like bunnies on heat I said."

"You didn't have to say that."

"Adds to the message, don't it?"

"So you've arranged to meet him?"

"Yes. Place and time you said. He was excited and annoyed at the same time. Said he was going to put the images on social media, email them to your boss, the works. Then he started spouting stuff like '*how could she do that to me*' and '*we had such a wonderful life together*'. He even said '*I love her and she told me she'd love me forever*'. Load of bollocks of course. He's an out-and-out nutter."

"Thanks for this, Misty."

"No problem. That wanker deserves whatever he gets. If you need more help give me a buzz."

He hung up and made his way to the Ethics Room where Sam was just finishing her call.

She looked up.

"Has Misty done the deed?"

"She has and it's all set up. What did Maj want?"

"He saw Shannon on TV this morning talking about her experience at Beacon. She named Erebus…"

"That's great."

She held her hand up. "No, unfortunately she didn't give Erebus's real name. Maj said that Shannon's identity was hidden, but the journalist she told Josh about was on the programme as well. Her name's Rhianna Bandicoot."

"That's got to be our way to track Shannon down. Could you…"

Sam smiled. "I'll get straight onto it after my Glen ordeal is over. I need to go now to finish preparing with him and Andy."

"Good luck."

"You too."

She left and he turned to Helen.

"Shall we start? It looks like Maj might be a few minutes yet."

Maj turned up fifteen minutes later looking flustered.

"Sorry guys," he said as he joined them at the table. "I had to drop Sabrina and a friend at school."

"Not what we heard," Helen said with a smile. "Sam told us you couldn't drag yourself away from the telly. I did nae have you down as a couch potato."

"Ha, ha." He turned to Luke. "I take it Sam's told you about Good Morning Britain?"

"She has, and she's going to see if she can get hold of Rhianna Bandicoot's contact details as soon as we've got the Board meeting out of the way."

"Great." He glanced at the laptop that was open in front of them, "How are you getting on?"

They spent the next hour refining their pitch and deciding which parts they would each take.

"I think that'll do," Luke said when they'd finished. "If

there are questions I'll take them and pass them over to one of you as appropriate. Can you email the presentation to Ellie please, Helen, then we ought to be heading up."

The Board Room was on the Executive Floor next to Ambrose's office and Luke, Helen and Maj arrived to find Sam and Andy already outside.

"Where's Glen?" he asked.

"Changing his clothes," Sam said.

"What? Why is he changing his clothes?"

"Don't ask me. He muttered something about power dressing."

"Probably putting his pouch on," Andy said with a grin. "The one he uses for his Chippenmales appearances."

Helen wrinkled her nose. "I'm feeling a wee bit nauseous at the thought."

"Here's the great man now," Luke said, and they all turned to see Glen striding towards them, arms slightly away from his body so that his biceps didn't rub against his steroid-widened thigh muscles. He had a broad smile on his face.

"He's come as a penguin," Helen whispered.

"You've certainly dressed up for the occasion," Luke said. "Does that bow tie light up?"

As ever, the sarcasm flew way over Glen's head.

"No, it's plain black."

"Why the evening dress?"

"It's an important day today. You only get one chance to make a first depression."

"Impression," Sam said. "You mean 'first impression'."

Glen looked at her and nodded. "Exactly." He turned back to Luke. "You're looking sloppy, Luke. Not even a tie for…" He deepened his voice. "…The Board!"

"They're normal people like you and me," Luke said, then looked Glen up and down. "Well, like me anyway."

"They're senior people. Very important people. It's vital to put on a show, to be an exhibitionist."

"An exhibitionist?"

"Yes. By the end of my speech…"

"It's a presentation, not a speech."

"Indeed it is, and it will give them a full depreciation of my talents."

"And the large team you have."

"That too. Oh, here's Ellie. It must be time for my appearance."

Ellie's eyes widened as she took Glen's outfit in. She didn't comment but it was clear from her expression what she thought of it.

"Ambrose suggested you all go in together rather than wait your turn," she said, her eyes still on Glen's jacket.

Clever Ambrose, Luke thought. The more time they had to observe the directors the better.

"James should be finished soon," she went on. "Ah, here he is now."

Luke watched as Ambrose and James emerged from the Board Room.

"Well done, James," Ambrose said as he patted him on the back. He turned to Luke and the others. "We're having a short comfort break. Please go on in and set yourselves up."

Chapter 68

Luke, Helen and Maj sat along one side of the boardroom with their backs to the wall. The space was dominated by an oval conference table around which the CEO and seven Filchers directors were seated.

Luke watched as Ambrose, who was directly opposite him at the centre of the table, stood up and looked around at the other members of the Board.

"Thank you, everyone, for your patience. We'll now move on to the final two presentations from Internal Affairs."

He gestured to Edward Filcher who was standing next to Glen, Sam and Andy at the front of the room.

"Over to you, Edward."

Filcher cleared his throat and stepped forward.

"Thank you, Unc... Hah!" He coughed. "I meant, ah... Chief. That's it. Yes. As in chief executive officer. Not chief constable."

"On with it, please."

"Yes, uncle. Not much time. Must press on." He swallowed, glanced around the table, caught Meredith's eye, then quickly looked away again.

"Security. Always important. Needs fifty staff."

"Fifty-three," Glen hissed.

Filcher looked nervously around at him, then swung back to face the front.

"Our Head of Security, Glen..." He gestured to Glen, "...and our deputy Head of Security, ah..." He indicated Andy.

"Andy," Andy stage-whispered.

"Absolutely. Hah! Plus Sam..." He gestured to Sam. "...who is a woman, but very knowledgeable, will now present on, ah… Security."

He backed away to the corner, bowing almost to the waist as he did so, and Glen, Sam and Andy stepped forward.

"Thank you, Mr Filcher," Glen said, and puffed out his chest. He looked around the table. "And thanks to you all for bearing with me and my entry age."

"I think you mean entourage," Ambrose said with a smile.

Glen returned his smile, although in his case it turned into more of a maniacal grin. "Indeed I do." He turned to Andy. "First slide, please."

Andy pointed a remote control at the projector, clicked and Glen recoiled as the light hit him straight in the eyes. He moved to one side, blinked twice and then looked up at the screen.

SECURITY

Glen Baxter - Head of Security
Andy Collins - Deputy Head of Security
Sam Chambers - Deputy Head of Ethics

"We've covered that," Ambrose said.

"Next slide," Glen hissed.

Andy clicked again and Glen stared at the screen for a few seconds. It was clear to Luke that he'd never seen it before.

"Andy and I will take it from here, Glen," Sam said and stepped forward.

She and Andy spoke for the next ten minutes and Luke was impressed with their performance. They did an admirable job of running through the functions and benefits of the team, using real-life examples to make a fundamentally boring subject more appealing.

When Andy had finished talking, he clicked and a slide with a picture of a German Shepherd appeared. He nodded to Glen who stepped forward, pointed to the screen and grinned.

"This is a dog," he said, then unfolded a scrap of paper in his hand and read what was written on it in a monotone without looking up. "We considered alsatians to guard Filchers' office overnight but ruled them out for cost reasons."

He refolded the note, slid it in his jacket pocket then looked at Andy who moved on to the last slide

Security is a priority
...but also brings benefits

Any Questions?

Glen turned so that he had his back to the conference table and gazed up at the slide.

"Security is a priority," he read, "but also brings benefits. Any questions?"

"I have one," Meredith Holcroft said.

Glen spun back to face the Board members and peered around the table trying to guess which of them had spoken.

"Over here," Meredith said.

He started walking around the table towards her.

"I think she meant it was her who spoke," Ambrose said.

Glen stopped, turned on his heels and walked back to the front. He smiled across at Meredith.

"Yes, Miss, ah… Dame…"

"Meredith. Meredith Holcroft."

"You're in underwear."

Someone gasped and he realised what he said.

His next words came out in a rush, and Luke could see

beads of perspiration appearing at the edges of his buzz-cut.

"I didn't mean that you're wearing underwear, Meredith. Obviously not. Although you may be." He laughed nervously. "Probably are in fact. I can't imagine you'd come to a Board meeting having gone commando." He swallowed. "Although I sometimes…"

Sam stood up at that point and spoke over him. Mercifully, he shut up.

"What was your question, Meredith?"

She smiled at Sam, evidently pleased that someone sane had rescued the situation.

"You and Andy said that you keep a close eye on the latest technological developments. How do you do that?"

"I can answer that," Andy said.

His answer was concise and to the point.

"Thank you," Meredith said when he'd finished.

"No problem," Glen said, keen to take the credit. "We strive to please and, ah… please to strive."

"I beg your pardon."

"It's a well-known saying," he said condescendingly. "As in 'planning to fail is failing to plan'."

"I think you'll find it's the other way around."

"You mean 'failing to fail is planning to plan'?"

Ambrose stood up.

"Thank you, Sam, Andy and Glen. And finally…"

"Before we go," Glen said. "If anyone wants tickets to my…"

"Thank you, Glen," Ambrose repeated, louder and more forcefully this time. He looked over at Luke. "Luke, could you swap places with your colleagues, please?"

Chapter 69

After Filcher had introduced them, this time without any hiccoughs, Luke stepped forward.

He was taking a big risk with this presentation and hoped it paid off.

"What we thought we'd do," he began, looking around the Board members as he spoke, "is describe an investigation we completed back in November. It wasn't a complete success, as you'll see, but it will show you how the Ethics Team operates and why we're essential to Filchers' ongoing success."

He clicked the remote control.

The new slide simply read 'Project Turnbull'.

"This project came about as a result of an accusation of bullying," he began, although in reality there had never been any such project.

"A senior manager in one of our utilities sector accounts, who I'll call Mr Smith, had consistently belittled a graduate recruit. However, when we looked into it we discovered that he wasn't doing this because he liked wielding power, as is usually the case, but because Mr Smith himself was under immense pressure. Revealing where this pressure was coming from proved to be difficult and I'd liken it to peeling back the layers of an onion. The breakthrough came when Maj looked into his use of computers."

He turned to Maj.

"Maj, would you mind."

"Hi, everyone," Maj said. "I set about analysing audit logs and found that Mr Smith was accessing the utility's main database more than I would have expected. In addition, he had sent a series of emails with hundreds of individual utility bills attached to each of them. The destination appeared to be Ofgem, the UK industry regulator, but it was clear to me, from the IP address and message routing data, that the email recipient was in Albania. That was where Helen's role was crucial."

"I spent a couple of days looking through paperwork," Helen said, "and finally struck lucky when I spotted that the Albanian capital, Tirana, had been included in an appendix to the main contract between Filchers and the utility. It was a clause granting access permissions to the utility firm's offices." She smiled. "They don't have an office in Tirana."

"Thank you, Helen," Luke said. "Armed with what we'd found, we confronted Mr Smith. He told us that he'd received a request for sample utility bills from an Ofgem email address, had complied in good faith, and then deleted their email. He denied any knowledge of the inclusion of an unknown Albanian address in the contract."

"That might have been the end of it. However, I have considerable interview experience from my time in the police, and it was clear to me from his body language that Mr Smith was lying. With Ambrose's permission, I interviewed him again, pressing much harder this time, and he admitted that he was being paid to send utility bills, although he hadn't known about the changed appendix, and wasn't aware that the email recipient was in Albania. It had been easy money, he said, but he knew what he was doing was on the margins of the law and the pressure was getting to him. That's why he'd taken it out on the graduate in his team."

"I pointed out to him that what he was doing was not just on the margins of the law, it was illegal. Ambrose came into the meeting at that point and we offered Mr Smith an ultimatum. Either he resign or we would take our evidence to the police. He resigned."

"Before I invite questions, I need to explain why Mr

Smith was being paid to send bills abroad, and why we didn't involve the police."

"The second one is easy. We didn't have enough evidence. The Crown Prosecution Service wouldn't have taken the case to court without a confession from Mr Smith, and he made it clear to me that he wouldn't repeat his confession if interviewed by the police."

"As to why he was being paid, I am convinced it was because this Albanian entity is involved in identity fraud. Stealing someone's identity is complex and this will be a highly organised gang. They will use a variety of techniques to obtain financial data, biographical details and passwords. Once they have those, a utility bill serves as proof of identity and address to open a new bank account."

"Thank you, everyone. Have you got any questions?"

Janice Martin was leaning forward with both hands on the table, and had clearly been listening carefully.

"I have one," she said. "As you know, Luke, I have been dubious about the need for a dedicated ethics department. I can see now how your combined skills came to good use in stopping Mr Smith in his tracks. However, what concerns me is that you said that he was a senior manager, which suggests you and your team can investigate anyone in Filchers, no matter how senior they are. Isn't that an infringement of an individual's right to privacy?"

"That's a good question, Janice, and it comes down to competing rights. Yes, Mr Smith has a right to privacy, but so does the utility and so do the utility's customers. In this case, it was clear to me that Mr Smith was abusing the system for personal gain."

"And that would apply to anyone, no matter their seniority?"

"Yes, it would."

He looked around the room. "Anyone else?"

"I can see that ridding Filchers of Mr Smith was a good thing," Meredith Holcroft said, "but where are the tangible benefits? There are five of you in the Ethics Team and that's a big hit on our bottom line."

"I'll answer that, if I may," Ambrose said.

He looked across the table at Meredith and smiled.

"Our revenue from this utility company exceeds £2 million a year, Meredith, and the contract is up for renewal this August. I told the utility's CEO what Mr Smith had been up to and he was extremely grateful for our prompt action, hinting that a new five-year contract is very much on the cards. That would not have been the case if their Chief Executive had found out about Mr Smith through some other means."

She nodded. "Thank you, Ambrose."

Luke could see that Dame Sarah Chittock was keen to speak.

"Do you have a question, Sarah?" he asked.

She smiled. "That was an excellent presentation, Luke, and I'm intrigued by this Albanian organisation. What they're doing is awful, but how do they make money? They must have been paying this senior manager a significant amount for him to risk his job like that."

"Almost certainly through financial fraud. Once they have enough information, these thieves can take over bank accounts and credit cards, open new accounts, shop online, commit tax fraud, create fake driver's licenses to use or sell, even obtain welfare benefits. The list is almost endless."

"I see." She shook her head and tutted. "What terrible, terrible people."

"We'll have to call it a day there," Ambrose said. "Thank you, Luke, Maj and Helen."

There were a couple of voiced 'thank you's and nods of approval as Luke and the others left the boardroom.

Chapter 70

"Well done, everyone," Luke said when they returned to the Ethics Room.

"You deserve special credit, Sam," Helen said.

"Absolutely," Maj said. "Managing Mister Steroid is no mean feat."

"I think they fell for the whole Project Turnbull story," Sam said. "It was so convincing that I almost believed it." She paused. "I kept a close eye on our four suspects while the three of you were talking and the one whose reaction I found most odd was Janice Martin. I could have sworn her eye started twitching when she realised the Ethics Team had the power to investigate Board members."

"Gillian was oddly silent throughout," Maj said. "Given she's the Finance Director, I'd have expected her to be the one to probe on costs versus benefits rather than Meredith."

"What did you all think about Sarah Chittock's question at the end?" Luke asked.

"That was definitely weird," Sam said. "She seemed keen to explore the benefits of identity theft. Could she be our villain?"

"Ach, surely not," Helen said.

"I'm with Helen," Maj said. "She seemed horrified by what the criminals were able to do, that was all."

"I don't know," Sam said. "Are you all familiar with the characters in the Harry Potter series?"

Maj laughed. "Sabrina's mad on it so, yes. And I have to admit I've seen all the films. Enjoyed them too."

"Ronnie read all the books when he was ten or eleven," Helen said.

"Chloe too," Luke said, "Though Ben was more into

Marvel."

"Well," Sam said, "I can't help thinking there's something very Dolores Umbridge about Dame Sarah Chittock. She presents herself as filled with saccharine, fluff and girlishness, but I wonder if she's concealing a darker side."

"She's certainly doing a good job of hiding it if she is," Luke said, "but I agree that she remains one of our suspects. In fact, we've seen nothing to rule out Gillian, Janice, Meredith or Sarah. I don't know what I was hoping for with that presentation, but it doesn't seem to have moved us any further forward." He sighed. "What we need is solid evidence."

"I'll see if I can track that journalist Rhianna Bandicoot down."

"Good. Hopefully, she can lead us to Shannon."

"I'll give you a hand, Sam," Maj said.

Luke's phone rang and he looked down at his screen and then stepped away to take the call.

"Hi, Pete."

"Sorry for the delay, Luke. That Kia Sportage you wanted me to look into is registered to a Bradley Dawson."

"Great. Just a second." He walked to his desk and wrote the name on his pad. "Got an address?"

"76 Somerton Road, Street."

He added the address below the name, thanked Pete, hung up and walked over to Helen.

"Helen, please can you ring Josh and between the two of you work out how we might usefully take advantage of him being in Siem Reap. If you come up with anything run it by me first though. I want to be sure we're not putting him and Leanne in any kind of danger."

"Aye, I can do that. Are you going out?"

"Yes." He held his notepad up. "I've got an address for that man who was looking for Shannon Wilson. He's in Street and I'm heading there now. I'm sure he works for

Erebus and I'm determined to get a name out of him."

His phone rang again.

"Hi, Pete," he said automatically.

"This is Ambrose."

"Oh. Hello, Ambrose."

"Well done today, Luke. There are a few things I want to update you on, but a couple of the directors are hanging around up here. Is it okay if I come down to the Ethics Room?"

"Of course. I'll see you in a minute."

A couple of minutes later, Ambrose knocked on the door and Luke let him in.

"Well done today," he said to Maj, Helen and Sam as he walked to the table in the centre of the room.

He sat down and Luke sat opposite.

"I won't keep you long, Luke. First off, I spoke to Howard Carter, Portsmouth's Chancellor, yesterday evening. He was shocked by what I told him about Professor Gerald Saunders and promised he'd look into it."

"Thank you."

"I'll let you know when I hear back from him. Second, I spoke to Sarah and Meredith about the party on Saturday. They were delighted to hear your offer to bring your cocker spaniel. Wilkins, isn't it?"

"That's right."

"I asked if you could bring your partner. I thought two pairs of eyes would be better than one."

"My partner?"

"Partner, girlfriend… Whatever the word is that's currently in vogue. I find it hard to keep up, but that's my age."

"Ah… I'll have to check."

His relationship with Sam wasn't a secret, but he didn't want to tell Ambrose about it without running it past her first.

"Why don't we ask her now." Ambrose turned around.

"Sam, could you spare us a moment, please?"

"Certainly, Ambrose."

She walked over.

"I'm sure Luke's mentioned the party at Sarah Chittock's house on Saturday. Would you be able to attend as well?"

"Yes, of course."

"Excellent."

"One final thing," Ambrose said, "and I think you should hear this as well, Sam. After the meeting, one of the board members said something that struck me as odd. She must have overheard me talking to Sarah and Meredith about Saturday, because she suggested that you had made a mistake, Luke, in becoming so fond of your dog. She said that treating a pet like family makes you miss them all the more when they've gone to meet their maker.'"

Luke raised an eyebrow. "Was it Gillian?"

"No, it was Janice. It was a peculiar comment to make out of the blue." He stood up. "It probably means nothing, but I thought I should share it with you."

"That was interesting," Sam said when Ambrose had left.

Luke smiled. "Even more interesting is the fact that he knew you and I are an item."

She returned his smile. "I'm not surprised. Ambrose strikes me as someone who doesn't miss a trick."

Chapter 71

Luke climbed into the BMW and entered Bradley Dawson's address into the sat nav.

It told him that the journey would take an hour, which gave him enough time to get back into the audiobook he'd started at the weekend. With any luck it would help him relax. Presenting to the Board had taken more out of him than he realised.

Within seconds he was back in the world of DCI Bone, and enjoying every minute. This was book three in TG Reid's crime series, and as ever the story was dark and gritty, but also laugh-out-loud funny in places.

When he reached Street, he paused the book and drove past Dawson's house, a detached building dating from between the wars, and parked a hundred yards down the street. There was no sign of the blue Kia, but the house had a garage so it could well be in there.

He hoped Dawson was in.

Project What was stalling, and stalling big time. They'd made some progress, but at the moment were heavily reliant on luck.

He wondered how the fictitious DCI Bone would cope if it was assigned to him.

A damn sight better probably!

Was it possible that the challenges posed by the Non-Executive Directors that morning were justified? The Ethics Team was expensive and, aside from the small amount Avon & Somerset Police paid for some of his time, didn't earn any revenue.

Were he and his team a burden on Filchers?

He shook his head. Thinking like that was stupid. And besides, if he could get a name for Erebus out of Dawson, they'd be halfway to solving the mystery.

All he needed was one small piece of good fortune.

He mentally crossed his fingers as he climbed out of the car, walked back to the house and rang the bell.

After a few seconds, he heard footsteps and the door was pulled open by a woman in her mid-sixties. She looked slightly flustered.

"You'll have to excuse me," she said, and gestured to her apron, which was covered in flour. "As you can see, I'm baking. Two minutes and I need to check the oven. How can I help?"

"I'm looking for Bradley Dawson. Is he in?"

She shook her head. "I'm afraid you've got the wrong address."

"Oh. Sorry to have bothered you."

She started to close the door.

He turned away, then a thought occurred to him and he turned back.

"He owns a blue Kia Sportage."

She pulled the door open again.

"We sold our blue Kia a few weeks ago. Just a second." She turned around and raised her voice. "Kevin, what was the name of the man who bought the Kia?"

"Who?" a man's voice called in return.

She turned back to Luke. "Sorry. He's a bit deaf."

She raised the volume to eleven.

"THE MAN WHO BOUGHT THE KIA. WAS HIS NAME DAWSON?"

There was a pause, then, "Can't remember."

She turned to Luke again and shrugged. "Ah well. I guess there are lots of blue Kia's around. Probably a coincidence."

"Was he Australian?"

"I didn't meet him. My husband handled it." A pinger sounded behind her. "That'll be the bread. Sorry I couldn't be…"

"Could you ask him, please?"

She sighed, and turned back again.

"KEVIN," she screamed. "WHERE WAS HE FROM?"

"Who?"

"THE MAN WHO BOUGHT THE KIA. WHERE WAS HE FROM?"

"Bristol, I think. Or Bath. Might have been Wells."

She turned back, shrugged again and started to close the door.

"He had an Australian accent though," Kevin added.

*

Luke got back into the Beemer and reflected on what he'd learned.

Not a lot, if he was brutally honest.

He'd wasted several hours on a wild goose chase. It was clear that Bradley Dawson had bought the Kia and registered it in his own name, but hadn't changed the address. Whether he'd done this deliberately, or because he'd made a mistake, was neither here nor there. Either way, it didn't move him closer to discovering who Erebus was.

Since he was so close to Glastonbury, he decided he'd visit the address where Shannon's parents said she'd been staying. With the luck he was having today, Beacon would have moved on, but nothing ventured, nothing gained.

He parked in the car park off the High Street, then walked the short distance to Northload Street.

Number 13 was a three-storey red-brick building with a single grey door. Cream Venetian blinds were pulled down on the six windows visible from the front.

He pressed the bell and waited.

A minute passed before he heard the sound of bolts being drawn back and first one and then a second key being turned.

The door was opened as far as the security chain would allow and a pair of woman's eyes looked at him inquisitively through the gap.

"Hello. Can I help you?"

He smiled.

"Hopefully. Do you work for Beacon?"

She hesitated for a second before replying.

"I'm sorry, who are you?"

"I believe Shannon Wilson was kept here."

"I don't know what you're talking about. This is a private residence."

"Are you…"

The door was slammed closed and he heard the sound of the locks being re-locked and the bolts being drawn shut.

She could have been telling the truth but he thought it unlikely.

Luke stood back, looked up at the building and caught movement in one of the first-floor windows. It had seemed like a woman's face, but it was gone when he looked more closely.

Could it be one of the women that Yvonne and Patrick had told him about? The ones Shannon had shared a dormitory with.

He headed back towards the High Street and tried to remember their names. After a while they came back to him. They had been Celestina, Brenonna and Valmoria, but those had only been their assigned Druidry names. Celestina's real name had been Marie Cotton and she'd been the one supposedly elevated to the next level.

He stopped walking abruptly as he realised he'd heard the name Marie Cotton somewhere else. As he did so he felt a thump against his back.

He turned and looked down to where a very short, and completely bald, middle-aged man was glaring up at him.

He held his hand up and smiled apologetically. "Sorry."

The man tutted, and continued tutting and mumbling to himself as he moved away up the road.

Luke walked to the window of the nearest shop. It was called 'GreyWolf's Lair' and had various potions and masks in the window around a handwritten sign.

> Be ye Wiccan, Solitary,
> Ceremonial, Druid, Shaman,
> Healer, Vodoun, Occultist,
> Eclectic
>
> Whatever your path
>
> HAIL & WELCOME!

Luke hardly took in the words as he tried to recall where he'd heard Marie Cotton's name before.

And then it came to him.

It hadn't been Marie Cotton.

It had been MC, her initials.

He called up Maj's number.

"Hi, Luke," Maj said. "Any luck?"

"No, but listen. Did you say that Rhianna Bandicoot mentioned someone she called MC?"

"That's right. She was a social worker who committed suicide after she left Beacon. Why?"

"I'll explain later."

He hung up and rang Pete.

"Hi, Luke."

"Pete, you said that Anna Grayling was the second person to kill herself by jumping off Churchill Bridge. Is that right?"

"Yes. There was another woman about eighteen months ago."

"Was her name Marie Cotton?"

"I don't know, but I can check. Give me ten minutes and I'll ring you back."

Chapter 72

True to his word, Pete rang back as Luke was approaching Wells.

"You were right about Marie Cotton."

"Mmm. So she wasn't elevated."

Pete laughed. "More the opposite, I'd say."

"Sorry, Pete. I was thinking out loud. Were there any suspicious circumstances?"

"Not according to the notes. Very much the same as Anna Grayling last week. It's like buses, isn't it?"

"How do you mean?"

"Well, Churchill Bridge is sixty years old and used mainly by cars rather than pedestrians. No suicides in its first fifty-eight years then along come two at once."

"I suppose it could be a coincidence."

"How could it be anything else? I can't imagine those two women planning a double suicide and then spacing their jumps eighteen months apart."

"No, you're right, Pete. Thanks for the info."

"No problem."

Luke ended the call. Despite what Pete had said, he wondered if there might be some link between the two women's suicides.

On the face of it there was nothing to connect Marie Cotton and Anna Grayling, aside from the fact they'd chosen the same location to end their lives. Marie had been a social worker and Anna had managed a brothel, so it wasn't likely that they would know each other at work or socially.

The only other similarity was that they'd both left their businesses and gone off the radar.

Was that it though? Was it possible that Anna Grayling

had been a victim of Beacon as well? But, if that was the case, what would lead her to jump from the same bridge?

There was a link, he could sense it, but he couldn't quite grab hold of it.

His phone rang. It was Helen.

"Hi, Luke. I've had a wee chat with Josh and Leanne and we've come up with an idea. They both said that the woman who showed her around was very proud of the machines."

"The machines?"

"Yes. They automate a lot of the spinning, weaving and so on, and apparently the Operations Manager was quite nerdy about them. We thought Leanne could ask if she could visit again to find out more about the..." Just a second. "...MS-100 loom."

"Are they sure it's safe to return? After all, the company is going to a lot of lengths to keep their child workers out of sight, and they know what they're doing is illegal."

"They said Claire was charming and they didn't feel under threat nor uneasy in any way. According to Leanne, Josh and the man on the front gate didn't get on, but Josh insisted they'd had an excellent conversation about the weather and there was nothing to worry about."

"In that case, it sounds like a good idea."

"Great. I'll let them know. Their flight back is on Friday but with luck they can squeeze a visit in beforehand."

"Thanks, Helen."

He looked at the clock on the dashboard and saw it was almost 5 pm. He rang Sam.

"Hi, Luke. Any luck?"

"Not really. I'm going to head home now so I'll see you in the morning."

"Okay."

"Have a good time with Kate this evening. Give her my love."

"Will do. And good luck with Ollie. Take care."

"And you."

He hung up, set the sat nav to home, resumed his audiobook and was soon chuckling at the antics of four old men who'd sneaked out of their care home to visit a beach. What it had to do with DCI Bone's murder investigation he wasn't quite sure, but it was fun nonetheless.

Half an hour later he pulled up at the farmhouse. It was wretchedly cold, and he was certain there was going to be a heavy frost overnight. However, it didn't stop him from looking forward to putting on an extra layer and taking Wilkins for a walk around the field.

The poor dog deserved spoiling. He was going to hate Saturday's pampering session, although Luke knew that he'd be well-behaved, especially if he was given the occasional treat.

Smiling, he walked into the boot room, but almost did a double-take when he saw that the door to the dog crate was open.

He went through to the kitchen, calling the cocker's name as he went.

"Wilkins?"

He walked briskly to the lounge.

"Wilkins?"

Nothing.

Had he had an accident or fallen ill?

Had Marjorie had to take him to the vet?

He checked his phone to see if he'd missed a message.

Nothing.

Perhaps she'd decided to take Wilkins home. Yes, that was probably what had happened. There had been instances before where she'd kept him with her for the whole afternoon.

He set off for her house, taking big strides to help fend off the cold, and also because there was a stupid niggling worry at the back of his mind.

"Hi, Luke," Marjorie said when she opened the door.

"Is there a problem?"

He smiled. "Not at all. I've come to get Wilkins."

"Oh. Isn't he back yet?"

"What do you mean 'back'? Where's he gone?"

She laughed. "Not Wilkins. Your friend."

"My friend?"

"Yes. You sent someone to pick Wilkins up because there was someone you wanted him to meet."

Luke's heart sank. "I didn't send a friend."

"You didn't?" Marjorie put her hand to her mouth. "Oh, Luke. I'm so sorry."

"What did he look like, Marjorie?"

"He?"

Chapter 73

"It *was* a man, wasn't it, Marjorie?"

"I don't know. All I saw was the note."

"The note?"

She nodded. "I presumed it was for you and left it opposite Wilkins' crate."

Luke raced back to the farmhouse and, sure enough, there was a folded sheet of paper face down on the cupboard where he kept the dog biscuits.

He turned it over and read what was written.

> I've taken Wilkins to meet you-know-who.

That was it.

No name, no threat.

It wasn't Sam's writing. He was certain of that.

He returned to the front door and inspected it closely. There was no indication of a break-in.

He lifted the third plant pot to the left of the door. The spare key was gone, meaning whoever had taken Wilkins had known where he kept it.

Other than Sam, the only other person who knew was his brother. Could he have taken Wilkins somewhere, to see their mother perhaps?

He returned to the note and inspected it again. It could be Mark's writing, but surely he'd have added his name.

He decided to ring him to be sure.

"Hi, Luke."

"Mark, have you been to my house today?"

"No. I've been here all day."

"At Borrowham Hall?"

"Yes. Why?"

"Someone's taken Wilkins. You haven't told anyone else about the key, have you? The one I keep under the plant pot."

"No. Erica's seen me use it but she's been here all day as well."

"Okay. Thanks."

"Let me know when you find him."

"I will."

There was one other person who knew, but had he deleted her details? He searched his contacts and was relieved to find her mobile number.

She answered on the first ring.

"Hello, lover. Have you reconsidered my offer?"

He ignored the question.

"Cora, I don't suppose you've been to my house today, have you?"

"No. Why?"

"Someone's taken Wilkins."

"Oh, no!"

"You haven't told anyone where I keep the spare key, have you?"

"No."

"Okay. Thanks, Cora. Sorry to bother you."

"Don't be silly. Poor Wilkins. I hope you find him soon."

He hung up.

There might be a chance that Sam had told someone about his spare key. Her mother perhaps. Why she would do that, he didn't know, but he ought to at least ask her.

He was about to ring when something that Ambrose said came back to him. He'd reported that Janice Martin had made an odd comment after the Board meeting. She'd said that it was a mistake to treat a pet like family, because it made you miss them all the more when they died.

Only she hadn't said 'died'.

What she'd said was, 'when they've gone to meet their maker'.

He picked the note up again and the meaning became clear.

> I've taken Wilkins to meet you-know-who.

Was he reading too much into it, or…

But why?

What had he done?

Was what he had said to the Board too close to the mark?

Was this a warning to keep away?

He staggered to the kitchen and dropped onto one of the bar stools.

Should he contact Janice Martin, or find out where she lived and confront her face-to-face?

Or should he involve the police? Perhaps there were fingerprints.

He couldn't bear it if Wilkins came to any harm.

His phone rang.

It was Sam.

He had to tell her about Wilkins, but first he needed to check that she hadn't told anyone about the spare key.

"Sam, have you…"

She interrupted before he could finish.

"Ollie's here," she hissed.

"What?"

Things were going from bad to worse.

She kept her voice low. "He says he's sorry, but he's acting very strange. He keeps telling me he loves me and that I love him."

"Where are you?"

"I'm in the loo. Just a second." She raised her voice. "I won't be a second." He heard the chain flush and she lowered her voice again. "Are you at home, Luke?"

"Yes. I've just got here."

"You know then.'

"Know what?"

"About Wilkins. Ollie said he left a note."

"What! It was him?"

"Yes. He's been watching your house and saw where you keep the spare key." She raised her voice again. "Be right there."

The line went dead.

Chapter 74

Sam tried to plaster a smile on her face as she returned to the lounge but it was difficult. She didn't think Ollie would do anything to harm her but neither did she trust him completely. He was acting very strangely.

She tried to keep her voice light.

"You've said your piece, Ollie, but I think you should go now."

He was standing beside the armchair looking nervously at Wilkins and didn't respond.

The dog, for his part, was sitting with his back to the sofa and staring intently back. Every second or two a low growl issued from his throat.

"That thing doesn't like me," Ollie said. "He was fine when he thought I was taking him for a walk but now look at him."

Sam walked over, petted Wilkins on the back of his head and sat behind him. The cocker looked up at her, relaxed slightly, lay down, and then returned his attention to Ollie and growled again.

"Does he bite?"

She ignored his question.

"You need to leave."

"Can I stay the night?"

She couldn't believe what she was hearing.

"Can you what?"

Wilkins stood up when he heard this and took a step towards Ollie.

He stepped backwards until his body was hard against the wall and gestured at the cocker spaniel. "Keep him away."

"What do you mean, can you stay the night?"

He looked up at her while trying to keep an eye on Wilkins at the same time.

"We need time together. To talk."

"Talk about what?"

"Arrangements."

"Arrangements?"

"We should keep everything low-key. A registry office would make sense…"

She was only half-listening as he continued talking.

The man was off his rocker.

Luke would have set off as soon as the call ended, but it would take him twenty or twenty-five minutes to get to Bath from Norton St Philip. Could she keep this madman talking for that long?

Ollie cocked his head to one side and smiled at her.

"Well, what do you think?"

She was tempted to tell him exactly what she thought when the doorbell went.

Ollie jerked around to stare at the apartment door, and then turned his attention back to Sam.

"Are you expecting him? Is this one of your nights?" He sneered. "Oh, yes, I know about your affair. I've had my eye on you."

The bell went again.

"It can't be Luke," Sam said.

"How do you know?"

She swallowed. She didn't want to tell him she'd phoned Luke from the bathroom, but she had to tell him something.

"He's at his house. I know he is."

Her heart sank as she realised it could be her mother at the door.

The bell rang again, then yet again and this time the caller kept their finger on their buzzer for several seconds.

"You called him, didn't you?" Ollie hissed. "When you were in the bathroom. You told him I was here."

He started to move toward her, his voice growing louder with each word.

"HARLOT!"

He took another pace.

"WHORE!"

He drew his hand back to strike her.

She pulled her head away to try and minimise the blow, but before it landed a flash of brown hair and white teeth shot up from the ground and a pair of canine jaws clamped themselves around Ollie's wrist.

He yelped and tried to shake the dog off but the grip only tightened.

"Get off me, mutt."

Sam heard a thumping noise, then a smash which sounded like the front door falling to the floor. This was followed by the sound of someone bulky pounding up the stairs.

The apartment door was flung open.

"Well," Misty said as she took in the scene. "What the fuck is going on here?"

"Get him off me," Ollie said.

"Here, boy," Sam said.

Wilkins released his grip and backed up to Sam but his eyes remained fixed on Ollie and he resumed his growling routine.

Ollie was breathing heavily and holding his wrist.

He glared at Sam.

"That mongrel should be put down."

Despite the fact he was in obvious pain, he started to grin. "My colleague here has got photos."

He turned back to Misty who returned his grin, drew her fist back and let him have it.

His head spun ninety degrees and he staggered back two paces and then clutched his jaw.

"I ain't your fucking colleague, numbnuts. That'll teach you to lie to me. Your wife, my arse." She turned to Sam.

"Are you all right?"

"I'm fine."

"Luke rang and told me what was going on. Lucky I was nearby." She gestured to Ollie. "Want me to hit him again?"

"No!" Ollie squealed.

He was as big as Misty, probably bigger, but had been reduced to a shivering wreck by the actions of her and an average-sized cocker spaniel.

Sam almost felt sorry for him.

Almost.

"No, don't hit him, Misty."

"Thank you," Ollie said. "You do care."

Sam closed her eyes for a second then stepped towards him. He was six or seven inches taller but as she advanced he seemed to shrink to half her height.

"You're a stalker, Ollie Green. Your mind is twisted and you would have hit me if first Wilkins and then Misty hadn't intervened."

"I'd never hurt you, Sam. I lost it, that's all. You can see why, surely? We pledged to spend the rest of our lives together and the thought of your affair…"

"For fuck's sake, Ollie, are you listening to yourself?"

"You sure you don't want me to hit him again?"

Sam turned to Misty. "I'm sure. As to what to do with him though…"

"We could let Luke loose on him."

"No!" Ollie squealed again, even louder this time.

Chapter 75

"What time is it in Norton St Philip now?" Josh asked.

"Six in the morning," Leanne said.

"Gotcha. We're seven hours ahead, aren't we? You and I have had lunch and they haven't even had breakfast yet." He paused. "Unless you're an early riser like Luke."

"I've already said that you should wait. You're only guessing that he's up by six."

"It stands to reason though. He takes Wilkins for early morning walks, and he lives out in the sticks, and yet he's still in by eight most mornings."

"You're not going to let this go until I say yes, are you?"

He grinned, leaned over the table and kissed her on the lips.

"You're a star."

He pulled out his phone, dialled the number and it rang several times before he heard Luke's voice. It was more gravelly than normal.

"Hello."

"Hi, guv."

"What time is it?"

His voice was slower as well, and it dawned on Josh that he had indeed woken him up.

Buggery-boo-boo.

He heard a woman's voice in the background, although he couldn't make out the words, then Luke spoke again.

"It's Josh."

Leanne mouthed, "Did you wake him?"

Josh shook his head, but his eyes gave him away.

She raised one eyebrow. "He was asleep, wasn't he?"

"He, ah…"

"What do you want, Josh?" Luke yawned. "It's six in the

morning and I was asleep. Is it urgent?"

"No." There was no response "Shall I call back later?"

"No point. I'm awake now." He paused. "*We're* awake now."

"Is Sam there?"

"Yes, Josh. Sam is here. How can I help?"

"Leanne and I are going to Tease again this afternoon." He hesitated. "This morning."

"Make up your mind, son."

"We're going in an hour, so that's two in the afternoon, but for you…"

"I'm familiar with time zones. Get on with it."

"The thing is, what should I do? Should I try to engage one of the admin staff again, or talk to the children working in Building C?"

"Why don't you use your own judgement?"

"Gucci! Good advice, guv."

"Is that it?"

"That's it. You can go back to sleep now."

There was a deep and very vocal sigh from the other end and the line went dead.

"Was he helpful?" Leanne asked.

Josh nodded. "Uh-huh."

An hour later, their tuk-tuk dropped them off outside Tease's factory and, to Josh's horror, the same security guard stepped out of his cabin, put his peaked cap on and pulled it tight down over his forehead.

"Hi," Josh said as he advanced towards them. "Nice to meet again. Hot, isn't it? But then, it is the hot season."

The man grunted, but didn't say anything.

"We're here to see Claire," Leanne said.

He returned to his cabin, retrieved their visitor's badges, passed Leanne hers and then lifted the other badge to his face. After a few seconds, he walked forwards so that he was only a foot from Josh, stared into his eyes then raised an eyebrow and looked back down at the badge again.

"It's my passport photo," Josh said and tapped it with his index finger. "That's why I'm not smiling." He smiled his widest of smiles. "But this is the real me."

The guard looked down at the badge again. "This is not the real you?"

Josh shook his head. "No."

"Then you cannot come in."

Josh swallowed and his smile vanished. "Ah, but… I didn't mean…"

The guard didn't smile, but said, in the same flat, deadpan voice, "I am joking." After what seemed like an eternity of further staring into Josh's eyes, he grunted and passed over the visitor's badge, then returned to his cabin,. He rang a number, said "They're here," picked up a magazine and started leafing through the pages.

A minute or two later Claire Gibson appeared from the central building and walked towards the gates. She called over to the guard.

"Darany, could you open the gate please?"

The guard put his magazine down and clicked a button.

"Nice to see you again, Darany," Josh said as the gates started to slide open. "A friend of mine is called Darren. No 'ee' but kind of similar."

The guard looked up and frowned. "Is he Cambodian?"

"No, he's from Taunton."

The guard's frown deepened into a scowl, then he picked his magazine up again and resumed reading.

Claire led them back into the admin building.

"Thanks for letting us return," Leanne said.

"It's my pleasure. I'm not surprised you wanted to find out more about the MS-100. It uses 3D weaving technology."

"That's fascinating," Leanne lied.

"I've prepared a short presentation to outline its features and benefits."

Oh no, please no, Josh thought, remembering how long

Claire's previous 'short presentation' had lasted.

She led them back to her office.

"Good luck," Sonisay mouthed to Josh as he passed.

"Thanks," he mouthed back and was rewarded with a smile.

As before, Konya was asked to bring drinks, and Claire pulled the screen down.

"This shouldn't take long," she said and clicked on the remote control.

From one-cut to 3D weaving

Tease's transition to cutting-edge technology

Josh laughed. "Good pun."

Claire frowned, looked up at the slide and then back at Josh, one eyebrow raised.

He pointed at the screen. "You've said 'one-cut' and 'cutting-edge'. Clever."

"It's not meant to be a pun."

"Ah, right."

She clicked the remote control again and another slide appeared, this time with six bullets.

"I'll start with our historic use of hand dobbies," Claire began, "then move onto 3D woven nodal truss structures. If I'm too quick, please say. We can spend as long as you like."

We've got a plane to catch in twelve hours, was Josh's thought.

Ten minutes later, Claire was still talking about using a hand dobby, which sounded to Josh like some kind of house elf, and he was fighting a yawn.

He decided he couldn't wait any longer and shot his hand in the air.

Claire paused mid-sentence.

"Okay if I pop to the loo?"

"Of course. Do you want me to…"

"No! Ah… please carry on. This is mainly for Leanne."

He left the office to the sound of Claire warbling on about figuring effects.

"Congratulations," Sonisay said. "You escaped again."

Josh grinned. "I said I needed to go to the bathroom. Ah, I don't suppose we could have a chat, could we?"

"What about?"

"Do you have a staff room? I don't want to be where Claire can see me."

She laughed. "Follow me."

Chapter 76

Sonisay showed Josh into a small kitchen-come-seating area at the front of the building and gestured for him to sit at the table in the centre of the room.

"Coffee?"

"I've just had one thanks."

While she made herself a tea, he tried to think how best to play it.

Sonisay seemed nice, but she couldn't work there without knowing about the children working in Building C. Did that make her one of the bad guys? Would she go straight to Claire and tell her he'd been prying?

He had to approach their conversation in a way that suggested all he wanted was an excuse to escape Claire's presentation. Yes, that was the way to go about it. It wasn't as if he had limited time. Claire would drone on for at least half an hour, and even then she would take Leanne to see the MS-loom, or whatever it was called, in action.

He'd talk about everyday life and what they did in their spare time, then gradually lead into Tease itself.

Sonisay sat down opposite, and raised her mug to her lips.

Josh smiled, he hoped disarmingly.

"Have you got a boyfriend?"

She spluttered, put the mug down and started to push her chair back.

"No! I didn't mean…"

Pissedy-piss-piss. He'd made this mistake before. Why didn't he ever learn?

"Don't go… I was making small talk, that's all. I'm with Leanne and we're very happy together."

She was standing now, one eyebrow raised.

"Why?"

"Why are we happy together?"

"No. Why are you making small talk?"

"Ah…"

He sighed as he realised that the only option now was to just go for it.

"Please sit down, Sonisay, and I'll explain."

She sat back down but was looking at him warily.

"When we were here the other day," he began, though he wasn't exactly sure where he was going with this, "I wandered into Building C, and I saw what's going on in there."

"You mean the children?"

"Exactly. It's not right, is it?"

"Why not? They're paid."

"But they should be at school. Some of them look like they're only nine or ten and that's no way to spend your childhood."

"They come from poor families and have little choice. In most cases, their parents can't get work and need the money to survive."

"Aren't their unemployment benefits enough?"

Sonisay laughed. "There is no such thing in Cambodia. If you're unemployed, you get nothing."

He decided to try a different tack.

"Why don't Tease employ the parents instead? They could probably work faster."

"You sound like my brother."

"Your brother?"

She nodded. "My brother believes that children are used because they are cheap. He has ideas on how to change things, but whether they'll listen is another thing."

"Does he work here then?"

"Yes."

"Could I have a word with him? I'd like to hear his ideas."

She looked at her watch.

"You're in luck. He's due a break so I'll see if he can spare a few minutes." She pulled out her phone, clicked a button and waited while the phone connected. "I should warn you though, he's an introvert and can come across as somewhat severe until you get to know him."

"No problem."

"Ah," she said as someone picked up at the other end. "Could you spare a few minutes to chat to someone about Building C?" She waited for a second. "Thanks. We're in the staff room."

She turned back to Josh.

"Darany will be along in a minute."

"Great, that's... Did you say Darany?"

"I forgot, you must have met him when you arrived."

"With the peaked cap?"

She smiled. "That's him."

He took a deep breath. "Right. Gotcha. Ah... right."

She started to stand up. "I ought to get back to my work, if that's okay."

"Before you go, you haven't heard of a woman called Elizabeth Rebus, have you?"

She nodded. "She's one of our investors, and I've seen various communications between her and Claire about Building C. It was Miss Rebus's idea in the first place, and she provided the initial funding." She laughed. "Mind you, it's only been six months and she's already made a healthy profit on her investment."

"And is the money paid to an account in Miss Rebus's name?"

"Funny you should ask that because it's been recently changed to an offshore account. I know because it was complex setting up our system to cope with it and I had to help."

"Is the new account in the same name?"

"No, it's in a different name. Why?"

"I'll be honest with you, Sonisay," he lied. "I'm a private investigator and the woman calling herself Miss Rebus is cheating on my client."

"Having an affair?"

"No. She's been syphoning money offshore from their joint account, and in all likelihood to the account she's now using for payments from Tease."

"I see. I can't remember the new name on the account, but I can have a look when I get back."

"Thanks. Can you text it to me, please?" He gave her his number and she entered it into her phone.

They both turned at the sound of the door opening.

"Ah," Sonisay said. "Here's my brother now."

Chapter 77

Darany removed his peaked cap and placed it on the table.

"Hi again," Josh said.

Darany grunted and sat down in the chair his sister had vacated.

"Not so hot in here," Josh ventured, "despite it being the hot season."

"Air conditioning."

Josh gave him a double thumbs-up and grinned.

"Gotcha."

Darany's face remained deadpan. "You want to talk about Tease's child labour?"

"Yes."

"Why?"

Josh realised that everything he'd said to Sonisay would be relayed back to her brother so he needed to stick with the story he'd given her.

He puffed his chest out.

"I'm a private investigator."

Darany looked him up and down.

"I find that hard to believe."

"I know I'm young, but my boss sent me."

"His name?"

"Lu…"

Josh stopped mid-word as it occurred to him that he shouldn't reveal Luke's real name. He wasn't sure why, but it felt wrong somehow.

"Lou, ah… Reed. Yes, Lou Reed. Lou sent me because our client is being defrauded by the woman funding Building C."

"So your only interest is the money. You don't care about the children."

"No. I mean, yes. I do care about them. They should be at school not working here, and I'd like to help if I can. Sonisay said you had ideas on how to put a stop to it."

"My plans are controversial."

"That's okay. I can live with controversial."

"Very well." Darany leaned forward over the table and lowered his voice. "I will ask Claire and the other Tease managers to a meeting…"

"Yes."

"…and once they are all assembled…"

"Yes."

"…I will enter the room…"

"Yes."

":…and I will shoot them with an AK47."

"Eh?"

Darany sat back, and the tiniest of smiles formed on his face.

"I am joking of course."

"Phew. That's a relief."

"I will use a bomb."

"What?"

Darany's smile broadened.

"I am still joking. I like to make people laugh."

Josh didn't think he'd ever make a living as a stand-up comedian, but smiled and nodded all the same.

"Very funny. But in all seriousness, what are your ideas?" He put his hand up. "And don't tell me you're going to nuke them."

"Replace the children with their parents."

"But that would mean paying higher salaries."

"I have a spreadsheet."

"You have a spreadsheet?"

"Yes."

"And?"

This was like getting blood out of a stone.

"The children work hard, but parents will be more

productive. I have input this into my spreadsheet."

"And?"

"If Tease stops paying Miss Rebus then overall manufacturing costs will not increase."

"I see."

"I must return to work now."

Darany stood up, turned his back on Josh and walked towards the door.

"Thanks for the information, Darany. I'm hoping our work will remove Miss Rebus from the equation which should mean…"

The door slammed shut.

Josh shrugged, looked at his watch and realised he ought to be getting back to Leanne.

Claire was in full flow when he returned to her office.

"Ah," she said. "Welcome back, Josh. I've been telling Leanne about the CR-Intensifier."

"Have you? That's interesting."

"I'll run through it again for your benefit."

"No! There's no need. Honestly."

"I insist. I wouldn't want you to miss out."

An hour and a half later, Claire showed them to the gate.

"Hi, Darany," Josh said.

Darany looked up from his magazine, grunted and gestured to the waiting tuk-tuk.

"Your taxi."

"If you want to visit again, get in touch," Claire said as they shook hands. "You haven't seen our ultrasonic cutter in action. It's a Suntech A101."

"Is it," Josh said, a plastered smile on his face. "Gucci! An A101. Fancy that."

"We'd love to, Claire," Leanne said, "but we're flying back to the UK this evening."

"That's a shame. If you ever return…"

We'll keep a wide berth, Josh thought.

*

"Champagne or orange juice, sir," the stewardess said, a broad, but to Josh's eyes totally false, smile across her face.

He looked up at her and grinned. "Is the pope a catholic?"

She didn't flinch a muscle. "Yes, he is."

"Right. It was a… Never mind. Champagne, please."

She poured his champagne, passed it to him and then moved down the aisle to the passenger seated behind.

He turned to Leanne and raised his glass.

"Cheers."

She clinked her against his.

"Cheers."

His phone beeped.

"You need to turn that off, Joshy."

"I'd better see who it is." He clicked on his phone and looked up again. "It's Sonisay. She found the name of the new account Erebus is using. I'll forward it to the guv."

He was about to do so when the stewardess reappeared, the smile still plastered across her face.

"I'll have to ask you to turn that off now, sir."

"I need to…"

"We're about to set off."

"Can I just…"

"Turn it off please."

He turned it off.

Chapter 78

Bradley Dawson, also known as Skylar and occasionally as Silas, had been sitting in his Kia for a couple of hours. There was no sign of his target, but he was a patient man. She'd be back, and then he'd confront her.

He was pleased with himself.

Not only had he tracked down the journalist investigating Beacon, but he'd also uncovered something in her past that he could use against her. Once he confronted her with what he knew, he was sure she'd do what he asked.

And if she didn't... Well, he'd cross that bridge when he came to it. There were other ways of making her back off.

Fern, or Shannon as she now called herself, was a different matter altogether. She wouldn't return to her parents, he was convinced of that, but he suspected she was staying with Rhianna Bandicoot. Even if she wasn't, he was sure that Bandicoot would know where she was hiding, and he was proud of his powers of persuasion.

He decided it was time to share the good news with Erebus.

She was quick to answer the phone.

"Hello, Skylar. Have you resolved things?"

"Not yet, but I'm close. I'm sitting outside the journalist's house and I've found out something about her that will make it easy to stop her in her tracks."

"Good. What about the girl?"

"This Bandicoot woman is bound to know where she's hiding. If I'm lucky, Fern may even be staying with her."

"I fail to see how that would be good news. How will you deal with the situation if Bandicoot is there, given it has to appear as though Fern has taken her own life?"

"I'll find a way."

"You're going to have to tread very carefully, Skylar. This journalist cannot be left thinking Fern's death was anything but suicide."

"I understand."

"I'm at an event this afternoon and when I've finished I want these two problems to have been dealt with. Is that clear?"

"Yes, Erebus, it's clear."

Chapter 79

Erebus hung up, happy that Skylar had made significant progress.

She had a lot of time for him. He needed an occasional nudge in the right direction, but he was on the ball. She trusted him to do the right thing as regards both the journalist and the girl.

He'd also done a tremendous job for her at Beacon, taking on the role of principal 'mentor' while also keeping on top of earnings. He was quick to recommend action if any source of revenue was declining, as he'd proven with Celestina. She paid Skylar a significant wage, but he was worth every penny.

Lewis was also a good employee, but not as ruthless as she'd like. It was only a few months since she'd taken him on to manage her estate, but whether he'd ever be up to taking on the migrant business, as she had hoped, remained to be seen.

If not, she'd have to recruit someone. Dealing with intermediaries like Henri in France and Christos in Greece was both tedious and time-consuming.

There was also the issue with the Afghans and she decided it was about time she had an update.

After six or seven rings, Lewis's phone went to voicemail. She was about to leave a message when he came on the line.

"Sorry." He was panting. "I've just run up the hill."

"Have you resolved the problem with the new migrants?"

"That's what I was doing. It was Connor's idea, and I think it'll work."

"What have you done?"

"Dealt with their child."

"Dealt with it?"

"Yes, we…'

"Stop, Lewis. I don't want the details. All I need is your assurance that the couple will now pull their weight."

"Definitely, now they haven't got…"

"Enough. Well done, and please tell Connor I'm very pleased with him."

She hung up and smiled to herself.

Perhaps Lewis did have a ruthless streak after all.

Chapter 80

Claire was delighted with the way the week had gone. The new employees were beginning to get up to speed, and she'd had a brilliant time with the visitors from the UK.

She decided to call Miss Rebus to tell her how well the children were settling in.

The phone was answered after a couple of rings.

"Hello, Claire."

"Hello, Miss Rebus."

"Is everything okay?"

"More than okay. I'm ringing to tell you how well the children are doing, They're proving to be quick learners."

"That's excellent news."

Claire smiled, pleased with her reaction. "Yes, isn't it? There are two who are struggling, but I'm sure they'll catch up in the end."

"Why are they struggling?"

"I think they're not as quick to pick things up, that's all. It's not as if they're the youngest either. Ponlok is eleven and Thavary is thirteen."

"You need to replace them. We can't afford to be carrying anyone."

"It's hard to do that. The parents need the money, and they'd be heartbroken if they were asked to leave."

"This is a business, Claire, not a charity. There must be plenty of other families who would value the extra money."

"Very well, Miss Rebus."

"Have you any other news?"

"You remember I told you about that Tease fan who visited at the beginning of the week."

"Yes."

"She and her boyfriend came back yesterday because

she was keen to see the MS-100 in action and we didn't have time on Monday. It's lovely having someone so enthusiastic about what we do here, and Leanne asked no end of questions. I'm not sure Josh was as keen, but she was ever so excited."

There was silence at the other end.

"Miss Rebus?"

"Did you say their names are Leanne and Josh?"

"That's right."

"What did they look like?"

"Why?"

"What did they look like, Claire?"

"They... Actually, they sent me photos for their visitor's badges. Do you want me to email them to you?"

"Yes. As soon as possible."

"You sound like you might know them…"

Claire stopped talking when she realised the line was dead.

Chapter 81

The BMW was, in Luke's opinion, a car more suited to a sales executive. However, it was comfortable.

Normally.

But not today.

It was at times like this that he wished he'd been given a choice of company car. A hatchback or estate would have coped much better.

He flinched as he felt a tongue in his ear. This was the third time and they'd been on the road for less than five minutes.

"Sorry, Luke," Sam said from the passenger seat, though he could sense amusement in her tone. She wrestled Wilkins away by the collar and pushed him to the back seat. "Stay, boy."

Luke glanced in the rearview mirror to see the cocker sitting bolt upright on the back seat and tilting his head to one side. It was as if he was saying, *'She said something but bugger if I know what it was'*.

He spotted a sign indicating a parking area half a mile ahead.

"I'm going to pull over. Would you mind sitting in the back with him?"

"Good idea. With any luck, that'll calm him down."

They stopped and Sam joined Wilkins in the back. She belted up and he lay down on the seat beside her with his head on her lap. He seemed content but she grabbed his collar in case he had a sudden desire to revisit his master's ear.

"That seems to have worked," she said after a couple of minutes. "How are we going to play it today?"

"I've been thinking about that. I'm going to need to

deal with Wilkins while all this pampering is going on, which means I'll be with Sarah Chittock and Gillian Ley since their dogs are also taking part. That leaves you free to try and strike up conversations with Janice Martin and Meredith Holcroft."

"That makes sense."

"Yes. We'll split up at the first possible opportunity so that we can divide and conquer."

Half an hour later they reached the gates to Rockington Manor where, after a few seconds, the ornate black gates started to swing open.

After a few hundred yards, the road curved to the right and the house came into view. It was almost as big as Borrowham Hall, but there the similarity ended. Rockington Manor was a Victorian reinterpretation of a castle, the main block lying between two octagonal towers and the whole building turreted.

"Wow," Sam said. "Andy said it was grand."

Luke pointed to the statues at the corners of the walled terrace fronting the house.

"And look, the Dame's put her mark on it." He laughed. "I'm not sure the architect had statues of poodles in mind when he designed this a couple of hundred years ago."

He parked the car around the back and they put Wilkins on his lead and walked him to the front.

Dame Sarah Chittock was standing by the door clad in a dusky pink gown and with five rings of pearls around her neck.

"I hope we're not too early," Luke said.

"Not at all, my dear. It's lovely for you to come at all." She bent down to stroke Wilkins. "This must be your delightful poochie-baby."

Wilkins drew back his head for a second, then relented and let her pet him.

"What's his name?"

"Wilkins."

"Is that a family name?"

"It is, but not my family. It's the surname of the man who makes my favourite cider."

"Interesting." She stood up again and offered her cheek.

Luke obliged by giving her a quick peck and Sam followed suit.

"Come on in. I want you to meet my bunny bears."

They followed her inside where a man was holding the leads of five toy poodles. All of them were white and appeared to Luke to have been coiffeured within an inch of their lives. He wondered what they were going to look like *after* their pampering session.

"Do you like their necklaces?" Sarah asked. "I had them especially made with aquamarines and blue topaz."

Luke could sense a smile appearing on Sam's face and tried to avoid catching her eye.

"They're very pretty, Sarah," he said.

"Aren't they just? My darlings are very excited about today and want to welcome you. This is Roxanna."

She indicated the first poodle and Luke looked at her blankly.

"Hold your hand out to her."

He bent down and held his hand out. The dog raised her paw and he shook it.

"And this is Bonnie."

She led him along the line until he'd shaken the paws of all five dogs, after which he glanced at Sam who had her hand over her mouth and immediately looked away.

"Please go in," Sarah said and smiled. "I'd join you but I need to welcome our other guests."

Luke and Sam walked through the hall to a large chandeliered room where they were immediately approached by a man in a tuxedo.

"Is it okay if I take your dog to our kennels until the event, sir?" he asked.

"Sure." Luke said, and passed Wilkins' lead over.
"Thank you."

He led Wilkins away and Luke glanced around. There were a dozen or so people in the room, Meredith Holcroft among them. She spotted him and walked over.

"Thank you for coming and rescuing the situation," she said, "although to be honest Sarah would probably be happy if it was just her five dogs here today. That would guarantee her a win in this stupid pampering event and she's unbelievably competitive."

"You don't have a pet yourself then, Meredith?" Sam asked.

She shook her head violently. "I'm not fond of animals." She laughed. "Nor of people, to be honest, but in your case, I'll make an exception. By the way, I hope I wasn't too hard on you when you presented on Tuesday."

"Not at all," Luke said. He spotted Gillian Ley at the far end of the room in conversation with Ambrose. "Ah, there's Gillian. Please excuse me, you two. I want to have a word with her about her labradors."

Chapter 82

"I'm sorry it has to be on a Saturday," Maj said, "but this was the only time she had available."

"That's okay," Asha said. "It's not as if you'd have enjoyed going into Bath shopping with us."

He smiled. "Yes, that's definitely a side benefit."

Asha walked to the bottom of the stairs and called up. "Are you ready, Sabrina?"

"Nearly, Mum."

She returned to the lounge. "Why didn't this journalist want to meet at her house?"

"She said it would be easier to talk in a cafe, but I suspect it's because Shannon's staying with her."

"And Shannon can identify the woman behind this cult? What's it called?"

"Beacon. Yes."

They both turned at the sound of footsteps on the stairs, and a few seconds later Sabrina appeared. She smiled at them both and twirled around.

"What do you think?"

"You look lovely," Asha said as she looked her outfit up and down

Maj nodded his agreement, but his heart skipped a beat. How did they grow up so quickly? It seemed like only yesterday she'd been a little girl, holding his hand to cross the road and begging for an extra story at bedtime.

Now look at her, very much a young woman.

Sabrina kissed him on the cheek.

"Bye, Dad. See you later." Her smile broadened. "Mum's got a credit card, so don't worry if we're late back."

Maj watched them leave, then grabbed his coat and headed outside.

Forty-five minutes later he parked in the Cattle Market car park in the centre of Frome and walked the short distance to the River House Cafe. Brightly decorated, and somewhat quirky, every table was taken but as he scanned the room he recognised the journalist from her appearance on Good Morning Britain. She was seated at a table by the window gazing out, deep in thought.

He walked over.

"Rhianna?"

She turned and looked up hesitantly.

"I'm Maj Osman." He held his hand out and she shook it. "Can I order you a coffee?"

"Yes, please. Skinny latte."

He ordered their drinks, returned to the table and sat down opposite.

"Thanks for saying you'd see me."

She smiled hesitantly. "I almost didn't. It was you mentioning Josh that convinced me you were genuine."

"Shannon told you about Josh?"

She nodded. "Another man has rung me twice asking to meet, and my sister told me this morning that he rang her too saying he needs to speak to me as soon as possible. His story is that he wants to make a television documentary, but I'm sure he's spinning a line."

"You think he's from Beacon?"

"I suspect so, yes."

"Has he got an Australian accent?"

Her eyes widened. "How did you know that?"

Maj explained about the man calling himself Silas who had been waiting for Shannon outside her parents' pub.

Rhianna sighed. "It has to be the same man. What do you think he wants?"

"Your coffees," a smiling waitress said.

Maj returned her smile. "Thanks."

She placed two mugs in front of them.

He waited until she had returned to the counter before

continuing, and kept his voice low.

"It may be that all he wants is to talk to Shannon to convince her that Beacon is genuine. However, when my boss confronted him in his car he spotted on the passenger seat what looked like a knife wrapped in a tea towel."

"But why would he want to harm her? Even though Shannon can identify Erebus, and what Beacon is doing is clearly immoral, I haven't uncovered anything illegal."

"Not yet, Rhianna, but I suspect it's only a matter of time. We believe that Beacon is one of several dubious, if not downright illegal, organisations led by the woman calling herself Erebus."

She raised an eyebrow. "What makes you think there are more?"

"We know for a fact that she's also making money out of child labour in Cambodia."

"You do? It sounds like this is even bigger than I thought. I need to…"

Maj held his hand up. "I admire your reporter's instincts, but it's vital we stop what Erebus is doing as soon as we can. Shannon hasn't returned home since she met Josh last week, and I need to speak to her. Is she staying with you?"

Rhianna hesitated, which told Maj all he needed to know.

"Please, Rhianna. You need to take me to her so that she can identify Erebus. Once she's done that, we can put a stop to the misery she's causing, and you can write your story."

"Will you guarantee me an exclusive?"

"Yes."

She stood up. "Come on then. My house isn't much more than half a mile from here."

He paid for their drinks and they left the cafe.

Rhianna led them left on Bridge Street. "I'm on Windsor Crescent. It's less than a fifteen-minute walk."

Her phone started to ring and she pulled it out of her pocket.

"It's my sister. Excuse me, Maj." She accepted the call. "Hi, Kandy."

She paused to listen for a few seconds, then put her hand over the microphone and turned to Maj.

"The Australian guy has rung her again."

She returned her attention to her sister. "What did he say this time?"

Kandy talked for longer this time.

"You did what?" Rhianna said after a while. "When?" Another pause. "I'll have to go, Kandy."

She hung up and turned to Maj.

"My sister gave him my address."

"When?"

"About an hour ago."

Chapter 83

Sam accepted the offer of another glass of champagne from the waiter even though, as with the first, she had no intention of drinking it. The bubbly would disappear into a plant pot a small amount at a time.

She hadn't managed to bait Meredith and decided to try to corner Janice Martin.

After a few minutes she spotted her returning from the bathroom and wandered over.

She smiled. "Hi, Janice."

Janice forced a smile in return. "Hello."

"It's lovely of Sarah and Meredith to invite Luke and me."

"I believe Luke brought his dog," was Janice's cold reply, "but I hadn't been aware he was bringing you."

Sam resisted the urge to rise to this double insult. Janice clearly believed that the only reason Luke was there was because of Wilkins, while she was nothing but an unfortunate appendage.

She decided to keep the tone of their conversation light, then see if she could draw the other woman out.

"Yes, it was lovely of Luke to ask me. He and I have been seeing each other since just before Christmas."

"You're a couple?"

"Hadn't you realised?"

"He recently made you his deputy, didn't he?"

Here was another not-so-subtle blow to the solar plexus, the suggestion that she'd only been promoted because they were a couple.

Sam smiled again, determined not to be riled.

"A few months ago, yes."

"I see."

"Sarah has a lovely house."

Janice looked around the room as if seeing it for the first time.

"It's big, I'll give you that. I don't know how she can afford it."

"Didn't she inherit the family business?"

"I wouldn't know. Have you been researching her?"

Keeping the tone light was proving difficult, not to say impossible. This was one snappy woman who seemed intent on goading her at every opportunity.

Sam decided to stop messing about and go for the jugular.

"Yes, we have. I believe Luke told you that someone senior in Filchers is involved in highly unethical business offshore."

"Yes, but my understanding was that it was a full-time employee, not a Non-Executive Director."

"Not necessarily. We need to rule everyone out."

"And am I ruled out?"

"We haven't completed our investigation, but I'm sure you're not involved, Janice."

Janice frowned but didn't respond.

Sam decided to push some more. "We now know where the unethical offshore business is."

"Cambodia."

This was said as a matter of fact rather than a question.

"How did you know, Janice?"

"You need to stop prying," she snapped. "You could be stepping into dangerous territory."

She turned abruptly and walked over to Meredith, who appeared to have been watching both of them with interest. They exchanged a few words after which Janice looked briefly back at Sam, a scowl on her face.

Janice knew about Cambodia. Did that make her Erebus, or had she heard it from someone else?

Sam decided to step outside for some fresh air. The

brief conversation with Janice had been exhausting, not least because she found the woman spiteful and rude.

She stepped through the ballroom's double French doors, walked along the side of the house for a few paces, emptied her glass into a jardiniere, realised she was going to freeze without a coat on, and was about to return inside when she heard someone talking around the next corner.

"It's only until Thursday and the money's good," a man said. He paused and she realised he was on his phone.

Who was this man? Could he be Janice's husband? What he said was probably innocent, but it sounded suspicious. He was out of view and she decided to stay where she was to listen some more.

"You'll have to put up with it," he went on. "Send me a photo."

Then she realised that she recognised his voice from when he'd taken Wilkins away.

There was silence for a few seconds and then a beep. She heard footsteps and smiled as the waiter appeared.

He stopped when he saw her and raised one eyebrow.

"You must be cold, miss. Do you want me to fetch your coat?"

She forced a smile. "I'm fine, thanks. I'm going back in now."

He indicated her glass. "Can I top you up?"

"No, thanks."

He nodded and returned to the ballroom. She followed him and watched as he retrieved his tray from a side table and left through the door that led back to the hall, presumably heading for the kitchen or wherever it was that the champagne was stored.

Sam shrugged as she reflected on what he'd said on the phone. He was probably talking to his partner about a new job, that was all. It was nonsense to assume that everyone she encountered was up to no good.

She watched people milling around the room. Luke had

disappeared, presumably because the pampering had started since Dame Sarah Chittock and Gillian Ley were also nowhere to be seen. Meredith and Janice were still talking.

Sam didn't feel like trying to strike up a conversation with anyone else and decided she would do what the waiter had suggested. She returned to the hall, retrieved her coat from the rack and this time headed straight out of the main entrance and turned left thinking she'd return to her spot beside the French doors via the terrace.

After a few paces she spotted the waiter again. This time he wasn't on his phone but was talking to a younger and much bigger man. Their body language suggested a manager-employee relationship, but the newcomer was dressed in jeans and a jumper rather than a dinner jacket, so he certainly wasn't a waiter. Could he be one of the kitchen staff?

She was debating what to do next when the younger man nodded agreement to something his boss had said and headed towards her, their conversation over. The waiter headed away towards the ballroom.

She smiled as the man approached but he was walking quickly and hardly noticed her. As he drew nearer she spotted what she thought was a smear of muck on his neck, but when he passed she saw that it wasn't dirt at all but a tattoo of a rat with its mouth open and teeth bared. Above the rat, picked out in black, were the letters 'RRMC'.

He turned away from the house and headed at pace down the hill towards what looked like rows of grapevines.

Sam waited until he was out of view and then, with a quick look back at the house to check no one was watching, headed off after him.

Chapter 84

"Rhianna, stop!" Maj said.

"What is it?"

He pointed to the car parked outside number 83.

"Is that yours?"

"No. I've never seen it before."

Maj remembered Luke saying that Silas had been in a blue Kia Sportage.

"It's his. It has to be."

"Should we call the police?"

"Yes. You do it, but move away out of sight." He looked around, and then gestured to the next house along. "Go behind that wall." He held out his hand. "Give me your keys."

"What are you going to do?"

"I'm going to go in and confront him."

"But you said he might have a weapon."

"Shannon's in there and we can't afford to wait until the police arrive."

He marched across the road, his mind working overtime. Should he proceed quickly and use surprise, or should he make as much noise as possible and call out to make himself known?

What would Luke do?

He'd move quietly at first, and then play it by ear, that's what he'd do.

And that was what Maj was going to do.

As he approached the front door he saw that it was slightly ajar. After glancing back to check that Rhianna wasn't in view, he gently pushed and heaved a sigh of relief when the door swung silently back on its hinges.

He stepped softly inside and stood stock-still, listening

for the slightest sound.

Nothing.

He could see two doors off the hall, both closed, while at the end of the corridor was an opening to what looked like a kitchen. He stepped towards the first door then stopped in his tracks when he heard a creak.

The Australian was upstairs.

They were upstairs.

He stood in silence, waiting for another noise so that he could identify their location.

Instead of a creak, a woman screamed.

Maj dashed to the stairs and took them two at a time.

She called out again, a single word this time.

"NO!"

It was coming from the door directly in front of him.

Maj leapt for the handle, pressed it down and pushed.

The door didn't budge, but he heard a grunt followed by another screamed "NO!", even louder this time, then a splash.

Maj took a step back, turned side on and charged at the door shoulder first.

There was less resistance than he had expected and the door fell inwards onto two people.

The woman, who had to be Shannon, was on her knees with her head over the side of the bath and her hair soaking wet.

The man had been standing over her but was knocked to his knees by the falling door. He pushed it aside and stood up in one movement, then snarled and ran at Maj, shoving him with all his might. Maj fell backwards and the man darted past him to the stairs.

Maj clambered to his feet and turned to Shannon.

"Are you all right?"

She looked up at him, her eyes red and full of tears.

"He… he…"

"It's all right, Shannon. You're safe now."

He turned his head at the sound of the front door slamming.

"Wait here."

"Be careful," she said, her voice hoarse. "He's got a knife."

Maj hesitated, but only for a second.

If Rhianna had stepped away from her hiding place and approached the house Silas might attack her. He needed to ensure she was okay.

He raced down the stairs, grabbed the handle of the front door, pulled it open and stepped outside to find Rhianna on the pavement by the front gate, her phone to her ear.

There was no sign of the Australian.

She looked over at him.

"Is Shannon…"

She stopped without finishing her question and her eyes widened in horror.

"WATCH OUT!"

In that instant Maj realised he'd been duped and that Shannon's attacker hadn't left the house. Rhianna was looking over his left shoulder and he leapt to the right as an arm swung down.

He felt what seemed like a punch to his left arm, just above the elbow, but adrenaline kept him going and he turned as the Australian faltered in his follow-through, stumbling slightly to regain his feet.

Maj drew his right arm back and threw a punch, catching the man on the ear.

Silas snarled and lifted his knife arm to strike again, but Maj was quick and his fist struck him a second time, a better blow that caught him on the jaw.

He rocked back, stunned.

Maj heard a noise behind him.

"YOU BASTARD!" Shannon screamed.

This seemed to decide things for the Australian who

turned away and ran to the road. For a frightening second Maj thought he was targeting Rhianna, but he sprinted in the opposite direction to his car.

Maj started to follow, but stopped when he felt a hand on his shoulder.

"No," Shannon said as he turned to face her. "Let him go."

Her eyes moved to his arm.

"He's hurt you."

Maj looked down to see that his shirt was ripped and blood was dripping from his elbow.

"It's only a nick," he said.

They both turned at the sound of gears crunching and watched as the Kia accelerated away.

Chapter 85

After a couple of hundred yards, Sam saw two small wooden buildings at the bottom of the valley in amongst the trees. It was clear that the man was heading for them, and she veered sideways into the wood where she could hide without fear of being seen.

She'd followed him out of sheer adrenaline, fired up by the sight of the RRMS tattoo, but was she being stupid, following a man who was in all likelihood a murderer?

Yes, absolutely.

Luke would be furious if he knew what she'd done, but she had to find out what the man was up to. After all, it could be a coincidence. This ex-gang member might be totally innocent, and not the person who had taken a dead Syrian to Bath Spa's Lost Property office.

Who was she kidding?

It had to be the same man but what did that mean? He appeared to be an employee, working for the waiter who in turn must surely be working for Dame Sarah Chittock. Did that mean that she was the villain of the piece and was involved in child labour in Cambodia and a therapy cult in Glastonbury? If so, was this man part of some other immoral and probably illegal venture under her leadership?

The very thought seemed ridiculous. Yes, Sam had joked about the Dame reminding her of Dolores Umbridge, but did she really believe that the lady in pink was an evil mastermind?

The two buildings, no more than sheds really, were about 100 yards apart. She watched as the man walked to the left hand one, opened the door and started talking. She was too far away for the sound to carry, but he looked angry and after a few seconds held his phone up for whoever was inside to see what was on it.

He said something else and then retraced his steps, evidently returning to the house.

Sam squeezed herself behind a trunk and waited until he was out of sight before scrambling through the trees towards the shed.

She walked to the door, which was slightly ajar, and opened it to reveal a young woman seated on the floor, her back to the corner and a plain red scarf over her hair.

The woman stared up at her, her eyes rimmed with red.

"Who are you?" Sam asked.

There was no response and the woman started waving her hand, indicating that she should leave.

Sam tried to get her head around what was happening. It looked like this woman was being kept prisoner and yet the man hadn't locked the door when he'd left. Did he have some other kind of hold over her?

She tapped herself on the chest. "My name is Sam." She smiled. "I can help you."

"No."

Sam pointed to the woman. "What is your name?"

"Jamila." Her eyes widened. "Go. Go."

"Come with me." Sam stood up and gestured for Jamila to do the same.

"No. Bibi."

"Bibi?"

Jamila folded her arms across her chest and rocked them from side to side. "Bibi."

"Your child?"

She nodded.

"Where is Bibi?"

Sam heard a noise behind her, turned and darted for the door but was too late as it was slammed shut.

She pushed against it but it remained closed.

"Let me out!"

There was no response and she heard first one bolt and

then a second being drawn across.

Sam reached for her phone and swore as she saw that there was no signal.

She turned back to Jamila, a flickering oil lamp now the only illumination in the enclosed space.

"Who is he, Jamila? Who is that man?"

"Connor."

Sam closed her eyes for a second as it dawned on her how stupid she had been.

What was important now was to keep her wits about her. Connor would be back and she needed to be ready for him. She lifted the oil lamp and used it to search the tiny shed. After a few minutes, she realised that the only item even halfway usable as a weapon was the lamp itself.

She sat down by the door with the oil lamp on the floor and smiled, a much more forced smile this time.

"Don't worry, Jamila. We'll get out of this."

She hoped.

Chapter 86

It was Wilkins' turn to be cosseted, coiffeured and curled and to Luke's surprise he seemed to be enjoying the whole experience.

The cocker spaniel was lying on his back, his head to one side with his tongue lolling out, while a middle-aged woman, who herself had deep pink hair, was trimming his toenails.

Luke looked at his watch, wondering when this whole fiasco would be over. Trixie et al, as well as Gillian's labradors and two other dogs, had already been 'done' and he wanted to get back to Sam to see if she'd had any luck with Meredith or Janice.

After what seemed like an eternity, but was probably only another four or five minutes, the woman turned to Luke.

"He's all done," she said.

Wilkins promptly scrambled to his feet, then sat down as she fed him first one, then a second dog biscuit.

Luke clipped the spaniel's lead onto his collar and Sarah Chittock walked in.

"He looks absolutely charming," she gushed as she bent down to pet Wilkins.

Luke couldn't have agreed less. That pink bow in the hair at the top of his head was going to disappear as soon as he got in the car. As for the pastel green body suit…

She stood up again. "Don't you agree, Luke?"

"Well, I…"

He was saved from lying by the tuxedo-clad waiter who walked in looking distressed.

"Could I have a word, Dame Chittock?"

"Of course, Lewis." She turned to Luke. "Excuse me

for a second."

She stepped outside.

Luke gave her a few seconds and then said goodbye to the nail-trimming-lady-in-pink before following her.

"That should do it," she was saying. "Make sure he does a thorough job, won't you."

Luke watched as the waiter left via the main entrance, a large jerrycan in one hand.

"Is there a problem?"

Sarah turned around to face him.

"Not really. There's some deadwood at the bottom of the vineyard and I've told Lewis to burn it. He's an excellent man and he'll make sure it's all gone, and gone for good." She smiled and grabbed him by the hand. "Come on, let's move into the ballroom for the judging."

"Oh dear," she said once she had led him inside. "I've forgotten my handbag. Will you excuse me for a moment, Luke. I'll be back in a second."

Chapter 87

Skylar was halfway back to Bath when his phone rang.

"Have you dealt with her?"

"Yes."

"Once and for all?"

He hesitated before replying. The girl was too frightened to say anything, but should he tell Erebus that she was still alive?

Yes, he decided. She'd find out anyway in due course, so he might as well tell her now.

"She's still alive, Erebus."

"Why?"

"A man came into the house before I could… before *she* could end her life. I had to leave."

"Who was he?"

"He must have been that journalist's boyfriend."

"Mmm. We can't leave it like that. There's the Bandicoot woman herself to deal with as well." She paused. "I wonder if a car accident might be the best way of dealing with them."

"That would require careful planning."

"That's what I pay you for, Skylar."

Was that how she thought of him? A hired hitman, prepared to do her dirty work for her, no questions asked? It was understandable, he supposed, given he had 'helped' first Celestina and then Wynna to end their lives. He'd have finished Fern off too if he hadn't been interrupted.

And besides, the money was good.

"I'll put some thought into it when I get home," he said.

"I have another problem I want you to deal with first. How far are you from Walcot?"

"Fifteen minutes. Why?"

She laughed.

"Fire, I think. Yes. Fire in the woods and fire in Walcot. It has a certain ring to it. Symmetry."

"Erebus, what are you talking about?"

"There's a young couple who…" She stopped. "Skylar, do you have the means to start a fire?"

"What? No. Why?"

"I feared as much." She went quiet again. "You frightened Fern, you said?"

"Yes. I'm certain she won't say anything."

He wasn't by any means certain, but what else could he say? And besides, if Fern and Bandicoot died in a car accident that would remove the problem.

The enormity of what they were discussing suddenly hit him. First, he'd pushed people over bridges, then he'd agreed to arrange a fatal car crash, and now Erebus was suggesting he start a fire to end a young couple's life.

There was a part of his brain telling him this was getting out of hand. Was it his conscience?

Did he even have a conscience?

Or was it plain common sense, the recognition that Erebus had lost control?

"…frighten them and deal with them later."

"What was that, Erebus?"

"I want you to scare them, tell them they mustn't share what they've found out about me. Make it clear what will happen if they do."

"Is this about Beacon?"

"No, it concerns another of my businesses, but it's important to act now. This couple only returned from Cambodia today so they won't have had a chance to tell anyone yet."

"Cambodia?"

She laughed. "Yes, Cambodia. I have another operation there which is almost as profitable as Beacon. If you do well, Skylar, I'll let you in as a co-investor."

She gave him the address in Walcot and the couple's names and ended the call.

He looked down at his notes.

Leanne Kemp and Josh Ogden, you're in for a big surprise.

Chapter 88

Luke was smiling down at Wilkins' pink bow and shaking his head when Dame Sarah Chittock reappeared.

"Found it," she said, holding her handbag up. "Shall we go in?"

Luke's phone rang.

"Please go on in, Sarah. It's my daughter. I'd better see what she wants."

He accepted the call.

"Hi, Chloe. How's everything?"

"Dad, sorry for the late notice, but could Denver and I come down this evening and stay overnight?"

"Of course. Is there a problem?"

She laughed. "Far from it. We've got some exciting news to share?"

"What is it?"

"Can we tell you when we see you?"

"Yes, of course. I'd better go. Wilkins is in a beauty contest."

"He's what?"

"I'll explain this evening."

"Okay. We should be there around seven."

"Bye, Chloe."

"Bye, Dad. Love you."

He smiled as he hung up, then frowned as he thought about what she'd said. 'Exciting news to share'? Could they be getting engaged or… No, surely she couldn't be…

His phone buzzed and he saw a WhatsApp message had come in.

Sorry, guv. No wifi on plane. Home now and need to sleep. Erebus's new account is in the name Bonnie Tinch.

Luke stared at the phone, then at the door to the ballroom. Finally, he knew for certain who Erebus was. The name on her new account was drawn from the names of two of her poodles.

His phone rang again. It was Maj this time.

"Hello, Maj."

"I showed Shannon the photos."

"And she identified Sarah Chittock?"

"Yes. How did you know?"

"I'll explain later. Sam and I are at her party."

"That Australian tried to kill Shannon, Luke. I saw his car outside and burst in on them in the bathroom. He was holding her head underwater."

"My god!"

"She knows him as Skylar. He's one of the senior people in Beacon."

"Where is he now?"

"He got away, but the police are here and I've given them a description and told them the registration number of his car."

"Good. Hopefully, they'll catch him before he does anything else."

He hung up as the door to the ballroom opened and Ambrose appeared.

"You're needed for the judging, Luke." He smiled and pointed to Wilkins. "Or at least, he is." He looked back up at Luke and saw the expression on his face. "Is everything okay?"

"It's Sarah."

"What is? You don't mean she's Erebus?"

Luke nodded. "There's no doubt it's her. Is Sam in there? We need to decide what to do."

"I can't believe it's Sarah." Ambrose put his hand to his mouth. "Oh no! They could be in danger."

"Who could?"

"Have Josh and Leanne just got engaged?"

"No. Why?"

"I went into the office this morning and spoke to Carys on reception. She said how nice it was for one of the Board to want to send them an engagement present."

Luke was one step ahead. "She gave Sarah Chittock their address?"

"Yes."

"I'll ring Josh."

It went to voicemail. He tried Leanne and the same thing happened.

"Maj is in Frome so he's a long way away," he mused. "I know." He looked up at Ambrose. "Would you mind asking Sam to join us while I make this call?"

Ambrose returned as Luke was hanging up.

"Sam's not there," he said.

Luke thought back to what he'd seen earlier. "I saw Sarah talking to the waiter. He was carrying a jerrycan. I hope Sam hasn't followed him."

"She might have followed that workman the waiter was talking to outside."

"I haven't seen him. What does he look like?"

"Well-built, with a tattoo on his neck. The waiter called him Connor."

Chapter 89

Josh came to with a start, sat up in bed and rubbed his eyes which seemed to be full of grit.

Was he in their hotel bedroom in Siem Reap? No, that didn't make sense because a faint light was coming through the curtains on the wrong side of the room.

He lay down again, was asleep instantly, then shot upright again when he heard a loud bang.

It came back to him then. Their long flight, the taxi ride home, he and Leanne deciding to grab some shut-eye despite it being mid-afternoon.

He was back in their apartment, though who knew what time it was. It was dark and his brain was telling him it was the middle of the night, but surely...

There was another thump.

He grabbed the duvet and pulled it towards him.

"Leanne," he hissed. "Did you hear that?"

There was no response.

He put his arm out to prod her, but she wasn't there.

There was another thump, then another almost immediately afterwards.

He jumped out of bed, turned the light on and screamed at the sight of Leanne immediately in front of him.

"Did you hear that?" she whispered. "I was in the loo when it started."

The thumping started up again, then they heard a man's voice.

"LET ME IN!" he shouted. "IF YOU DON'T OPEN THIS DOOR I'M BREAKING IT DOWN!"

Chapter 90

Sam was sitting next to Jamila and holding the woman's hand.

Her shoulder was sore from repeated attempts to barge the door open, but she had more important things to think about than a little bruising.

The oil lamp was on the floor at her feet, still the closest thing she could find to a weapon.

He was a big man though and if, when, he came back for them she wouldn't have the element of surprise in her favour. She had to hope he had seen sense and would release her.

But why had he locked her in there in the first place? And why was he keeping this woman captive? If only Jamila could speak more than a few words of English.

She heard a noise, climbed to her feet, picked the lamp up and moved to the door.

"HELLO!"

There was no response.

"LET US OUT!"

She could hear him moving around, then the sound of splashing.

What on earth was he up to? Why was he spreading water around the base of the shed?

Her nose wrinkled as she smelt something in the air. It was slightly sweet and pungent.

"WHAT ARE YOU DOING!"

There was more splashing, then she realised what the smell was.

Petrol.

Chapter 91

Connor drained the jerrycan and stood back to admire his handiwork, pleased with how much coverage he'd achieved from four gallons of fuel.

He wasn't stupid though. Petrol wasn't to be messed with and the fumes were highly flammable. The last thing he wanted was to put himself at risk in what was going to be an impressive inferno.

He stepped back and placed the empty container at the base of one of the trees, deciding that he'd wait for the fumes to disperse before stepping forward and putting a match to the base of the shed.

As he put the can down, there was another muffled shout from the building.

"LET US OUT!"

He moved to the door to reply.

"YOU SHOULDN'T HAVE INTERFERED!"

There was a pause before the woman called back.

"YOU DON'T HAVE TO DO THIS!"

Connor smiled to himself.

Yes, he did.

He'd set out to end the problems created by the Afghan woman, but it made sense to kill two birds with one stone. Besides, this interfering bitch deserved what was coming to her.

She shouldn't have followed him.

And this time he wouldn't make any mistakes. He'd panicked when the Syrian had died, thinking that removing him from the estate and hiding him in the Lost Property office was his best bet. What he should have done was bury him deep in the woods.

That's what he'd do with the women's corpses once the

building had burned to the ground.

Not that there'd be much left of them.

He sniffed the air. There was still a distinct acrid smell but it was less than it had been. He pulled the box of matches from his pocket.

"DON'T!"

The shout came from behind him and he turned to see Lewis running out of the trees.

"What do you mean 'don't'? You gave me the jerrycan, Lewis. What did you expect me to do?"

"You were meant to scare her into working, that's all."

"This is a better solution."

Connor took a match out and made to strike it against the side of the box.

Lewis reached out but he shoved him in the chest sending him backwards and to the floor.

Grinning, Connor lit the match and threw it at the base of the shed.

The petrol-soaked wood immediately burst into flame.

Chapter 92

"Sarah," Luke said, "would you mind stepping into the hall for a moment? Ambrose and I would like a word." He smiled apologetically to the other dog-owners and the judges. "I'm sorry about this, but we won't be a second."

Sarah smiled. "Very well, dear.' She handed the leads of her poodles to Gillian and followed them out.

Luke closed the door behind them.

Ambrose looked at her sternly. "We know, Sarah."

She furrowed her brows. "Know what?"

"About Beacon," Luke said, "and about your role in Tease as well."

"I don't know what you mean."

"Are you denying your involvement?"

"Why would I deny it." She giggled. "They're legitimate business interests of mine. There's nothing illegal in what I'm doing."

"But Tease is using child labour," Ambrose said.

"Those children are bringing money home to their poor families, Ambrose. As you know, everything I do is aimed at helping the less fortunate. The same is true with Beacon where hundreds of mixed-up individuals have benefitted from the counselling we offer." She turned back to Luke. "Now, do you mind if we return to the ballroom?"

"What about Skylar?" Luke said, and noticed her flinch when she heard the name. "Who was he trying to help when he held Shannon Wilson's head underwater?"

"I don't know anyone called Skylar."

Luke decided a white lie was in order.

"Yes you do, Sarah. He's in custody, and he's told the police that he works for you and that he attacked her at your request."

"That's absolute nonsense."

She was trying to blag it, but he sensed that she knew the game was up. He decided to push a little further.

"Was he also acting on your orders when he murdered Marie Cotton and Anna Grayling, pushing them to their deaths off Churchill Bridge in Bath?"

She swallowed, seemed to be in shock for a second and then her beatific smile returned.

Had she seen a way out? Was there one more trick up her sleeve?

With a shock, Luke recalled the conversation he'd overheard between Sarah and the waiter.

"What was that about burning deadwood earlier, Sarah?"

"Oh, Lewis and Connor will have completed that errand by now. I do hope no one was caught up in it." Her smile widened further. "Fires can be so dangerous, can't they? Where's Sam, by the way? I haven't seen her for a while."

Luke felt like throttling the woman, but instead turned to Ambrose.

"Don't let her out of your sight, Ambrose."

He dashed out of the hall and sprinted towards the vineyard.

Chapter 93

Luke was halfway down the hill when he saw flames. They were rising twenty to thirty feet in the air and there was smoke too, thick black fumes rising through the inferno and blowing away to the east.

He increased his pace.

Seconds later he heard the crackling of burning wood.

As he drew nearer he saw that what was on fire wasn't deadwood but a building. It looked to have been a shed, but the walls had collapsed inward and it now looked like nothing more than a large bonfire.

The fire was intense.

He stopped six or seven yards away, unable to proceed any further, and held his hands in front of his face to shield the worst of the heat.

The burning planks hadn't fallen to the floor. They were supported by something or someone.

Was it Sam? He couldn't bear it if…

He flinched as he felt a hand on his shoulder.

"The body is there," a voice said sadly.

Luke turned to see a young man with his arm around a woman of about the same age. She was in anguish, tears running down her cheeks and deep sobs issuing with each outward breath.

"It is terrible," the man said. "I am Nabi and fortunately my wife wasn't injured, but…"

He pointed twenty yards deeper into the wood, but all Luke could see were the backs of two men. Beyond them, something lay on the ground.

Not something, someone.

He stopped breathing.

They'd had so little time together. How could it come

to this?

He wiped below one eye.

"Luke?"

He swung around.

"Sam?"

He turned back to the tree, then back to her.

"I thought that was you. That you…" He leaned forward and kissed her, then stepped back again.

"I love you, Sam."

She smiled up at him. "I love you too, Luke."

Chapter 94

Luke turned around and he and Nabi walked towards the two men who parted as they drew near. Sam remained behind and grabbed hold of Jamila's hand.

There was enough light from the still-burning shed for Luke to see that the man prostrate on the ground was Connor Iverson. His eyes stared up unseeingly and there was blood pooled around the back of his head. Luke knelt and pressed two fingers against Connor's neck. As he had anticipated, there was no pulse.

He looked up at Nabi.

"What happened?"

"I do not know. Someone must have hit him and then released both Jamila and…" He pointed to Sam. "…your wife. I am sorry, I don't know her name."

"Her name is Sam. You don't know who hit him?"

"No. We ran here when we saw the flames, but Connor was already dead."

"We?"

Nabi gestured to the other two men. "Hene and Idris are my fellow workers."

"Could it have been the waiter?"

"The waiter?"

"His name is Lewis."

"It could have been Lewis, but he and Connor work together. Why would he save the women, and…" He pointed to the dead man. "…why would he do that?"

"NABI!" Jamila screamed. She seemed to be becoming more rather than less distressed.

"I must comfort my wife," Nabi said.

He went over to her and they exchanged a few words, but it didn't seem to calm her.

"Is she worried about Lewis returning?" Luke asked.//
"No. She is fearful of what he might do to Bibi."
"Bibi?"
"Our daughter." Nabi was struggling to hold it together himself. "They took her from us because we did not work hard enough."
"How old is Bibi?"
"She is two."
Luke pulled his phone out of his pocket.
"What are you doing?" There was panic in Nabi's voice.
"I'm calling the police."
"No! You cannot."
Luke put his arm on the man's shoulder.
"Nabi, I can see what's going on here and it has to be stopped. Don't worry, I'll make sure you're looked after."
"But we…"
"I know you're illegal immigrants, but that doesn't mean you can be exploited like this. Please, you have to trust me."
Pete answered the phone straight away.
"Hi. Having a good time?"
"Far from it. I'm standing in a copse looking down at Connor Iverson's body. He was attacked but his murderer has got away."
"Whoa, Luke. I thought you were going to a party on an estate in the middle of Somerset."
"I'm in the grounds." He looked over at Nabi and Jamila, and then at the two Eritreans. "This is complex, Pete. We're talking people traffickers, modern human slavery and child labour."
"What! This is not some kind of joke is it?"
"I wish it were. Right now, the most important thing is tracking down a two-year-old girl who's been abducted. You need to get as many officers here as you can."
He gave Pete the address then ended the call and turned to Nabi.
"The police are on their way. Right now, we have to get

you up to the house where it's warm."

"We have the other shed. There is a heater."

Luke's heart went out to the man. He had been cowed by Sarah Chittock and her thugs, forced to work for little or no money and to live in squalor.

"No, Nabi, you need to come with me."

Chapter 95

Luke tried Josh's phone again as they walked through the vineyard towards the house. Again there was no answer and he left a message.

He tried Leanne. Her mobile rang four or five times and he was about to leave a second voicemail when there was a click and a man spoke. His words were hissed, as if he was afraid he'd be overheard.

"Who's this?"

It wasn't Josh but it was a voice that Luke recognised immediately.

"It's Luke. Are Josh and Leanne okay?"

"They're completely out of it. Just a second, his gag is slipping."

There was a short pause and then a woman's voice came on the line.

"We arrived just in time," Helen said. "The wee bawbag was outside when we arrived."

"Where is he now?"

"He's trussed up like an oven-ready turkey."

"And Josh and Leanne?"

"They've fallen asleep again. We're in their lounge and the police are on their way."

"Good work, Helen. Thank Bob for me, will you?"

"Aye, I can do that."

Luke hung up and turned to Sam.

"Josh and Leanne are fine."

"What do you mean? Why wouldn't they be?"

He smiled. "I'll tell you later."

They walked into the house to find Dame Sarah Chittock seated in a flamboyant chair in the hall, Ambrose standing a few feet in front of her, while two men that

Luke had seen at the party earlier stood to either side.

She was smiling and enjoying what she saw as a position of strength. It was almost a regal tableau, the queen in the centre while pages flanked her on either side.

Her smile vanished when she saw Nabi, Jamila, Hene and Idris follow Luke and Sam in.

"Who are they?" she asked.

"Don't pretend you've never seen them before, Sarah," Luke said. "They work on your estate."

"Then Lewis must have employed them. I've never seen them in my life."

"She's telling the truth."

Luke turned around to see that it was Lewis who had spoken. Next to him stood a woman Luke had never seen before. She held a toddler in her arms.

"Bibi!" Jamila screamed.

She dived forwards, took her daughter and cradled her to her breast.

"I've had enough," Lewis said. "Connor was going to kill them and I saw red."

"Don't say any more, Lewis," Sarah said. "You'll incriminate yourself."

Before Luke could do anything, Lewis walked over and spat in the Dame's face.

"I don't know how I got sucked in so deep, but I'm going to make you pay."

She wiped her face. "I don't know what you're talking about, Lewis. I'm innocent." Her smile was back now and she'd turned it up to maximum.

Lewis sneered at her.

"I've got evidence, *Dame* Chittock." There was something in the way he said 'Dame' that made it sound like an insult. "I recorded you talking to Henri, and I've got documents as well that prove what you've been up to. You're going to spend a long time inside, you evil bitch."

It was then that Luke heard the sirens.

Chapter 96

Luke shook hands with Denver, then walked to the Mazda's passenger side when Chloe emerged and gave her a kiss on the cheek.

She bent down to pet Wilkins who was desperate for her attention.

"I thought you said he had a bow, Dad?"

"That came off as soon as we got home."

"His new curls are nice though."

She stood upright again, and the cocker sensed she'd finished and rushed to Denver's side in pursuit of more strokes.

Chloe smiled as she watched her boyfriend indulge him.

"So, was Wilkins well-behaved at the party?"

"Yes, he was very good, especially given how much was going on."

"Was it lively then?"

"You could say that."

He exchanged a look with Sam, who mouthed 'ask her', before turning back back to his daughter.

"What's the exciting news, Chloe?"

"Let's wait until we're inside. Denver's brought the bubbly."

She smiled and seemed for an instant to look down at her midriff, or was it his imagination?

Once inside he sat back on his Dad chair and tried to relax but it was hard, ever so hard. His instinct was to perch on the front edge, to ask more questions, to find out what her 'exciting' secret was.

Sam fetched four champagne flutes and handed them out while Denver opened the bottle.

"Are you okay to have some, Chloe?" Luke asked, trying

but failing to keep his eyes from her tummy.

She saw where he was looking and grinned.

"You mean, because I'm going to have a baby?"

There it was.

She was expecting.

His little girl was…

"You are funny, Dad." She was laughing now. "I'm not pregnant."

"You're not? Then what are we celebrating?"

She turned to her boyfriend. "I'll let you tell him."

Luke looked at Denver and saw how relaxed he seemed, much more so than when they had visited before.

"Gerry Saunders has been sacked," Denver said with a grin. "The Dean called him in yesterday, and the Chancellor was there too. I was told that someone from security walked him straight to the door afterwards."

"That's brilliant news."

"Thanks for your help, Dad," Chloe said.

"Yes. Thanks, Luke," Denver added.

Sam raised her glass.

"Cheers."

The others joined in the toast and Luke sat back in his chair, finally able to relax.

"So you said the party was lively," Chloe said. "Was that because there were so many dogs?"

He laughed. "It was nothing to do with Wilkins and his furry friends. In fact, there were more police cars than dogs."

"More police cars? How come?"

His phone rang and he looked over at Sam and then gestured to the screen. "It's Helen, and hopefully it's good news."

He accepted the call.

"Well?"

"I'm at home, Luke, and Bob's just got back."

"What about Nabi and his family?"

"I'll put him on."

There was a short pause and then a man came on the phone.

"Thank you, Luke," Nabi said.

"Nabi! I wasn't expecting you to be there."

"It's down to Migrant Plus, and in particular to Bob and Shannon. They helped me complete the application forms, and Helen has said we can move in with her until our asylum claim is processed."

"That's wonderful news. Can you put Bob on, please?"

After a few seconds, he came on the line.

"Hi, Luke."

"Thanks for everything, Bob. What about Hene and Idris?"

"Their papers are in, and they've been put up in a hotel but it looks like they'll be granted asylum as well."

"Where's Shannon?"

"Back with her parents."

"Good. I think you deserve a drink."

"After everything that's happened today, I'm sure that you do as well."

"Don't worry. I've got one."

He ended the call.

"That sounded promising," Sam said.

He smiled, nodded then updated her. They continued talking to and fro for several minutes.

"What on earth have you two been up to?" Chloe asked when they'd finished. "I heard mentions of Afghans, Eritreans, Tease, which as far as I know is a fashion retailer, and two people called Erebus and Skylar. And what was all that about a Glastonbury beacon?"

"It's complicated," Luke said. He drained his glass and held it out to Denver. "Top that up, if you don't mind, and I'll explain everything."

*

"Wow, that's some story," Chloe said when Luke had finished. "It sounds like Nabi and his family are going to be okay. The two Eritreans too. But what about those poor children working at Tease's factory?"

"Sam and I spoke to Josh earlier," Luke said. "He met with someone in Siem Reap who has a plan that sounds like it will work. Most, if not all, of the children working there have parents who are unemployed and this man, his name's Darany, has calculated that, with Sarah Chittock not taking a cut, an adult taking their place will be cost-effective."

"I'm going to ring Darany tomorrow," Sam said, "and help him finalise his spreadsheet for presenting to Tease's Board."

"What's going to happen to the Operations Manager?" Denver asked.

"It's difficult to say," Luke said. "I think we'll have to leave it to Tease to decide, but it's likely they'll replace her."

"And the therapy cult?"

"I'm confident Beacon won't last long. The leader and her deputy are now in police custody and likely to be spending many years at His Majesty's pleasure. The head of the snake is gone and, once Rhianna Bandicoot publishes her findings, I don't think the body will be hanging around for long."

"Which only leaves my ex, Ollie, to worry about," Sam said with a dry laugh.

"Your ex?" Chloe said. "Was he working with Chittock?"

"No, but he's proving to be a challenge."

"More than a challenge," Luke said. "We'll have to wait and see what happens, but at the very least he'll be given a restraining order."

He stood up.

"Right. That's enough talking shop for today. Let's grab our coats and scarves and walk to Tucker's Grave. Wilkins needs the exercise and I could murder a cider."

Afterword

As with all my books, this is a work of fiction. That said, there are areas where I have attempted to build plausibility into the story by using, or in some cases bending, facts. With that in mind, I thought it worth clarifying what is true and what is made up.

Beacon is my invention. Unfortunately, however, therapy cults are thriving. The one in this book is based on Lighthouse, founded by multimillionaire Paul Waugh, which was the subject of a BBC documentary.

One woman the BBC interviewed, who rented a six-bedroom house to Waugh, said she ended up with eight Lighthouse team members living there and that the house became "absolutely filthy" with every bedroom converted into a bedsit. The BBC also found that over £1 million - roughly half the firm's income - had been paid to Paul Waugh himself over the preceding four years.

On 28th March 2023, following a request by the UK government, a judge at the Royal Courts of Justice decided it was in the public interest to close the firm behind Lighthouse.

The following day Paul Waugh wrote on Twitter, 'I asked the judge to close our old company down'.

As I write this, Lighthouse continues to drain money from its unfortunate victims, but now calls itself Lighthouse Global and has rebranded with a new emphasis on Christianity rather than self-help.

Channel dinghies are of massive concern, not least for the danger they put asylum-seekers in. Over the past few years over 100,000 illegal immigrants are believed to have crossed the English Channel in small boats. Nationals of five countries (Iran, Albania, Iraq, Afghanistan and

Syria) accounted for two-thirds of those.

Rescued asylum seekers are usually served papers, detained for a few days, and then released into the community while their asylum claim is processed. They are provided with housing and basic living expenses by the Home Office, but are not allowed to claim welfare benefits or work.

Over 90% of people arriving in small boats have claimed asylum and around three-quarters of those applications have been successful.

Child Labour is prevalent in many countries. Children in Cambodia are subjected to the worst forms, including commercial sexual exploitation. Children as young as 5 have been found working in many sectors, including brickmaking, agriculture, construction and the manufacture of alcoholic beverages and textiles.

Boohoo was investigated in 2020 by The Sunday Times. Their undercover journalist worked at the factory that Boohoo used in Leicester and was told he would be paid £3.50 an hour, well below the UK minimum wage which at the time was £8.72.

Boohoo disengaged with the Leicester company which then closed down its UK operation before opening up a new factory in Morocco under a different name. In November 2024, The Telegraph reported that Boohoo had started working with them again.

This is despite a so-called 'ethical overhaul' with Boohoo reporting, also in November 2024, that it had scrapped over 400 suppliers after allegations of low pay and poor working conditions.

The Road Rats Motorcycle Club originated as a London street gang. After evolving into a motorcycle club, members were involved in violent clashes with other groups, most notably the British chapters of Hells Angels and Satans Slaves. Two RRMC members have been imprisoned, one for a shooting and the second for murder.

Beacon of Blight

Thanks for reading 'Beacon of Blight'. I would greatly appreciate it if you could leave a review on Amazon.

This is book 7 in my Luke Sackville Crime Series. If you read it as a standalone, I invite you to look at the first six books: Taken to the Hills, Black Money, Fog of Silence, The Corruption Code, Lethal Odds and Sow the Wind.

Want to read more about Luke Sackville and what shaped his career choices? 'Change of Direction', the prequel to the series, can be downloaded as an ebook or audiobook free of charge by subscribing to my newsletter at:
sjrichardsauthor.com

Acknowledgements

Thanks must first go to my wife Penny for her help, support and critical feedback on my first draft. She knows her crime fiction!

My beta readers provided excellent feedback as always. Thanks to Chris Bayne, Deb Day, Denise Goodhand, Jackie Harrison, Sarah Mackenzie, Allison Valentine and Marcie Whitecotton-Carroll.

Thanks also to my advance copy readers, who put faith in the book being worth reading.

Yet again Samuel James has done a terrific job narrating the audiobook, while Olly Bennett designed yet another tremendous cover.

Last but not least, thanks to you the reader. I love your feedback and reading your reviews, and I'm always delighted to hear from you so please feel free to get in touch.

TIGER BAIT

Stiffen the sinews, summon up the blood

Luke Sackville's Ethics Team has several projects on the go ranging from environmental negligence to social media trolling. As they start to investigate these apparently minor misdemeanours, Luke begins to see a link between them.

Further work reveals connections to an organised crime cartel, but before Luke can act a trap is laid and more than one of his team find themselves fighting for their lives.

Tiger Bait is the eighth book in the series of crime thrillers featuring ex-DCI Luke Sackville and his Ethics Team.

Out 6th May 2025 - Order your copy now

mybook.to/tigerbait

ABOUT THE AUTHOR

First things first: my name's Steve. I've never been called 'SJ', but Steve Richards is a well-known political writer hence the pen name.

I was born in Bath and have lived at various times on an irregular clockwise circle around England. After university in Manchester, my wife and I settled in Macclesfield before moving to Bedfordshire then a few years ago back to Somerset. We now live in Croscombe, a lovely village just outside Wells, with our 2 sprightly cocker spaniels.

I've always loved writing but have only really had the time to indulge myself since taking early retirement. My daughter is a brilliant author (I'm not biased of course) which is both an inspiration and - because she's so good - a challenge. After a few experiments, and a couple of completed but unsatisfactory and never published novels, I decided to write a crime fiction series as it's one of the genres I most enjoy.

You can find out more about me and my books at my website:
sjrichardsauthor.com

Printed in Great Britain
by Amazon